She knew something was wrong—things weren't where they were supposed to be...

Julie opened her side door as always, dropping her keys on the kitchen table along with her books from school and her pocketbook. She reached into the refrigerator and grabbed a Pepsi. She did this almost every day, even when she was in college at Brown. Habits were not easy to break. She then hung up her coat and went into her makeshift office. It certainly was roomier since they threw out all the junk before finding the money. As she looked around, she had a funny feeling that someone had moved her stuff. Who? Why? How?

She went back to the kitchen and looked at the door. There were no marks of a break-in. Same with the front door. No jimmy marks or scratches on the lock. The chain was still on the front door. Everyone came in the back. She looked at her desk. The computer was not sitting right.

Yes, she knew she was anal retentive, but that's not exactly where her computer went. Files were not lined up straight, one on top of the other. The top page was from yesterday's work. She always left her work for the next day on top with her little notes attached. Those notes were not where she put them.

She opened her drawers and went into her files. The files were slightly out of sequence. She kept her documentation for the book in precise alphabetical order, not one file out of place.

Now three of them were not where they were supposed to be. The history files with the dates were out of sequence. The interview files where she kept her comments were at the bottom of the drawer. She was starting to get a little panicky.

Julie Chapman grew up in Key Largo, a tenth-generation Conch, raised in the Florida Keys by her grandmother, Tillie, since Julie's parents were deceased. Then one night Tillie has a car accident and ends up in a coma, leaving Julie and her best friend Joe to wonder if it really was an accident. As Julie and Joe start digging for the truth, they uncover some dark and desperate secrets that can not only cause them a good deal of trouble, but also cost them their lives.

KUDOS for *Conch Town Girl*

In *Conch Town Girl* by Daniel J. Barrett, Julie Chapman is writing a book as part of her requirements to receive her MFA in Education from Brown University. The book, coincidentally, is called *Conch Town Girl* and tells of Julie's life growing up poor in Key Largo and the Florida Keys. While writing the book, Julie is also taking care of her grandmother who has been in a hit and run accident, working as a teacher's aide, falling in love with her best friend, Joe, and coaching the cross-country track team. When Julie and Joe find $300,000 in the attic, they begin to uncover some dark secrets that could put Julie, her grandmother, and Joe in real danger. The story is charming and gives you a good glimpse into what like was like for a poor white girl growing up in paradise. There is a sense of community and authenticity that add a nice touch to the story. ~ *Taylor Jones, Reviewer*

Conch Town Girl by Daniel J. Barrett is about Julie a young girl who grew up in the Florida Keys. She has had to overcome losing her parents at a young age, being raised by her widowed grandmother, and poverty to make something of her life. She managed to get a scholarship to Brown University and got an MFA in Education. As part of her requirements for the MFA, Julie is writing a book about her life in the Florida Keys. Woven through the story of her life is the present in which Julie has her hands full taking care of her grandmother, Tillie, who is in the hospital after a hit and run accident. She also has to finish her book, solve the mystery of illegal money found in her attic, and work full time at her old school. There's a sweet little romance woven in with all the other subplots, and the overall story is quite touching. There is a definite ring of truth to the book that tells me the author has spent a great deal of time in the Florida Keys. The plot is strong with a number of surprises to keep you guessing. ~ *Regan Murphy, Reviewer*

ACKNOWLEDGEMENTS

Thank you to Black Opal Books for making this book possible. A special thanks to Lauri Wellington, Acquisitions Editor and to Faith for making *Conch Town Girl* come to life. Your dedication and hard work went beyond the call of duty.

CONCH
TOWN GIRL

Daniel J. Barrett

Daniel J Barrett

A Black Opal Books Publication

To Martha
Thank you. BEST wishes.

Dan

DEDICATION

To Alice Fox

And to my wife, Sandy, and those many friends who served as readers and advisors.
Thank you all. You are greatly appreciated.

CHAPTER 1

Tillie was asked to fill in for the dinner crowd. She backed out of shifts as much as she could, covering only breakfast at the Waffle House for the time being. Her friend and fellow waitress, Martha, had to take her mother to the doctor's office for a 4:00 p.m. appointment and would not be back on time. Tillie switched with Martha for tomorrow's breakfast shift. *No problem* she thought. She left a note and some dinner for Julie, who would be in later after practice. There was nothing like routine to keep the day going smoothly. *Another day in Key Largo.*

It was getting dark and closing in on 4:30 p.m. when Tillie hopped into her Escort and headed out to the restaurant for the evening shift. She never drove fast and got there in twenty minutes, right before the shift began. She parked in the lot and started toward the front door. As she turned to open the door, she saw a white truck parked across the street with a tall man getting out of the driver's side. For some reason, he looked familiar but she could not place him. The man turned and looked at Tillie. She held his gaze for only a few seconds but it felt like a lifetime. He turned around, hopped back into the truck, started it, and took off like a bat out of hell.

Tillie was shaken. She ran through the front door and told the manager that she had to go home for a minute. It was an emergency. She said she would be back in less than a half an hour. She had to speak to Julie. She ran out of the restaurant with the manager shouting at her, "Is everything all right, Tillie?"

She turned. "No."

She started her car and took a left out of the parking lot, going south on the Overseas Highway, heading toward home. She was speeding for the first time in a long time. She had to see Julie.

In the meantime, her manager Phil called Julie at home to let her know Tillie was on her way and she was very upset about something. He'd just caught her coming into the house from cross-country practice.

"Hi, Phil, what's up?" she asked.

"I really don't know, Julie," he said. "Tillie was very excited, almost in distress, and she said she had to rush home to see you. She said it was an emergency. I have no idea what the problem is but she said she would be back in a half an hour."

"Thanks, Phil. I am sure she is okay. She should be here in a minute. I'll wait outside for her," Julie said, wondering what was wrong.

Tillie tried to control her emotions and held on to the steering wheel for dear life. *Please Lord, don't let me get a speeding ticket,* she thought. As she headed out of town toward home, a big truck, with its high beams on, came up behind her and started to tailgate her. She couldn't see who it was or even what kind of vehicle was behind her. She sped up even more. It was a desolate one-mile section, just south of town, with nothing but highway and sand ditches on both sides of the road, and one lane both ways. The vehicle behind her—she could now see that it was a pickup truck—pulled out, so, she slowed down to let it pass. As soon as the truck's passenger door met her driver's side door, she looked over and saw a face that she'd thought she would never see again. The driver immediately jerked the truck hard to the right, hitting the Escort on the front driver's side, and pushed the car toward the ditch. Tillie tried to keep the car straight and hit the gas but it just made the car swerve more to the right and fly off the road. She was going almost sixty miles an hour when she became airborne. She hit the ditch and the car rolled over and over and then stopped. The truck slowed, stopped, backed up, and then took off again. Tillie's car was at least fifty feet off the road, upside down, with the lights facing into the wetland area. It was partially submerged in the bog.

❧❧❧

Julie could wait no longer. Tillie should have been here by now. It was less than seven miles door-to-door, even as slow as Tillie drove. Julie got into her car and went toward the Overseas Highway, heading north to the restaurant. She'd barely gotten onto the highway when she noticed two police cars on the west side of the road, parked in a southern direction. The lights were flashing and Julie's heart sank. *Oh, my God, please don't let it be Grandmother. Oh, God.* She parked off to the side of the road and ran across the highway to the sheriff's vehicles. Moving behind the police cars, she saw a car upside down with the lights on. Tears formed in her eyes.

She knew one of the deputies, Sam Parker. He ate breakfast regularly at the Waffle House. He saw Julie and said, "Julie, stay where you are, please."

"Sam, is it my grandmother?" she asked.

"Does Tillie have an old Escort?" he asked.

"Yes," she said.

They walked gingerly through the field and saw Tillie hanging upside down, still fastened in her seat belt.

"Tillie, can you hear me?" Sam said. "Tillie, Tillie? I think she is unconscious."

"Oh my God." Julie tried talking to Tillie but she got no response. It was clear Tillie was in trouble.

The ambulance was on its way. As soon as the deputies saw the car, they had called the Mariner Hospital to let them know they had a very bad accident. The EMTs were able to get Tillie out of the vehicle and onto the stretcher. She had a weak pulse but they were only a few miles from the hospital. The emergency room was ready for her.

Julie followed one of the deputies and the ambulance while the other deputy took care of the crash site. They pulled into the emergency room exit. Julie parked to the side and watched the EMTs rush Tillie to the emergency room. Julie followed them in but she had to see the admitting room staff to complete the admittance paperwork. Thank God Tillie was now covered under her policy from the school. A couple of months earlier, Tillie would have lost everything, including the house, which she had owned for over forty years.

As Julie sat there, all she could think about was fifteen years ago when she and Tillie saw Annie Chapman die right in front of them at the same emergency room exit door. With the image flashing before her eyes, she thought, *If Tillie dies, I'll be alone. It's been the both of us together, and now, it may just be me. Why?*

With that, she burst into tears, covered her face, and used her jacket to dry her eyes. *Tillie was always there for me, and now I'll be there for her, God willing.*

CHAPTER 2

S am Parker came up to Julie after she completed the paperwork to admit Tillie. "Do you have any idea what happened, Julie?" he asked. "Fortunately, we were driving by when we saw the headlights pointing out into the field. If we had been going any faster, we would have missed the accident completely. I would hate to think what would have happened to Tillie if we'd missed it."

"I really don't know what happened," Julie said. "I got a call from Phil, the manager at the restaurant, who told me Tillie was in a panic and on her way to see me at home. He said Tillie said there was an emergency and she would be back in a half an hour, then she rushed out."

"Well, we will get to the bottom of it, but let's hope she pulls through. Our prayers are with her," Sam said.

"I better call Phil at the restaurant and let them know what happened," Julie answered.

Julie called Phil at the Waffle House. "Where is Tillie?" he asked.

"She is at the Mariner Hospital in critical condition, Phil," she said. "She went off the road, less than a mile from our house. She almost made it home. We have no idea what happened to her. We won't know until she wakes up," she said.

"I'll close as soon as our last customer finishes dinner, and we'll meet you at the hospital before 8:00 p.m. You are not alone, Julie. We want you to know that."

The surgical team rushed Tillie to the operating room. The preliminary report showed that she was unconscious, had a broken left ankle and pelvis, and a fractured skull. They immediately put her into an induced coma to stop the brain from swelling. Pressure was building up and they needed to stop the process before operating on her for her other conditions. They took her vital signs and the doctor asked Julie if Tillie was retired. "She's in remarkable shape," he said.

"She has been a waitress since she was fifteen years old, almost forty-eight years," Julie told him. "She was slowing down, just taking a few less shifts every now and then to work toward her retirement at age sixty-five."

"How old is she now?"

"Sixty-three."

"If she wasn't in such good shape, this accident could have been fatal," the doctor said. "I believe she'll pull through but she'll have a long time convalescing."

"Whatever it takes," Julie assured him.

The surgeon went back in and completed the procedure to save her life. Then over the next few days, they would take care of her broken bones. Tillie would not be waking up for a while.

The only thing Julie could think of while waiting for Tillie at this point was to call Joe. *Who else do I have to call?* She would call her school in the morning. There wasn't much she could do in the hospital and working with the kids would take her mind off of it. Perhaps Joe could come down for a while. Only until Tillie got out of her coma and they knew what else had to transpire for her to get well. Julie really didn't have any money for a treatment facility while Tillie got better. She needed help.

I guess I can kiss my book goodbye for a while. I could take Tillie's place at the Waffle House for the dinner hour and still work at the school. I can't quit the school because I have to have the school's health insurance to cover Tillie's hospital bills. She sighed. *It's amazing what goes through your mind when trauma strikes.*

Julie called Joe on his cell. He was just finishing up work at his job in upstate New York.

It wasn't Wednesday so the call surprised him. Joe had spoken to her every Wednesday since she was a little girl. "Hi, Julie. To what do I owe this honor?" he asked.

"Tillie was in a very bad automobile accident tonight and she's in the hospital in critical condition. They put her in an induced coma to combat the pressure buildup on her brain and she has several broken bones they can't get to until the pressure subsides."

"Oh, Julie," he said. "Are you all right?"

"No, but I'm better than Tillie," she said cautiously.

"Are you sure you're not Irish?" Joe asked with a chuckle as he thought about his family's sense of humor drifting to the dark side. "That's something I would have said."

"Yes, I know that," she said.

"Do you want me to come down?" he asked.

She broke into tears. "Yes."

"It may be a day or two but I will be there as fast as humanly possible, Julie. I'm working on two projects for the Troy Consulting Group and I have one investigation going with the Coast Guard up in Troy. I'll make some calls and see what I can do," he told her. "If nothing else,

I'll fly into Fort Lauderdale International, see Mark Silva for a brief moment, and then head right down to your place in Key Largo, or I'll come right to the hospital, depending on what time I get in. You've got my cell phone number, so call me. Or I'll call you as soon as I get everything ready so I can leave."

"Thanks, Joe. I don't know what I would do without you."

"We'll get through this," he promised. "I'll let Mary know as well. Tillie will be in our prayers."

Julie thanked him and hung up her cell phone.

A little before 8:00 p.m., Phil and the crew came into the surgical waiting room. They had coffee and dinner for Julie, knowing she would probably be there all night. They stayed for an hour and a half and then said their goodbyes. There wasn't much they could do, so Julie told them to leave and get a good night sleep. Without Tillie at the restaurant, things would not go as smoothly. She was a fixture there.

Thinking ahead, Julie called Phil to the side. "If Tillie is laid up for a long time, I'll cover her shifts as best I can." The novel she was writing would be just a fond memory for a while. She needed money to help with Tillie's recovery.

"No, Julie, you don't need to do that. I'll cover Tillie's salary and tips as long as I can."

The others told her not to worry. They would chip in as well. They wanted Julie to complete her book as much as she did. "Hell, it's our life story as well as yours."

❧❧❧

The surgeon came out around 1:00 a.m. "Your grandmother's stabilized. We'll fix her broken ankle and pelvis by the end of the week. The fractured skull will be carefully watched, but there isn't much we can do. It should heal on its own. We'll need to get her out of the induced coma before the week's over, ten days at the most. At that time, we'll determine if there's any residual damage or any long-term effects—longer than expected, I mean. Her recovery from the broken ankle and pelvis will determine if her working days are over or not."

"Thank you, Doctor." Julie had tears of joy in her eyes. Tillie was okay but not out of the woods. Joe would be here in a day or two and they could figure out together what had to be done to take care of Tillie, the house, and everything else.

Julie fell asleep about 2:00 a.m. She tossed and turned on the waiting room couch until a few minutes after 7:00 a.m., when Sam Parker walked in with the chief of detectives of the Monroe County Sheriff's Department.

"I would like to introduce you to Mike Kenny our chief of detectives for this area," Sam said, after gently shaking Julie's shoulder.

"Hi, Mike, it's nice to meet you," she said.

"Can we take a few minutes of your time?" Mike asked. "We have a few questions to ask you. We would prefer to ask Mrs. Carpenter but obviously it would be a little premature at this time."

"Sure, fire away. It looks like I'll be here for a long time."

"Well, first," he said, "this was no accident."

"Are you sure?" she asked.

"Yes," he said. "Our technicians have been at the site for the entire night. We finally removed your grandmother's car to our sub-station in Islamorada for further analysis. Other than the rolling effect that crumbled the roof and dented the doors, there was damage to the driver's side. It looks like your grandmother was a victim of a sideswipe hit and run. There is a racing stripe of white paint from the driver's door to the front driver's side headlight. It was very clear your grandmother was pushed off the road at a very high rate of speed. I understand she was racing home to see you, which certainly didn't help. She had to be going at least sixty miles an hour when she left the road."

"Tillie never sped in her whole life," Julie protested. "And if that was the case, I have no idea what the emergency was that she was racing home to tell me about. Phil called me from the restaurant and told me she was on her way home and she was very upset, but he had no idea what the problem was. She never said anything other than that she would be back in a half an hour. Phil's her manager."

"We know. He called in as soon as he left you to tell us the exact same thing."

Julie sighed. "Well we won't know anything until she wakes up and tells us exactly what happened."

"Be very careful now that you're alone in the house," Mike told her. Sam nodded in agreement.

"I'm not afraid for myself, but for Tillie. Are you going to assign anyone to guard her while she was in the hospital?" she asked.

"We don't believe she's in any danger, and we really don't have the manpower to cover her twenty-four/seven," the detective said.

"What if someone was trying to kill her?" Julie asked.

"Again, we think this may have been road rage or something," Mike said. "We will find whoever did this but we're certain she'll be safe in the hospital."

"I'm not so sure," Julie argued.

"Once we know the status of the car and really check it out, then we can determine if it's a hit and run road rage, like we think, or something else," Mike said. "Until then we can't provide coverage. We're really thin now and we can't allocate even one officer to the hospital. The Mariner Hospital does have guards on duty all day long. We have notified them of the situation and they'll walk by her room every hour, if needed."

Sam cleared his throat. "Julie, perhaps some of Tillie's friends can stay here until she's better."

"I'll ask," Julie said. Tillie had a lot of friends in town and Julie was sure they would help out for the short term.

"You be very careful," Sam repeated.

"I will be. And my long-time family friend, Joe Traynor, is flying down from Troy, New York, to be with me, hopefully within the next few days."

"Thank you for your time, Julie," Mike said.

"Call us at any time, day or night, if you get any information whatsoever," Sam added. "In the meantime we'll be going over Tillie's car with a fine toothcomb and analyzing the paint scraped on the car from the hit and run driver. There are so many places the driver can hide in the Florida Keys, but we'll do everything we can to find out what happened." Sam gave Julie his personal cell phone number. "Tell Joe to call me when he gets in."

Now I guess all I can do is wait and pray. I should call Tillie's friends from St. Justin Martyr Church. I'm sure they will want to know as well. I hope they catch the son of a bitch who did this to Tillie. She never hurt a fly in all her years. No good deed goes unpunished, Julie mused. *Joe will be very pissed when he hears that this was no accident.*

Julie went down to the hospital cafeteria and got

some breakfast. The dinner they brought her last night was left untouched and cold. She couldn't eat. She was too upset. After breakfast she left the hospital, went home, and immediately called Jan, her fifth-grade teacher, in charge of the class in which she was a teacher's aide. She called her principal as well and told her she would be out for a few days until Tillie woke up.

The hit and run had flown through the Key Largo grapevine like wildfire. No one knew what was going on. No one saw a thing. It was lucky the deputies were going by only a few minutes after the crash or Tillie would now be lying in the morgue, and this would certainly be a long day.

She took a shower, packed an overnight bag in case she had to stay the night at the hospital, and went back to see Tillie. In the meantime, Joe called her and left a message while she was in the shower. He was on the 6:40 a.m. flight the next day, from Albany to Fort Lauderdale, arriving before noon. He would rent a car, stop and see Mark Silva, his best friend, at the Coast Guard facility in Fort Lauderdale, and then drive to their house to see Mark's wife, Louise, and the kids. It had been a while since he had been back in town. Joe would be at the Mariner Hospital before 4:00 p.m.

CHAPTER 3

After Joe got off the phone with Julie, he was also worried about Tillie's safety in the hospital. He told her that he would talk to the sheriff's department when he got there. He also asked, just to be safe, if Tillie had any friends that could at least stay with her in the hospital, until the situation was resolved.

He figured Julie would contact Father Schmidt, the pastor at St. Justin's, and ask him if they could supply volunteers to be with Tillie, at least until she woke up.

Joe had a lot to do before flying out the next morning.

He called his brother Pete. He was two years older than Joe, unmarried, and worked for their father in his contracting business.

"I'm leaving in the morning, very early," Joe told him.

"Do you need a ride to the airport?"

"No, Johnathon Mills will take me. I'll call regularly, not every day, but I'll let you know how things go in Key Largo."

"Good. And I'll do the same," Pete said. "Don't worry about anything here. I know what Tillie and Julie mean to you."

Since Joe was in the Coast Guard he had to contact his superior officer to let him know of this current situation. He was a special investigator assigned as a Coast Guard Special Agent for Investigative Services. He was then promoted to Warrant Officer.

Joe would be an officer in Islamorada with a special assignment. Due to his officer's status, he would stay at Tillie's house and fill in at the Islamorada facility as needed. This would free him up to help Julie settle everything she needed regarding Tillie's care. Next, Joe called Southwest Airlines and was able to get an early flight in the morning. He was also able to carry his weapon on board since he was part of Homeland Security and would be dressed in full uniform as a Warrant Officer, with his weapon fully secured.

After he packed and made a list of what he needed, he would call Mary Lynch, his girlfriend since last December, and let her know he was leaving for the Keys for an emergency. He hoped she would be okay with it. They had not been getting along especially well over the last few months. Work, her work, got in the way, so it seemed.

Joe booked a rental car at the Fort Lauderdale International Airport for only a week. If he had to stay longer he hoped he could get a government car for the duration of his stay. Maybe it would only take a week. Joe got a ride from Johnathon Mills to the Albany International Airport. He got there about an hour before the flight. He bypassed the line and went right to the Southwest gate for his flight. He introduced himself to the crew. They were expecting him. He had one suitcase and a carry-on. They put his luggage in the front, right next to the pilot and stewardesses' overnight bags. He sat in the front seat and closed his eyes. He' hadn't gotten much sleep last night, going to bed at 2:30 a.m. and getting up at 5:00 a.m. His conversation with Mary hadn't gone well and all the calls he had to make had his head spinning. At least he was on his way.

By the time he awoke, the plane was descending, right over the top of the Seminole Casino in Hollywood, Florida. He saw the large Hard Rock Café sign to the right. *Welcome to Fort Lauderdale.* He had made this journey quite a few times in the last thirteen years. While deplaning, he thanked the crew for their hospitality and headed toward the Hertz rental office in another section of the airport. His car rental paperwork was ready. He hopped on the shuttle bus for the short ride to the parking area and opened the door to his 2013 Ford Fusion. *Nice car*, he thought.

ɛ∕ɔɛ∕ɔ

Joe walked into the main entrance of the FBI head-quarters and met the guard at the door. He went through security and handed the guard his weapon before going through the scanning machine. Paul Philips met him at the door. Paul and Joe were friends from the old days.

"Hi, Paul, how are you?" Joe asked.

"Great, welcome back. Don't you look spiffy in your dress uniform? I never thought I would see the day."

Joe smiled.

"Come on up," Paul said. "Terry Owens is still here as the Florida Regional FBI Director and I'm still the Miami Director."

"Some things never change," Joe said. He followed Paul up the stairs and to the back toward Terry's office.

"Hi, Joe, welcome back," Terry said. "You look very handsome."

"Your making me blush, Terry," Joe quipped. "Great to see you."

"You, too. What brought you to sunny Florida? Got out before the cold hits up north?"

"I wish it was that simple," Joe said. "Do you remember the family that befriended me many years ago when I first got to Miami and then when I went down to Islamorada?"

"It's been a long time, Joe. Why don't you refresh our memories?"

"Well, after my mother died a few years ago from breast cancer, Tillie served the role of a second mother to me. And I became a big brother to her granddaughter, Julie. Now Tillie's been in an accident and I need to help…" Joe began, filling the other two men in. After about an hour, he said his goodbyes.

"If it is more than it appears to be, call us," Terry said. "And we'll be glad to help out in any way we can."

"Thanks, guys. I really appreciate it." Joe headed out the door to the parking lot, got into his car, and pulled back out onto the highway. He headed south to the end of I-95 to the Dixie Highway and took Route 1 all the way to Key Largo. He was about an hour and half away, and it was around 2:15 p.m. so he should make it to the hospital by 4:00 p.m., just as he'd promised.

CHAPTER 4

Joe arrived in Key Largo around 3:45 p.m. and had about ten miles to go to get to the Mariner Hospital in Tavernier, just south of Key Largo. The driving was fine. It was a straight line from Miami, but it was raining as usual in the Keys. The rain picked up and he had to be especially alert in stop-and-go traffic. Rear end accidents during rainstorms were a way of life in Florida. Traffic was backed up getting into Tavernier and he got in around 4:10 p.m.

Not bad, close enough.

He parked in the visitor's lot, went to the front desk, and asked for Tillie's room. She was on the special trauma care floor, which had limited visitors. He showed the young lady at the front desk his badge and she called up to the floor. Tillie was in room 505 and Julie had let the floor nurse know Joe would be arriving around 4:00 p.m. He got a special visitor's pass for the floor and headed toward the elevator.

Julie met him on the fifth floor just as the elevator opened. She gave him a big hug and kissed him on the cheek.

"Hi, Joe, how was the trip?" she asked.

"Non-eventful," he said. "The weather wasn't too

kind but it slowed me down and made me more conscious of my lack of driving skills."

For ten years, Joe really hadn't had to drive while in the Coast Guard. He went everywhere with others, and someone else usually had the keys. He didn't have a car all that time. He still had a New York driver's license so he was especially careful with Florida cops. "You forget about accidents until you start driving Route 1 south."

"Yeah. Let's go see Tillie," Julie said.

"How is she?" he asked.

"She's in an induced coma," Julie told him. "They will operate on her by the end of the week for her broken bones, but only if her heart rate remains normal and all of her vital signs are good. They said the fractures could be fixed without any internal surgery. There were no bones exposed. The fractures and breaks are not major—as if there is anything non-major about breaking your ankle and pelvis."

He laughed. "My father once told me, after a fall from a ladder and a broken wrist, that he would consider all surgery on himself, major surgery."

Julie smiled. "Welcome back, Joe."

They walked into room 505. Joe had not seen Tillie in quite some time. He thought she had aged quite a bit since Julie's graduation from Brown University in early May. *It's probably just the condition she's in.* Her face was covered with black and blue marks. There were tubes clinging to her arms and she looked like she was sleeping. Joe's father had looked exactly like this only a little while ago. John Traynor had been put into the same exact coma after being beaten by intruders in a home invasion. Joe certainly hoped they had good doctors in Tavernier just like at the Samaritan Hospital in Troy. If not, Jackson Memorial Hospital had a state of the art emergency trauma center. If needed, he could probably get a helicopter sent from Islamorada to Miami from the Coast Guard facility to take Tillie to Miami.

"Well, Tillie, how are you," Joe asked. He knew she was out of it but just maybe she would know he was there for her.

"Joe, do you expect her to answer you?" asked Julie.

"No. Wouldn't it be nice, though?" he said.

Julie smiled. "Your mouth to God's ear," She quipped. "Sam Parker and Mike Kenny will be by to say hello and let us know if they have found anything new. Joe, Sam told me this was no accident," she said. "He and Mike Kenny, the detective, told me at 7:00 a.m. this morning. You were already on your flight to Fort Lauderdale."

"Wow. Do they have any ideas why?" he asked.

"Not at this point. There was a large stripe of white paint that extended from the driver's side door to the front headlight," she said. "They were checking it out now. I don't know what the results were but we will find out hopefully when they arrive."

"Tillie didn't have an enemy in the world," Joe said. "Maybe it was an accidental hit and run."

"It was a hit and run, but it appears to be deliberate. She left the road at a high rate of speed. She never drove fast. You know that, Joe."

"Let's get something to eat. I'm starved," he said. "When can we see the doctor?"

"He said he would be in for rounds at 7:30 p.m."

It was now around 5:00 p.m. and they went down to the cafeteria for a quick dinner. Joe thought the hospital cafeteria food was actually very good or else he was so hungry, it just didn't matter. The prices were right at $3.95 for dinner, $2.75 for employees. It fell right into his current budget. Julie had a salad, moved it around her plate, picking at the tomatoes. Joe inhaled his dinner and went back for a cheeseburger for $1.50 with pickles and chips.

"Jeez, I didn't know you ate so much when you were under stress," she said.

"Stress? What stress? I'm hungry." Then he shrugged. "Okay, I guess I'm a little stressed," he said, coming clean. "She looks terrible."

"It's quite a shock, seeing her, isn't it?"

"Yes, it is," he agreed.

They sat there for a while. It was getting close to 6:00 p.m. as they awaited the arrival of Sam and Mike.

Joe hesitated. "Julie, perhaps this isn't the best time to bring this up, but we, more likely you, need to make some plans."

"I can barely make it through the day. I have to go to work or I'll get fired and then we will lose our health insurance. We still need to pay the bills."

"I know," he said. "But we still need a plan. Okay? Before they come, we have to think about a few things." He sighed. "Does Tillie have a will?"

"I don't know. I don't think so," Julie said.

"Do you have a will?"

"No."

"Do you have power of attorney for Tillie or vice versa?" he asked.

"No," she said.

"I don't mean to be crass, but we need to fix these things now if we can," he said. "As soon as she awakens, we need her signature on your documents and your signature on hers."

"Why?" Julie demanded.

"If she needs short term care or long term care,

someone has to sign her in if she is incapacitated at that time. When Tillie awakens, and then if she has a relapse, you could lose the house. You would have to sell it. If, God forbid, it's worse, and she does not have a will, you'll have to prove you are her only relative. If she dies intestate, it causes major complications."

"I guess you're right. Can you handle the paperwork in the meantime? You know I am not familiar with any of that."

"Yes, I just went through the same thing with my father and now that he's recovering, Pete and I are pleased everything is in place. Pete gets the house. I don't need it," he said. "He'll live there forever. I have the Coast Guard and my Rensselaer degrees as my inheritance. You have your Brown University degrees and your writing skills." He frowned and ran his hand through his hair. "This is about Tillie, not us. I'm sorry. I know I am preaching to the choir. I'll call Dan Simmons, my friend running the Coalition in Albany. He is a lawyer, a very good lawyer. If you want, he can draw up everything you need. I might add it's for free. He owes me. He can come up with two wills, leaving everything from Tillie to you, and everything from you to Tillie. He can draw up two separate powers of attorney for the same reason. If you want, I can serve for free as the executor of both estates so there will be no complication or claim of interference over either one. I can call him as soon as we get back to your house."

"Good," she said. "Do that."

"I still need to check in with Joan Talbot at the Coast Guard in Islamorada. I am now officially stationed there for a while," he said.

"Really?" she said, pleased.

Julie and Joe were sitting near the cafeteria door

when Sam and Mike walked in, almost on the dot of 6:00 p.m.

"Could you be a little more punctual?" Joe said, laughing.

"Hi, Joe," Sam said. "I would like you to meet Mike Kenny. He's the detective assigned to Tillie's case. He works out of the sheriff's sub-station in Islamorada."

"Nice to meet you, Mike," Joe said.

"Have you been promoted, Joe?" Sam asked.

"Yes, I am now a warrant officer, but it was a strange set of circumstances that brought me back into the Coast Guard," Joe said. "I had to re-enlist to work on a case in Albany, on a temporary basis, and was promoted, and was asked to continue to work with the FBI and Homeland Security on some special cases. I wasn't really full time and I still work for an educational consulting group in Troy, New York," he told Mike. "I was assigned to Islamorada and the Keys as a favor to help Julie and Tillie as best I can. The assignment is for two months at the most."

He paused and looked each man in the eyes. "Julie told me this was no accident, guys. Is this true?"

"It looks that way," Mike said.

"So what's going on?" Joe asked.

"The paint is still being examined and we will probably know something within the next few days. The work is being done out of the Key West headquarters."

"Do you think Tillie is safe here without a guard? What if whoever hit her came back and found her here in the hospital?"

Sam frowned. "I don't believe that would be the case," he said, and Mike nodded in agreement.

"I just want to be on the record that it was brought up," said Joe.

"We acknowledge your concern, but we don't have the manpower to cover her room, Joe," Mike said.

"I have full access to Coast Guard investigative services and the best technology in the world, if you need assistance," Joe informed them.

Mike more than Sam was a little reluctant to get help at this early stage. "We're on top of it and we won't let it go until we catch whoever did this to Tillie. We still have no idea why anyone *would* do this to her," he said. "We're going back to the Waffle House in the morning to talk to Phil and the staff to see if we can make any sense out of why she left in such a hurry and why she was so upset. We're also going back to talk to the regulars at the dinner hour to see if anyone saw anything. We're also checking up and down the street, to see if we can find anyone who saw anything at all. The main cameras on the entire stretch of road were in the bank parking lot and in the front and sides of the bank. We don't know what it shows at this point but we're looking everywhere."

"Sounds good," Joe said. "We're meeting with the doctor during his rounds and then we're headed to Julie's place. She has her own car. Julie, you should be home, right?"

"Yes," Julie said. "However I may go with you to see Joan. It's been a while and I want to see the kids as well." *Anything to break the hospital routine.* "We can pick my car up on the way back."

"Sounds like a plan," Joe said.

Julie and Joe said goodbye to Mike and Sam and headed up to Tillie's room to see the doctor.

"Please remind me to call Dan Simmons when we get back," he said.

"Will do," she promised.

Doctor Robinson was making his rounds as Julie and

Joe got off the elevator, walking toward Tillie's room. "I will be right with you, Julie, as soon as I stop into see another patient." A few minutes later Doctor Robinson, the neurosurgeon assigned to Mariner Hospital, walked into Tillie's room. "Hi, Julie, who's this?"

Julie introduced Joe, who was standing in his wilted warrant officer's uniform and starting to get a little more fragrant as time passed. He'd gotten dressed at 4:30 a.m. this morning for his flight out of Albany.

"Nice to meet you, doctor," Joe said.

"How's she doing?" Julie asked.

Doctor Robinson told Julie and Joe exactly what he'd already done and what was coming up to address all the issues caused by the crash. "When she got to the hospital, she was in and out of consciousness. When I arrived, less than a half an hour later, I scrubbed and went into surgery, immediately. I decided to keep Tillie in an induced coma at this point." He paused to gather his thoughts before continuing. "A person goes into a coma for a variety of reasons such as severe blood loss, epilepsy, shock, brain tumors, misuse of over-the-counter or prescription drugs, and inflammation of the brain from accidents, to name a few. In this case, it was the accident and a severe blow to the head. From what I heard the paramedics say, as the car rolled, she hit her head hard on the steering wheel."

Julie nodded. "Her 1990 Escort didn't have air bags and no one ever thought about it until now. She never drove very much and she could hardly afford to upgrade a car that performed rather well as far as she was concerned."

"I put Tillie into the coma in an effort to reduce brain swelling which allowed her brain to rest. The bones are easy to fix after the fact." Robinson paused for a breath.

"The immediate treatment is directed at maintaining Tillie's respiration and circulation. Intravenous fluids, as well as other supportive care, are needed to keep her healthy, hence all the tubes stuck in her arms to keep her hydrated and fed," he said. "Tillie is totally stable and out of immediate danger. Other considerations are addressed first, such as infections and pneumonia, and then her broken bones. Usually a coma does not last for more than a few weeks, but since this was induced, a week to ten days is probably all that will be needed to make sure the swelling subsides. Most people coming out of a coma, induced or not, can make a full recovery, but they may suffer from confusion, speech problems, and memory loss or partial paralysis until fully recovered."

With that explanation, it was clear Tillie would live. That was the most important thing to Julie and Joe. The quality of her life afterward would be up to them in helping her fully recover. Both felt the weight of the world, but mostly Julie. It was her grandmother, her flesh and blood, and the woman who'd raised her.

"Thank you, Doctor," Julie said. "We'll be back here early tomorrow morning.

Joe had to check in at Islamorada and see about getting his government car as well. He was a little compulsive about the car because in the service if you didn't ask, you didn't get. He was also compulsive about getting the rental car back within a few days or the cost would start to mount. He'd lived on such a small amount of money over the years that he was always on top of money issues. It was just the way he'd been raised.

They left in Joe's rented Ford Fusion and headed for Joan's living quarters at the Islamorada Coast Guard facility. Joe had called and asked if he and Julie could stop by around 9:00 p.m.

"Of course. Everyone, including my husband, Jeff, and the kids, Jeff Jr. and Lucy, will be here. Did you eat yet?" Joan asked.

"Yes, is the beer cold?"

CHAPTER 5

Joe and Julie pulled up to the Coast Guard housing units adjacent to the main facility. He'd forgotten to ask Joan where her new quarters were now that she'd had several promotions, amazingly all at Islamorada. Every time the command asked her to move to another location, she reminded them of her husband's importance to the facility and the marina housing the facility, her family's ties to the area, and that her age was getting close to fifty now. Instead, they moved several key functions to her instead of moving her to the functions. Her specialty was technology and operations and she could do it for the entire Florida Keys organization from anywhere.

Islamorada was almost half way down the Keys, so the location was perfect. In fact, the new radar infrastructure was moved to Islamorada to catch low-flying planes manned by drug runners who previously flew under five hundred feet and were never detected. The Coast Guard had difficulty with the old system picking up pilots who were aware of the limitations and flew around the radar detection system. Joan was in charge of keeping the technology state-of-the-art which manned the new radar system. With the new system, they had been quite successful in tracking low-flying planes and caught them as they landed. Before, it was a crapshoot and more illegal flights passed through than were ever caught. Now, the odds had changed.

After parking near the administration building, Joe and Julie went to the front gate, asked for Joan's quarters, and were shown the way to her front door.

"Hi, Joan, it's been a while," Joe said.

"Welcome back," she said, while giving him a big hug and a kiss. "Hi, Julie, how's Tillie?"

"She's holding her own for now," Julie said. "They medically induced a coma to keep her brain from swelling. They'll have another surgery by the end of the week to fix her ankle and pelvis. Her wrist appeared to be okay."

"Want a beer, Joe?" Jeff asked.

Joe smiled. "I thought you'd never ask."

"Yes, it's been almost one whole minute since you arrived. Some things never change," Jeff added.

"Hey, guys," Julie said, as she watched the kids come in to the room.

"Hi," said Lucy. "How are you doing? Are you coming back to school soon? Our cross-country meet is Saturday, you know."

Joan was mortified. "Lucy, for God's sake, give her a break."

Julie laughed. "Yes, Lucy, I will be there. I didn't recruit you to not see you run, you know."

Joan just shook her head at her daughter. *Kids,* she thought.

Julie told Joan what had happened and how it was no accident. As they spoke, Joan had Joe complete all his paperwork to be assigned to Islamorada. All the necessary documents were prepared and ready for him. She put it together, knowing he would need it to get a car assigned and a place to hang his hat so he could get paid. She had a schedule already prepared for him with days on and off so he could work around the schedule to help Julie and then Tillie, if and when she was able to come home. Joan was also prepared to keep Joe for any additional time they needed. She already assigned him several cases that were under investigation. In fact, she was short-handed and Joe would be a godsend to work with her and the chief warrant officer at the main facility in Islamorada.

Joe didn't know the chief warrant officer in charge but a meeting was set up for the next day to meet and greet. His friends at the Coast Guard, the FBI, and Homeland Security paved the wave for a smooth transition. Joe just wanted to ensure the man in charge at Islamorada that he was no threat to his job, even though they had about the same rank. He wanted to fully explain why he was there and what he could do to pull his weight, especially in the areas of intelligence, investigations, and Spanish language intercepts.

Joe and Julie stayed about an hour. They had to get home and Joe had to call Dan Simmons. They got home before 10:00 p.m. Joe dropped his bag off in Tillie's room, since the spare room, where he used to stay, was now Julie's office. He would sleep on the couch. Once Tillie got home, Joe would see about getting a room somewhere on the Coast Guard grounds if possible. He really didn't want to sleep on the couch for a long period of time.

He called Dan Simmons at home, but he wasn't there. Joe left a message that he would call him in the morning and told him what he needed. After the call, Joe hopped into the shower, said good night to Julie, and hit the couch. He had been up since 4:30 a.m. that morning and had traveled over 1,500 miles, while driving almost one hundred miles in the pouring rain. He was exhausted. He fell asleep as soon as his head hit the pillow.

∽∾∽

Joe woke up around 7:00 a.m. He had been dead to the world when he fell asleep and sleeping through the night made all the difference in the world. He was re-freshed and ready to go, but go where? He got up and made coffee. He wondered if Julie had stayed up all night. She was wired. She came into the kitchen just as the beeper on the coffee machine came on.

"Cream and two sugars, please," she said.

"Yes, madam," he said, teasing. "Was there anything else, madam?"

"A toasted bagel with butter would be nice," she said. "I'm going to take a shower."

"Yes, madam," he repeated with a chuckle. "It will be prepared when you return."

Joe called Dan at the Albany Coalition for Families. He knew he got in around 7:30 a.m. and wanted to catch him before his day got away from him. *Me too*, he thought.

"Hi, Dan, it's Joe."

"Got your message, two simple wills and two powers of attorney coming up."

"Mighty chipper this morning, Dan," Joe said.

"Well, it's all fun and games until somebody loses an eye."

"Quoting from *Christmas Story*, I see?"

"How are you, Joe? How're Julie and Tillie?"

Joe went on to tell him about the crash and how it

wasn't an accident. Dan was well aware about non-accidents—his father had just died in the spring under similar circumstances.

Joe said his goodbyes. "Dan will FedEx everything as soon as he can," he told Julie

"How is Dan?" she asked.

"He's good. Mary, my girlfriend who works with Dan, is not happy, however."

"Was she mad at you or mad at me?" Julie asked.

"I don't know. I suspect she's mad at me. Things have not been going smoothly because of her new job with Dan and my situation, but I'll talk to her again soon and see what was going on."

"I certainly liked talking to Mary better than Jennifer," Julie said. "Jennifer has hated me since I was ten years old."

"Are we going to discuss my girlfriends now, Julie?" he asked.

"Why not?" she said.

"Because I don't want to. Let's head out to the hospital," he said. "I also have to figure out how to get the rental car back to Fort Lauderdale. Maybe I can get a ride back with Mark."

His compulsiveness to check things off never ceased to amaze Julie. She grinned at him.

Joe chuckled. "I know. I can't help it. Oh, by the way, we need to find the deed to the house for Dan, as well and the original paid up mortgage. It will ensure that Tillie owns the house free and clear and there are no liens against the property. We may have to update a title search since it was 1971 when it was last done. We can go to the Key Largo Town Hall after we get the deed and make sure everything's in order."

After breakfast, Julie locked the doors and looked

around as usual. Then they headed out. As they drove into Key Largo, they stopped at the Waffle House and said
hello to Phil and the crew and let them know how Tillie
was doing. Julie had called the hospital earlier before
they left the house and found out that Tillie was stable
and still in the coma. On Friday, they were going to fix
her ankle and pelvis. She would be taken out of the induced coma no later than the following week.

Phil shook Joe's hand. "Mike Kenny came by and
asked about Tillie's abrupt departure before the accident," he said. "He wanted to know if anyone on the staff
had any ideas why she was so nervous and in a panic."

"Did anyone?" Julie asked.

Phil sighed. "No, not that I know of," he said. "Mike
came back for the dinner crowd and asked the same questions. A few saw her leave in a hurry but no one knew
why. Mike said he was checking to see if there were any
cameras in the area, and if anything was captured on video, up and down the road at the same time Tillie left. I
don't know the status of what he found. Perhaps you
should call him."

"That's a good idea," Julie said, pulling out her cell
phone. "Maybe he found something out. Mike said Tillie's car had some white paint scraped on the side and he
wanted to know if anyone saw any suspicious white vehicles in the area." She dialed Mike's number. "Hello,
Mike, it's Julie Chapman."

"Hi, Julie."

"Anything new?" she asked.

"We were working on two avenues without much to
go on right now. First, we were analyzing the paint to see
what kind of vehicle it came from, and second, we're
checking for video cameras up and down the main street
in Key Largo to see if there were any white vehicles in

the area around the time your grandmother left the Waffle House and headed south," he said. "She was there around 5:00 p.m. but we checked a half hour before up to 5:15 p.m. just to be sure. You never know what we might find." Mike said. "We knew the bank had several cameras and the gas station, a few doors down from the bank, had a couple aimed at the pumps and at the front door. I'll let you know."

"Thanks," Julie said and hung up.

She and Joe left and headed to the hospital. They stayed for a short while in Tillie's room at the hospital. Julie held Tillie's hand but knew there was nothing she could do but pray and hope for the best.

Joe stood by the bed, brushing Tillie's hair. *God, she has aged since I saw her last. I guess I've probably aged, too.* When he got shot in Albany in his last case, he thought it aged him a lot. They left the room, said goodbye to the duty nurse, and headed for Joe's meeting in Islamorada. They had time and Joe dropped Julie off at the house so she could have her own car if needed. It wasn't far, maybe twenty minutes at best.

e/ɔe/ɔ

Joe walked into the Islamorada station and met with Joan Talbot and Jacob Cramer, the chief warrant officer for the facility. Joe thought he was a nice guy and Jacob fully understood why he was there. There was a little apprehension on his part and Joe didn't blame him in the least. Jacob was a lifer and knew the score. He was accommodating, but not overly so. Joe got a basic olive green government car assigned to him for the duration.

At the meeting, Joe got a run down on all the cases under investigation, mostly those to which he had already been assigned. Jacob wanted Joe to be involved with those cases where his fluency in Spanish would be helpful. Joe was not just fluent, but knew all the idioms and nuances of the language.

He was given a tiny office toward the back of the administration wing. *It must have been a broom closet before becoming an office.* He had a computer, a Coast Guard encrypted password, and was ready to go. He would come in every day and work every afternoon until dinnertime. He'd visit Tillie in the morning while Julie went back to work at her school and helped out with the cross-country team. They would both go visit Tillie in the evening together. Julie would work on her book on the weekends since she already had a good start. Maybe she would only be a few weeks behind schedule after all. It all depended on Tillie waking up and the kind of care that would be required afterward.

ɞʚɞ

Joe got home for dinner at the end of the day. Just as he walked in the door, Mike Kenny called to let them know the paint chips analyzed by his investigative department in Key West came from a white 2002 Ford F-150 pickup truck.

"That's great news," said Julie.

"It is and it isn't," he said. "The good news is that we know what we are looking for now but the bad news is there are over 750 Model 2002 white F-150 pickup trucks registered in all of Florida," he said. "That's the most popular truck in America and white is the most popular color. I also checked online and 65% of the pickup trucks for sale in Florida are Ford F-150s with the next closest being a Dodge and a Toyota at 10% each. It's quite a challenge to look at every truck to see if there was any damage before the truck was fixed. We're also putting out a bulletin in all of the South Florida sheriff departments asking the officers to contact their local repair shops to see if they worked on any Ford pickup trucks, specifically the 2002 F-150. We will have to wait and see what happens."

"Well, thanks for the update, Mike," Julie said.

"We collected all the camera videos from around the Waffle House area to see what we could pick up. We have the gas station and the bank and an ATM right before you leave town, going south. We can't find any others. If you spot any let us know."

Julie hung up and told Joe what Mike had said. "Where does it leave us, Joe?" she asked.

"It doesn't give us much, but remember it hasn't been that long. It is still a small town and when the word gets out about Tillie, someone may remember something. Maybe they were unaware of what happened and when they find out, they may come forward."

Julie frowned. "Has anyone contacted the local paper and asked to put something in about the hit and run?"

"Let's ask Mike tomorrow. If not," Joe said, I can make an official request from my Coast Guard office. But right now, let's eat."

Over dinner, Joe gave her the rundown on his meeting with Jacob Cramer and Joan and he outlined his schedule for her. She was pleased they could take turns visiting Tillie, she could get back to work, and still have time to get the girls' cross-country team ready for the meet.

"By the way, Joe, I dumped a lot of stuff from downstairs into garbage bags. Do you think we could get one of those small dumpsters to leave by the side of the house? It would be easier and it would go more smoothly if we could. We can only leave out five bags a week at the curb for the garbage pickup. They are really cracking down here in the Keys about garbage and illegal dumping. It would take six months to get rid of everything at the rate of five bags a week."

"See if they'll take my Visa card," he said. "If not, we will have to wait until I get paid in two weeks. I'm running a little low, Julie."

She understood. "I know, it's just that getting rid of this junk and cleaning up takes my mind off of everything."

"I know. Ask tomorrow, and if they take Visa, have it delivered by Friday afternoon. We can put what you've already accumulated into the dumpster and take a look at the attic after your cross-country meet."

Just having a plan seemed to settle Julie. She smiled. Joe's compulsiveness had started to rub off on her. *Maybe it's not such a bad thing.* She had never been in the attic, not in her entire life, and was curious as to what they would find.

They ate and headed out to the hospital. Julie had spent the day cleaning the downstairs thoroughly. She was tired but felt a great sense of accomplishment. She didn't want Tillie coming home to a dirty house. During her cleaning time, she found the deed to the house. *Thank God.* She'd taken it to the town hall and reconfirmed that Tillie was the sole owner of the property. Evidently, upon her husband's death many years ago, the deed and the mortgage had both been transferred to Tillie, and then the mortgage was subsequently paid off. *At least this is a step in the right direction.*

CHAPTER 6

The FedEx package arrived at 8:00 a.m. the next morning. Julie signed for it, and opened it as Joe came into the living room.

"Good morning," he said. "Is this the package from Dan?"

"Yes, everything is here. Dan even has a cover letter outlining exactly what we have to do. There are color-coded Post-Its where my signature, Tillie's, and yours must be signed to make it official. All the signatures have to be notarized so when we get to the hospital we can ask if they have a notary available. If not, I can ask Marlene at the bank to notarize the documents for us. She will be glad to come to the hospital to get our signatures, including Tillie's. Remind me to call her and let her know what's going on."

"Sounds good," he said. "Let's get our schedules straight before we leave. You were going into school today, a little late, but I am sure they will be glad to see you. I'll take the rental to my office at the station." He paused to gather his thoughts. "I called my old partner Mark last night and he is all set for Sunday. I'll drive up, drop off the car, and get a ride back with Mark and his family. He wants to have a cookout, so I can pick up food for it before we go to see Tillie. Is she still getting her pelvis and ankle taken care of on Friday?"

"Yes as far as I know," she said. "They are doing it early, around 6:30 a.m. in the morning. By the time we get there, she will be in recovery."

They each said goodbye and left for the day. Joe went to visit Tillie before he headed to the Coast Guard station. Julie would be at school all day and then at cross-country practice later on. They would meet at 5:00 p.m. and then get dinner at the hospital. Julie said she would call Mike Kenny to see what the video cameras produced, if anything.

While she was at practice, Mike called Julie. "The bank cameras did not produce anything of value, but the gas station had a few pictures of a white truck, pulling out from the curb about one hundred feet from the pump," he said. "There are no direct pictures of anyone getting gas, but it's quite clearly a Ford F-150 and there was a man in the driver's seat. You couldn't see the man's face but, with the window open, it appeared that the man's arm was white. He did not look young or old. He was maybe in his late 30s or 40s. It's hard to tell. There were no pictures of a license plate from the gas station camera angles."

"Does it cut down the number of vehicles you have to look at?" Julie asked.

"I don't think it will cut it down a lot, especially since men owned ninety percent of the pickup trucks purchased in Florida. If the man was white, and we'd really have to look closer at the picture to make sure, then there's a chance to eliminate those non-white owners, but we have to compare the truck registrations to the picture IDs on the owner's Florida driver's license. It won't be easy. There are over 750 trucks in all of Florida identified as a 2002 Ford F-150. I'll start looking at registrations by county, Monroe County being first, and then on to Broward and Dade Counties, the closest counties to Key Largo."

"Thanks, Mike. I appreciate all your hard work." Julie hung up, called Joe on his cell phone, and conveyed the message.

"Hey, it's a start," Joe said. "Don't get discouraged. After less than a week, this is a good start, at least a beginning to the puzzle. If the driver's found, he will be arrested for hit and run and, at least, Tillie will be paid for her hospital bills left uncovered by insurance."

"Are you sure?"

"Absolutely. All automobile insurance policies issued in Florida offered uninsured motorist coverage, which allows policyholders or their survivors to recover damages due to injury or death caused by an uninsured motorist, that includes hit and run drivers. But uninsured motorist coverage does not cover damage to a vehicle. Her car won't be covered unless they locate the driver who hit her. The Escort was probably only worth about $500.00 but Tillie will have to spend five times that just to get a car equal to the Escort. A junker would cost at least $2,500.00 and you couldn't count on it running very well. Whatever we get for Tillie, we'll make sure Jeff Talbot takes a look at it before we buy it for her. Jeff will look around for her in the meantime."

It might be premature, preparing for Tillie driving again, but it was the only way Julie wanted to think about the future.

She wanted to have Tillie back to normal, maybe not working, but alive and well.

એજ્જ

The dumpster arrived early Friday afternoon. The company left a message for Julie, so she came right home from school. She had to pay them in person or they would not leave the bin. Joe's Visa card was accepted. She would miss practice today but it couldn't be helped. She needed to get this behind her so she could feel they had moved forward. The cross-country meet Saturday was early so Joe could put everything she had accumulated into the dumpster and then they could tackle the attic around noon when she got back.

Since Tillie was laid up for what appeared to be a long time, Julie wanted to clean the house thoroughly, before she came home. It had not been done in quite some time. Julie had been away and Tillie still worked full time. There really wasn't any free time. Julie thought this would be the perfect time to catch up on cleaning, it would keep her busy, and maybe stop her from worrying about Tillie and the future.

On one of their trips into town, Julie had purchased cleaning supplies including several pails, a new mop, glass cleaner, and tons of cheap paper towels from the dollar store. She needed large trash bags to get rid of junk accumulated over the years.

After tackling the first floor, the main part of the house, she and Joe would then head up to the attic to see what was there. She had never been in the attic but Tillie told her there was a bunch of stuff she stored from Julie's father and mother.

Julie's grandfather had some old fishing equipment and tackle boxes as well. Tillie had not been up there since before her husband George died.

There must be two inches of dust alone, Julie figured. She would open the attic windows and air it out before tackling any cleaning or junk removal.

e⁄ɔe⁄ɔ

Both Julie and Joe were at the hospital right after Tillie's operation. It went well. Her ankle was in a cast and her pelvis only had a slight fracture so there was little the doctor could do without causing more severe problems at her age. Rest and recovery was the best thing that could happen for Tillie. The burden was not on Tillie but on Julie to make sure Tillie would do what was necessary while at home recovering. It was not going to be an easy task. Tillie was very independent minded.

As soon as they heard everything went well, Joe went to Islamorada for a meeting and started a new investigation in the Keys. For the next few months, he would be involved in the Columbian end of the drug delivery system—or, rather, the beginning of it—which started in South America and wound up in the Florida Keys. Now, the Cubans were involved in drug running but it was the Russian mafia that moved up the ladder and took over the drug trade in South Florida, especially in the Florida Keys. Russian organized crime groups, flush with dollars, had formed alliances in the early 1990s with Colombian drug traffickers in the Caribbean. They acquired cocaine for delivery to Europe and the United States through Key West and provided weapons to Latin Americans. The Russians, operating out of Miami, New York, and Puerto Rico also opened up bank accounts and front companies across the Caribbean, largely used to launder hundreds of millions of dollars from drug sales and other criminal activities.

The original base for the Russians began many years ago in Cuba before the fall of the Soviet empire. The current Russian government might have cut ties with Cuba but the new emerging economy in Russia, developed by the Russian Mafia, had not. They had continued to supply both Fidel and his brother Raul Castro with cash that maintained their lifestyles while everyone else was left to starve.

Joe had at least five cases to work on and he would start by trying to understand what others could not. He would read the English and Spanish versions of the intercepted chatter and attempt to put two and two together. The Russian end would be a challenge but Joe was prepared to learn Russian as soon as possible to make life easier for everyone.

Julie went to school, knowing she had to leave early to pay for the dumpster around noon. Jan, the classroom teacher, told her not to come back because they had little to do that afternoon, and she could see Julie was stressed.

Julie spent the afternoon dragging out bags of accumulated treasures to hurl into the dumpster. She knew Tillie would be upset that she'd cleaned up without asking her for permission, but it was clear that if she didn't do it now, it would never happen. *Asking for forgiveness is easier than asking for permission,* Julie reminded herself as guilt churned her stomach.

Once again, she met Joe at the hospital, had dinner, saw Tillie, and made it home by 8:00 p.m. When Joe pulled up, he saw how much Julie accomplished once she got started. He was quite impressed.

Julie got up early Saturday morning and went to the cross-country meet that started at 8:00 a.m. She felt good, slept through the night for the first time in a week, and was completely refreshed. Since Tillie's surgery had gone so well, they would wake her up on Monday and then the fun would begin. *Will she be normal? Will she remember what happened?*

Joe reminded Julie that his father still had not remembered everything that happened to him during the home invasion in Troy.

"What home invasion?" she demanded.

"Oh, don't you remember? Or maybe I didn't tell you. Anyway, a short time ago, while Dad was at home alone, there was a break-in. They assaulted him and left him unconscious. Nothing was taken and Dad remembered nothing of the incident once he was awake and stable. They rushed him to Samaritan Hospital after someone reported the break-in. My brother, Pete, wasn't anywhere around. But he will be now. He has to be." Joe sighed and ran a hand through his hair. "I got the original call about Dad from Samaritan Hospital, at my apartment in downtown Troy, since I am the official contact person. Mary and I rushed to the hospital. It was touch and go for some time. It's been a long recovery but Dad's seemingly on the mend and getting better every day. Pete called yesterday and said Dad has just started remembering other things around that time and, hopefully, he will remember what happened. It's been little a while since the break-in."

"Oh, Joe. I'm so sorry. That must have been so hard for you and Pete."

"Yeah, it was hard on both of us. Pete stepped up and now runs the construction crew for Dad's construction business, something he was unprepared to do until this incident. Pete seems to have come into this role of protectorate and is overseeing three small jobs in the meantime. Pete, as the oldest, was always closer to Dad, especially since he never worked for anyone else since graduating from high school." At thirty-five going on thirty-six, Joe thought it was about time. "Pete seems to have the situation under control and he knows if anything else happens, I'll return immediately."

Family was family after all. Joe and his father didn't get along very well. Both of them were stubborn. It didn't mean that Joe didn't love him. It just meant they had to take each other in small doses. That was why Joe went away to MIT and then into the Coast Guard. He was raised to be independent. Evidently, Pete never got that lesson plan.

Julie called and asked Jimmy Smith if the cross-country team was ready.

"They're as ready as they can be. So get your rear in gear and get here."

She laughed. "I'm hustling as fast as I can."

They were competing against three other teams from the Keys and it looked like they had a good chance to do well in both the boys and girls events. Julie was counting on Lucy doing well this meet. She was new at cross-country but she had good potential. She came in tenth the first meet and seventh in the second. She'd improved her time greatly since then. Her running technique was better and she'd learned to pace herself better.

Joan was there, watching, and so were Jeff and Jeff Jr., so at least Lucy had encouragement from her family. Joan was closing in on fifty years old and was getting close to retirement. Her son, Jeff Jr. was a senior and he would graduate this spring from Coral Shores High School. Lucy was now sixteen and she was a sophomore at the same high school. Julie had recruited Lucy to the cross-country team after seeing her run across campus one day. It was hard to turn down your only babysitter, ever.

Lucy began to love running and began to excel. Julie went from being Lucy's babysitter at eleven years old to her cross-country coach at twenty-three, now just turned twenty-four.

It shocked Joan when her daughter came home and told her about it. She smiled. *Full circle,* she thought.

When Julie was running back in high school, as good a mother as Tillie had been to her, she had only gone to one of her events in four years. Tillie had to work and Julie understood. When Julie won her events way back then, she had to receive the trophies, standing alone all by herself. Lucy would never have a problem.

High school cross-country races were five kilometers, or 3.1 miles long. When Lucy first started running, she could barely run a mile without being totally winded. As she built up her stamina to meet the other girls' physical running capacity, her times began to improve. She was only sixteen and not out of shape, just not in running shape. And there was a vast difference between the two.

Daily team practices varied greatly in distance, depending on when meets were schedules, with lighter workouts the day before the event. Daily workouts were as much as three to four miles of warm-up, including hills, two to three miles of workout, and then a cool-down of maybe one mile. However, that was usually only for stronger runners. Lucy had to build up to compete on an equal level. She did, and then started to excel. Julie was really proud of her.

The meet started and would be over in less than a half an hour. Boys ran first and then the girls followed up a few minutes later. There would be an award ceremony at the end with patches handed out to the winners.

Julie would go to the hospital in her formal coach's track outfit and then back home before noon to help Joe.

ତଡେଡ

Julie pulled up and parked in the lot near the emergency room exit. At the same time, an ambulance raced in with its light flashing and the emergency siren going full blast. She stopped to see what was going on and, in a split second, Julie's whole life flashed in front of her eyes. She was back as a child, watching her mother die in the back of the ambulance. She stumbled on the curb, caught her balance, and then sat on the bench just outside the emergency room door.

Julie started thinking about Tillie and what she had meant to her over her lifetime. Tillie Carpenter was the strongest woman Julie had ever known. Tillie had always been her mother. She had raised her since Julie was eight years old. You would never even know she had grown up, had been away for five years of college up north at Brown University, and had just reached her twenty-fourth birthday. She was now back home in Key Largo, living with Tillie, just starting as a teacher's aide at her old school, Key Largo Elementary. Tillie still had to get used to Julie being an adult.

Julie got the job as a teacher's aide to supplement her income while she wrote her first novel *Conch Town Girl*, at home, in the Florida Keys she loved. Tillie was still "helping" her, just like when she was eight years old, making sure everything was okay before she left for her new job at the school. Julie laughed to herself, remembering her first day home after graduating from Brown University and getting this new job, telling Tillie, "Yes Tillie, I have my lunch. Yes Tillie, I'm leaving now. I promise I won't be late." *God, it's like I'm still back in fifth grade.*

Tillie was her grandmother, on her mother's side. She had always insisted on having Julie call her Tillie instead of Grandma because she was only forty years old when Julie was born. She couldn't possibly be a Grandmother at age forty. *I really do love her, but jeez.* Then

the memories came flooding back. Julie remembered everything that happened like it was yesterday…

℘℘℘

Julie's parents died very young. Her father, Tom
Chapman, was twenty-four when he was lost at sea. Her
mother, Annie, couldn't face life without him. She died
of a drug overdose two years later. They were married
right out of high school at eighteen. Both were native
Conch descendants, those raised in the Florida Keys for
generations. The original Salt-Water Conch people, the
natives, were originally British citizens who fled after the
War of Independence and settled in the Bahamas and
eventually migrated to the Florida Keys over the years.

Julie Chapman was a tenth generation Conch who
had come home to roost. So she thought. Tillie and Julie
had some rough times over the last fifteen years but Tillie
gave her a strong sense of pride, a strong character built
on a wonderful role model, and a will to succeed against
all the odds placed in front of her. From the pictures on
the wall, Julie looked just like her dad—blue eyes, light
brown hair, and a long lanky body. Julie was tall for a
woman at five feet, ten inches. She had a runner's phy-
sique so she appeared less imposing. Julie didn't remember her dad as well as her mom since he died when she
was only six. Her mom died when she was eight but Julie
saw her more and remembered her the most. Her dad was
away at sea most of the time and her mom, Tillie, and
Julie were the Three Musketeers most of the time. Julie
had taken her mother's death harder than her father's for
those very same reasons.

Julie had just finished her Masters of Fine Arts Degree from Brown University. After graduation from Coral

Shores High School, one of the highest rated schools in the nation, she received a full ride to study Literary Arts in the School of Humanities. For over forty years, Literary Arts at Brown University had been a creative and intellectual center for the United States literary avant-garde. Along with a handful of other writing programs nationwide, Brown provided a home for innovative writers of fiction, poetry, electronic writing, and mixed media. Upon graduation with an MFA after five long, around the clock, years, Julie came home to take care of Tillie, now in her early sixties—if it was possible.

Tillie was still a waitress at the Waffle House on Overseas Highway in Key Largo, the same job she had all these years. She had been cutting back now but she was still up at the crack of dawn for the breakfast crowd and was still dragging Julie out of bed after all these years. Julie really didn't know how Tillie did it, every day, day after day.

For her master's thesis at Brown, Julie was allowed to start her first nonfiction project, a book entitled *Conch Town Girl.* It wasn't much of a stretch. It was about Tillie and her, and about growing up poor in the Florida Keys. The research was all in her head. She'd had to go home and interviewed a ton of people, who knew her parents and Tillie, and get a sense of how she grew up—the way she and Tillie interacted in their daily lives and what they had to do to survive. Julie was fortunate because her first few chapters submitted to her advisor turned from a short story to a full book.

Her dean secured a stipend for her upon graduation to complete her novel. With the $75.00 a day as a teacher's aide, it almost paid the bills. Julie wanted Tillie to retire or at least work a hell of a lot less—it being Tillie's idea and all. If Julie eventually sold her book, she could then develop a writing career in a place she loved, with the people she loved, Joe included. She needed to remember to tell her readers about how Joe had affected her and Tillie's lives.

Julie's story, for her new book, started with her parents wedding. They had dated since they were fourteen years old as ninth graders in high school. They never thought about not being together. They planned to get married after high school graduation but that changed in the winter of their senior year. Her mother, Annie, got pregnant in January, not to the delight of everyone, especially Tillie. In those days this was not an acceptable situation.

The families kept it quiet and Julie's parents got married at St. Justin Martyr Catholic Church on Overseas Highway, just down the road from the Waffle House. Everything was just down the road from the Waffle House, the center of all activity in Key Largo, it seemed. Annie started to show in March but not enough to keep her out of school, which always ended in early May in the Keys, because of the heat. Julie was born in October of 1990 and baptized in the same church, St. Justin Martyr. They all lived with Tillie, especially since her father was always out to sea for days at a time. Tillie and Annie took turns taking care of Julie with Annie working the opposite shift from Tillie at the Waffle House, to make ends meet. Julie's grandfather, Tillie's husband, George, died many years ago, long before Julie was born. As a Conch, his parents named him after King George. He was the only one who could call Tillie "Matilda," her Christian name, and get away with it. That name died with him.

After a few years, they were all settled in at Tillie's cottage, Tillie, Mom, Dad, and Julie. It all changed when she was six. Her father was a fisherman on the boats out of the Keys, mainly down in Marathon, Florida. He kissed his family goodbye one early morning and never returned. He got caught in a storm. His two coworkers' bodies were found several days later on the shores of Big Pine Key. His body was never found. Her mother was so distraught, she fed her oxycodone addiction until she died, two years after Julie's father. Before Tom's death, Annie's only vice was having a few beers with him on the weekends. Times sure changed.

೭৲৩

How did you lose your father at age six and your mother at age eight? If it wasn't for Tillie and Julie's life-long friend, Joe Traynor, she didn't know how she would have ever made it. Back then, they looked for her father for months but the search was finally canceled. No funeral, only a prayer service at their church. Her mom's funeral was a different story. Close friends came, nobody else. No one mourned a drug addict except her own family.

Julie was too young to know what had happened. Tillie never explained the circumstances to her surrounding the deaths of Tom and Annie Chapman, not until she graduated from high school and was going 1,500 miles away, to Brown University. Then Tillie sat her down and explained to her all about her parents' deaths. It was not done to be morbid or cruel, but to let Julie know that Tillie would always be there for her, even if she were 1,500 miles away. This small step began Julie's journey as a writer, which developed into the *Conch Town Girl* novel she had now undertaken.

CHAPTER 7

Joe started cleaning what remained downstairs as soon as Julie left early Saturday morning. He had most of the junk accumulated by Julie the day before placed into the dumpster within two hours. He waited for Julie to do the attic with him because he was unsure what was up there and he wanted Julie to decide what she wanted to keep. Cleaning was no problem. Whatever she wanted was fine with him. He'd gotten boxes from the liquor store and he was ready to pack whatever she wanted to save. Joe was a minimalist. Julie was somewhere in the middle between he and Tillie. Tillie could have been on the new TV show *Hoarders*, not quite as bad but bad enough.

He had large trash bags and, after cleaning forty years' worth of accumulated dust, grime, and dirt this afternoon and loading up what was already done, they could place what was left by the attic stairs for easy moving to the dumpster. He was not looking forward to opening the attic drop down stairs and was sure Julie wasn't looking forward to it either.

He had a few minutes, so he ate breakfast and decided to call Dan and Mary, then his father, then Mark to confirm plans for Sunday, and finally Johnathon Mills at the Troy Education Consulting Group. It was one thing to say everything would be fine without him at the Troy group but it was another to mean it. He trusted Johnathon implicitly but Joe never believed absence made the heart grow fonder, just the opposite in fact. Out of sight, out of mind, he found, was more true than not. *Just ask Mary.*

Joe let the phone ring for what seemed to be infinity. Finally, Dan's answering machine picked up.

"Hi Dan, are you there?" Joe asked, instead of leaving a message. "Are you hung over or somehow incapacitated?"

Just before he hung up, Joe heard a "Hello."

"Did I wake you, Dan? I'm sorry."

"Sure you are, Joe. Did you get my package?"

"Yes, Julie got it and she found the deed and went to the Key Largo town hall. Tillie was the only one on the deed and the only registered owner."

"Great, it saves a lot of time, effort, and money. For now, you don't need to do a title search or get title insurance, not until, or if, she sold the place."

"That's good news," Joe said. "Julie and I are running out of money quicker than a sailor in port for a day."

Dan chuckled. "That bad?"

"Well, I just had to shell out for a dumpster, a car rental, and a ton of gas money but it was okay. We were cleaning out the house just to have something to do, which keeps Julie focused on her book and Tillie's recovery. They have been exceptionally kind to her at her school. She's at her cross-country meet this morning and will be back by noon so we can tackle the attic."

"If you need anything else, I have a friend in Miami who is a licensed Florida attorney and can be invaluable in filing your documents," Dan said. "Do you have a pen? I'll give you her name. Believe it or not, she went to Albany Law School and moved to Florida after graduation. Her fiancé, at the time, now her husband, was from Miami. He met her at Albany Med where he was an intern."

"Thanks, Dan, for all your help," Joe said, writing down the contact information. "By the way, before I call her again, how's Mary? Did you get a chance to talk to her this week?"

"I did. I have a feeling not everything is wonderful in Lotus Land, Joe."

"What did she say?" Joe asked.

"She didn't come right out and say it but I believe she was very upset that you left on such short notice and never really said goodbye to her."

"She never gave me the chance, Dan. She cut off my call and told me she was busy."

"I know," Dan said. "For what it's worth, Mary's fully involved with the Coalition, and it's good for me but bad for you. I think she thought she was handed the job as head of finance was because of you and no one considered her to be qualified, even though she was."

"We needed someone quick, Dan, just like we needed you to take over immediately. If it hadn't happened, and it wasn't approved by the FBI, then the Albany Coalition for Families would no longer have existed."

"You don't have to tell me, Joe. I am eternally grateful to you for what you did. When I say you would take a bullet for me and my family, I am not exaggerating." Dan sighed. "Mary's good at this job, Joe, but in the long run, I don't know if her personality will carry the day. She does not inspire people the way you did or even the way my father did. You know and I know, but I don't know if she could be convinced that her future success or downfall may be in her own hands."

"Thanks, Dan. I'll call her right now."

"I think she's at the office," Dan said.

Before calling Mary, Joe wanted to get it straight in his mind exactly what had transpired the day he left for Key Largo after receiving the call about Tillie's accident. Joe had been reluctant to tell Mary he was going away for a month or two due to Tillie's circumstances and his reassignment to Islamorada, possibly for the next few months. He remembered the circumstances of the call vividly because right before he called her, Southwest called back and assured him he would have a seat on the 6:35 a.m. flight from Albany, arriving at 9:50 a.m. in Fort Lauderdale. The airlines justifiably liked having protection for its flights and the seat was always free for qualified, screened individuals, especially those related to Homeland Security. Joe, being Joe, could then relax, knowing he would have plenty of time to see Mark and his family, stop at FBI headquarters in North Miami Beach, and still get to Key Largo by 4:00 p.m.

He remembered saying, "Hi Mary, I tried your apartment and left a message, so I thought I might catch you at the office."

"Hi, what's up?"

"Tillie had a bad accident down in Key Largo. Julie is now alone and I offered to go down there for a while to help."

"What happened?" she asked.

"Tillie was rushed to the hospital in critical condition and they had to induce a coma to stop her brain from swelling. It's touch and go at this point."

He also remembered the tenor of Mary's voice when she asked, "How long will you be gone, specifically."

"I don't know how long exactly, about two months. I hope it's no longer than that. I'll continue to be paid by the Coast Guard, and I asked for a temporary transfer to the Islamorada headquarters, which is only ten miles from Tillie's house. But as I said, the assignment is for no more than two months, maximum."

"Well, good luck to you."

"That's it, good luck?"

He remembered her saying, "What do you want me to say, Joe? That I'm happy about it? We don't see enough of each other as it is."

"That's probably both our faults."

Another sarcastic "probably" came out of the phone. At least that's the way Joe took it. "I'll call you when I get there."

"Sure, let me know how things are going. But I won't have much time to talk to you because the Albany Coalition for Families fiscal year end is coming up soon and our 'watchers' the auditors, are glaring down our necks."

"Well, say hello to Dan for me and tell him I'll call him from Key Largo."

They had exchanged icy goodbyes. *I remember not hearing the word love in there anywhere,* Joe thought. *If I don't get back quickly, I know our relationship will be in jeopardy.* When she'd hung up, he'd known Mary was not a happy camper. What did she expect of him? He remembered thinking it had gone pretty well, hadn't it? Not really. At the time he didn't think Key Largo, Tillie, or Julie were the problem. He was the problem for sure. He could not leave Julie and Tillie in this crisis, regardless of the outcome with Mary. It would resolve itself. He suspected how this conversation would go, but he owed it to her to call her once more.

Now being in the Keys for almost a week, he hoped Mary might just be thinking more kindly toward him, so he dialed her number and prayed for the best.

She picked up immediately. "Albany Coalition for Families, how may I direct your call?"

"Hi, Mary, it's Joe."

"I'm a little busy right now, Joe. I have to get our month end statements completed by noon for the board meeting."

"Listen Mary, if you don't want to talk to me, why don't you just say so? I've called you twice now and your unresponsiveness kind of tells me something. What's going on? Are you mad at me? What did I do to you? When I get back, I would like to know what I am coming home to. Will you be there, Mary?"

"I don't know."

"Do you want to talk about it?" he asked.

"Not now, maybe later," she responded,

"When is later?" he asked.

"When are you coming back?"

"I told you, I would be here no longer than sixty days. It's what my schedule is planned for and my current assignment," he said.

"How do I know this will happen?"

He had no idea how to answer her anymore. "What do you want from me, Mary? Do you want me to drop everything and come home while Tillie is still in critical condition? Is that what you want?"

"I don't want anything."

He was really getting mad and his Irish temper was boiling, but the little voice in his mind told him to slow down, to take a deep breath, and do nothing. *Do absolutely nothing. She will be there or not be there. It is her decision. I want to be with Mary but is this what I can expect every time there is an issue or an emergency? How can I work for Homeland Security, and be out of town for any length of time? Perhaps she needs to date an ac-*

countant, someone local who, like the old commercial, "*strives for middle management." Maybe then she'll be happy.*

"I have to go," he said. "The next phone call's yours, Mary. You have my number."

He politely hung up. *I think I see the bullet flying near my head, just like the real ones a while ago. The imaginary ones probably will hurt worse than the actual one that grazed my arm last spring,* he thought. He still felt the effects from that wound. Now this would be a new one he'd have to heal.

CHAPTER 8

Joe got back to cleaning. Julie would be home by noon. He almost forgot to call his dad, his brother Pete, and Johnathon Mills from the non-profit in Troy. He did so and spent the good part of an hour with the three on the phone. He had a good conversation with his father and his brother. It was the same with Johnathon Mills.

Johnathon was a man of his word. Joe didn't know why he didn't trust what Johnathon said. He guessed it was his own nature. Johnathon was a very good, honest, man. He wanted Joe back whenever he was available. They worked well together and, having the FBI in your building didn't hurt business. Johnathon, like Joe, was a man of few words, and his commitment to Joe was un-paralleled.

Julie got back around 11:00 a.m., earlier than they thought she would. She was all excited. The boys came in third out of four cross-country boys' teams. This was a rebuilding year for them with a lot of freshmen and soph-omores on the team with limited long distance running experience. The good runners were recruited by the foot-ball coach. He would slot them in as wide receivers or split ends because of their speed. These runners now played football in the fall but would be back for the spring track season. It was a good compromise, Julie thought. The girls came in second, which was a move up for them. Julie was really excited because Lucy came in second in a field of thirty girls, only thirty seconds behind the winner. She was also ten seconds ahead of the third place finisher, which was remarkable with the limited experience she'd had. Lucy had to really put it in gear to pass the third place finisher with two hundred yards left to go.

Jan was there. "You know, Julie, Lucy could be recruited early next year for the University of Miami cross-country team as a junior. Early commitment could take a lot of pressure off the family if she had a scholarship looking her in the face. The University of Miami is nationally ranked for women, but better yet, under Title Nine, they give full scholarships to young women on the team."

Jan had already made an inquiry at Miami to her old coach. He was retired now but he said he would come down, watch Lucy, and see what she really had. That was good enough for Jan and Julie. They had not told Lucy anything but Julie hinted as such to Joan. She feared Joan wouldn't keep a lid on it even though she promised. Time would tell.

☙❧☙

Joe and Julie grabbed a quick sandwich and started to pull down the hatch to the attic. There were fold-down stairs, which reached the floor when fully opened.

"Who wants to go first?" said Joe.

She laughed. "It should be my honor, Joe. My house, my problem."

There was a string near the top of the stairs that looked as if it was connected to a light socket. Julie pulled the string and miraculously the light went on. *A light bulb that lasted for forty years? Wow.* She looked around. The space was about the same as the first floor but it had a very low slanted roof and the beams were exposed, showing the nails which came through from the inside of the roof. There were piles of boxes near the center of the attic and not much toward the eaves because of the narrowness of the roof. There was less stuff than she'd expected, so that was good. Cleaning everything was another matter. There must have been at least an inch of dust lying on everything.

"Joe, can you hand me the vacuum cleaner. It might be easier to use the vacuum instead of raising all the dust by sweeping."

There was an outlet right next to the light switch above the opening to the attic so she plugged in the vacuum and cleaned near the stairs first. It must have been ninety-five degrees in the attic so they would have to work quickly with a lot of cooling off breaks in between. As soon as she cleared a dust free path, Joe came up and stooped next to her. His six-foot frame would not allow him to stand fully erect.

They cleaned off one box at a time and Joe started to bring the stuff downstairs so they could look at it more thoroughly in less heated conditions. After they removed the stuff, they thoroughly vacuumed, changing the bags several times. Thank God Tillie kept several vacuum bags on hand. Toward the end, all the bags were filled with dust so they finished sweeping out the entire attic floor. It looked good and it was another triumph and accomplishment. They measured triumphs in small doses.

They took a break and Joe opened a beer for each of

them. They sat there in the hallway and looked at thirty boxes of accumulated treasures from years ago. What they needed to do was go through all the boxes, keep mementos for both Julie and Tillie, and discard junk, clothes, and ratty equipment left for years.

They immediately dumped old fans and an old air conditioner. It looked as if Thomas Edison had invented it. There was a bicycle tire and a tire to car that probably no longer existed. Joe handed Julie the first box. She dusted off pictures and put them aside on the living room couch, formally known as Joe's bed.

They wanted to sort out the stuff so that when Tillie came home, she would be more pleased than irritated at what they'd done. About half way down the first section of boxes was a bunch of old clothes that either belonged to her grandfather George or maybe even her own father, Tom. The clothes looked like something from the early nineties not the 1950s, which would be the case with George's clothes.

She looked at the shirts and pants and folded the clothes neatly. She wanted to keep a few things so she could remember her family.

Under the shirts appeared to be a gym bag, it looked in very good shape and almost brand new or at least never used. Julie picked up the bag. It was heavy, not bowling ball heavy, but heavier than clothes.

She opened up the bag and looked inside. "Joe, can you come here a minute?"

"What's up?" he asked.

"Look in the bag," she said.

He opened up the gym bag sideways to get a better look inside, and his eyes widened. "What the hell's this, Julie?"

He turned the bag upside down and shook it. Packs

of plastic-wrapped stacks of hundred dollar bills flew out of the bag. He counted thirty wrapped bricks of hundreds.

"Oh my God, Oh my God," Julie cried. "What's this? Where did it come from? Oh my God, Joe. Oh my God!"

Joe looked dumfounded. "Has anyone been in your attic?"

"Joe, I've never been in the attic in my entire life, and I don't believe Tillie has either, not in a long time at least."

"Do you think she knew the money was here in the attic?" he asked.

"I certainly don't believe so," she said. "If it was stolen, Tillie would never have anything to do with it. If it was her money from George, I don't think we would have lived the way we did, as poor as we did, all this time. I don't think Tillie would be a waitress for close to fifty years if we didn't need the money."

"I believe that as well," Joe said. "If it were Tillie's, it would have been in the bank at least."

As Joe looked at the plastic wrapped bricks, he started to open one up then hesitated. "Julie, before I open these, get me a pair of your cleaning gloves and two gallon size Ziploc bags please. We might want to get someone to look at this money before we do anything. I don't think it's a good idea to leave it in the house now that we've found it. Do you?"

"I don't think so, but what would you suggest?"

"I think we should put it all in a double wrapped garbage bag and find a safe deposit box to put it in. I don't think it's safe to leave it here."

After Julie brought him the gloves, Joe cut open one brick and counted it. It had $10,000.00 in one hundred dollar bills—one hundred individual bills. As he looked at each of the thirty packages, all wrapped in plastic, he noticed each had a strap that looked like a bank strap but it didn't look like the strap was in English. It looked like a symbol that had a circle with almost a type of an A in the middle of it. It looked like a cursive A but the left side was thin and the right side of the A was much thicker. Joe drew what he thought the symbol looked like and showed it to Julie. She agreed.

He placed the one brick of hundreds—with the strap wrapped over it and around, glued at the back—into the double wrapped Ziploc bag, and then took the other twenty-nine bricks and put those into a double wrapped black garbage bag.

Julie looked at the clock. It was almost 12:30 p.m. Banks closed at 2:00 p.m. in town, and Joe didn't want to raise the alarm by going to her bank in Key Largo. He had opened an account to deposit his paycheck so he could also open a safe deposit box in Islamorada, at a bank about a block from his Coast Guard complex. If he—or they—needed quick access, they would not have a problem. Joe called his bank immediately and asked the manager if they had any boxes available. All they had were two regular size boxes. The larger ones had been taken for years. Joe asked him to get the paperwork ready for joint ownership and he would take both boxes. They would be there within a half an hour.

They left everything on the floor, jumped into the car, and headed out to the bank. Joe turned to Julie who was driving. "You know, there was $300,000.00 in one-hundred dollar bills."

"I know," she said. "I have no idea what's going on, but you're right. Having it locked up in a bank vault, regardless of who owns it, was a really good idea for now."

"Whose money do you think it is?" said Joe.

"My grandfather had only the house and died very young. You see the way we lived and you know what happened to my mother. If it was Annie's money, then she would have blown it all on drugs after my father died, and she would have died even sooner. It can't be Tillie's. It just can't."

"So it had to come from your father, but when?" he asked. "It had to be in the attic for at least the last seventeen years. Didn't he die when he was twenty-four and you were only six years old? That was at least seventeen years ago." He thought for a moment. "Well, we can figure it out, but let's get it in the bank first. I want to show Mark the money, quietly, tomorrow afternoon when he comes down with the family for the cookout. We better be careful in any case."

"I don't care whose money it was," Julie said. "I don't want it if it was illegally gained, or if it isn't Tillie's."

They would discuss that later on, when Tillie came out of her induced coma.

They got to the Islamorada bank by 1:35 p.m. in plenty of time to fill out the joint paperwork and learn how to use the boxes. Joe simply told the bank manager that Julie's grandmother gave her some items for safe keeping and she wanted to make sure they were, in fact, safe. Julie told him that Tillie was in the hospital but didn't tell him why.

Everything went smoothly. They brought both boxes out to a secured, locked room. The vault clerk told them to take their time and knock on the door when they were through. They wanted to ensure their privacy. No one knew what would be in the boxes, other than the owners.

Julie and Joe emptied the double, black garbage bag, dumping the contents onto the desk. They barely fit all twenty-nine bricks into the two boxes, leaving little room for Tillie's deed and the paid-up mortgage documents, which Julie remembered to bring as well. They knocked on the door, went back into the vault, and, with the clerk present, locked their portion of both boxes. Then the vault attendant did the same. They thanked her for her patience and left the bank.

They sat in the car for ten minutes, neither one speaking.

Finally, Julie started the car. "Let's go home."

"Sounds good," he said.

CHAPTER 9

They arrived back at the house before 3:00 p.m. Sitting on the couch, facing Joe in the chair, Julie sighed. "What does this all mean, Joe?"

Joe looked at the bills through the plastic. He noticed the top one hundred dollar bill was dated 1995. "Julie, this has to be from your father. The top bill is dated 1995. Your grandfather was long deceased before then. I really don't believe your grandmother had anything to do with it, and you're probably right, your mother couldn't accumulate that much. If she did, she'd probably have died from drugs even earlier," he said. "So, what was your father doing in 1996, when you were six years old?"

"That's a very good question, Joe," she replied.

"Not to disparage him, but there were a lot of so called 'fishermen' in the Florida Keys who didn't make enough money fishing to support their families, or even themselves," Joe said. "This is a lot of money, and it could not have been from a few small runs, meeting boats, and bringing back small amounts of dope. Besides, wouldn't he have only had a small amount of money, a few thousand or so, if he were paid for a few small shipments?" He shook his head. "In my experience from being in the Intelligence Division of the Coast Guard, this seems to imply he delivered a far greater amount of cash for coke or vice versa, probably in the millions of dollars, unless he'd just started. You know, looking at the cash strap on the bills, it certainly appears to be a foreign symbol, not English. It obviously stands for something and each pack has the same symbol. I checked all thirty blocks of cash before we went to the bank. I'll bet it stood for $10,000.00 in some foreign language. The script almost looked like Eastern European or something. It is definitely not any form of Spanish that I know of, so it probably didn't originate from Columbia, or if it did, there's a lot more to it." He stood. "You have a scanner, right?"

"Yes, I do, why?" she asked.

"Let's trace an exact replica of the symbol on a sheet of paper and then scan the drawing into your computer. We can go to specific money-search sites and then find the right words to ask if this symbol means $10,000.00 in any language."

Julie started up her computer, scanned in the drawing, and it popped up on her screen. She saved it as a PDF document. From there, they went to a search site and asked the question. What came back was both quick and amazingly accurate. The screen showed a website for Russian monetary symbols. The language was Cyrillic. She then typed in *Define Cyrillic* and it stated: *Of, relating to, or constituting an alphabet used for writing Old Church Slavic and for Russian and a number of other languages of Eastern Europe and Asia.*

Julie turned to Joe. "It looks like my father had something to do with the Russians."

They both sat back for a minute.

"When were the Russians in the Florida Keys? I know they took over the drug trade in Miami from the

Cubans but this would have meant they were probably here in the Keys back in the early 1990s. The money was clearly printed in the 1990s. Let's look at the rest of the bills in that stack we kept."

He put the rubber gloves back on and fanned the money. There were dates ranging from 1986 through 1995.

"In 1986, your father would have been only sixteen. It's unlikely he would' have been involved in anything illegal then, but you said when you were six he was gone for long periods of time and when he was home, he was never really home. Didn't you say that?" he asked.

"Yes, as I remember, he wasn't home a lot, and there were a lot of fights between my mother and Tillie. He also never bought a thing for us and relied on Tillie for everything. To think he had $300,000.00 all this time, the bastard."

"You might be getting ahead of yourself, Julie. We're not sure who owned the money, or how it got here. It's best if we wait until Tillie wakes up and, hopefully, she can tell us something, anything, that will help. I feel better knowing the money is in the safe deposit box in the bank."

"I feel less safe about this $10,000.00," she told him.

"We don't even know if the money is marked. If it is, and we needed to spend some for Tillie's sake, it could be even worse. We better not touch it except to have Mark or Jack trace the serial numbers through our sources."

They left around 5:00 p.m. and went to dinner at a nearby restaurant on the way to the Hospital. Joe was dying for ribs. He told Julie about his conversation with Dan and then about his being pissed at Mary.

"Unless she calls me this time, I'm not calling her back. Tag, she's it," he said.

"Do you love her, Joe?" Julie asked.

"I thought I did, but you know me, head over heels. How many times did you have to tell me about Jennifer Alvarez being jealous of a ten year old before I caught on?" he replied.

"I thought that was a whole different ball of wax," Julie said. "I thought then you were enamored about being in love with a Cuban girl. Mark had indoctrinated you to such a point, I didn't understand a word you said half the time. Seriously, you stepped back and realized what you'd become, and you didn't like it. That's why you got out of the Coast Guard. Now, you're older, and hopefully wiser," she said with a smile, "and you are now back in the Coast Guard for the right reasons." She shrugged. "Yes, Jennifer was beautiful but your temperaments never matched. I thought it was just an accident waiting to happen. But Mary seemed to be a different story. You just got out of a terrible relationship and you fell for Mary at first glance. It took you six months to build up the courage to ask her out. What was that about, anyway?" she asked. "Did you think you would get back together with Jennifer? Huh?"

Joe smiled at Julie's directness. God, she had him nailed and he knew it. "Now that you have me all figured out, perhaps you can tell me all about *your* love life, so we're on an even par," he stated with a grin.

She smiled back. "Well, since you have almost ten years on me—nine and a half to be exact, but who's counting, and since you are so much more experienced— I really don't have much to tell you," she said. "Do you want to know when and where and with whom I lost my virginity? Yes, the proper term is 'whom' in case you're interested. Would you like to start there? Or would you like to know about all the wild times at Brown University? You know, Brown was the number one party school of all the IVY's and probably in all of New England. Only freaks go there, *moi* included."

"I think I better let this topic go for now," he said. "No, I don't want to know about your love life, I just wanted to know if you are seeing anyone now. If you were and if it was serious, perhaps you should let him in on this ongoing saga. That's all," he said.

"Point taken," she said. "Are you sure, Joe?"

He seemed a little flustered with the statement and said nothing.

☙☙☙

After dinner, they went to see Doctor Robinson who said he would take Tillie out of her medically induced coma on Monday. It had been an entire week now and he thought it would be enough. All her vital signs were favorable.

Julie wanted to stop and see Lucy and congratulate her on her performance. It was around 7:00 p.m. so they headed over to Islamorada and then they would go back home from there.

"Hi, Joan, sorry to stop in like this, but is Lucy in?" she asked.

"Of course, it's pizza night and she's in stuffing her face in front of MTV. Lucy, Ms. Chapman, your coach, is here to see you," Joan shouted.

Julie laughed. "Ms. Chapman, how formal, Joan."

Joan grinned. "Want some pizza? There might be a half of a slice left."

"No, we ate regular food at a real restaurant tonight, not McDonald's for a change."

Lucy walked into the room. "Hi, Julie. Hi, Joe."

Julie hugged her. "Lucy, you were great today and I just wanted to stop by and let you know. If you keep up the good work, you can name your own ticket later on if you want. College isn't cheap, even with a scholarship, trust me, I know."

"Didn't you get a full ride to Brown?" Lucy asked politely.

"Even with a scholarship I was $3,000.00 a year short to pay for clothes, a car later on for grad school, plane tickets, and personal items. Those things are not covered, Lucy."

"Oh, I didn't know, sorry."

"No problem, just remember what I said, you could go a long way."

Joan's husband wandered into the room.

"Hi, Jeff," Julie said. "How are you and little Jeff, who's not so little anymore?"

"Good, everything is fine, the marina is fine. They keep trying to move Joan up and down the coast, but if she can stay two more years at least, she can retire, and then help me at the marina. Then everything will be better. Want a beer, Joe?" he asked.

"I thought you would never ask," as the running joke went.

The running reply was that it was under one minute from entry to beer. Joe had his beer. Joan and Julie caught up on what had happened to date—everything except the $290,000.00 tucked into the safe deposit box and the banded $10,000.00 in the glove compartment of Joe's car—but that would wait for another time.

On the way home, Joe and Julie stopped at the grocery store to get steaks, salads, and dessert for tomorrow's cookout. Julie looked forward to seeing Mark, Louise, and the kids.

ↄↄ℮ↄ

It was early Sunday morning and Joe had reluctantly promised Julie he would go to the 9:00 a.m. mass at St. Justin's with her before heading up to Fort Lauderdale. Joe was a "CE," Catholic-speak for those Catholics who only attended mass on Christmas and Easter. There were more and more Catholics doing just that after all the Church's trials and tribulations in recent years. Joe had gone more regularly before his mother died of cancer, but less often afterward. He didn't see the point as much as before. His father and brother felt the same. Joe had recently read that the largest religion, based on sheer numbers, in the United States, was Roman Catholic and the second largest was non-practicing Roman Catholics. Joe could certainly believe it.

He and Julie decided to get breakfast at the Waffle House first and pulled in before 8:00 a.m. They said their hellos, caught up with the staff and friends, and headed out to church, making it right before mass began at 9:00 a.m. on the dot.

Julie felt bad she didn't really inform her pastor about what was going on. But he was more Tillie's pastor than hers, anyway. As soon as mass ended, Joe headed out with his rental car and Julie stayed to say hello to her priest, Father Schmidt. He was the longest running priest St. Justin's ever had, twenty-five years, in fact. He had baptized Julie and was there for her confirmation as well. Julie didn't even remember who her godparents were. Tillie was her confirmation sponsor. Julie took Ann, for Saint Ann, as her confirmation name, after Mary's mother, the mother of Jesus, and her own mother, Annie. Julie wanted to start going back to church on a more regular basis once everything settled down, if it was to be. Also, the church sponsored home visits by church volunteers. She needed to involve Father Schmidt with regard to Tillie.

It would be nice, if Tillie was laid up at home and not in some facility, to have her friends and fellow church members call on her from time to time to relieve the loneliness and boredom was sure to happen, knowing Tillie.

"Hi, Father Schmidt, how are you?" Julie said.

"I'm fine. How's Tillie?" he asked.

She went on to apologize to him for not keeping him informed but since Tillie would not be out of the coma yet, hopefully on Monday, there was little reason to visit.

"Let me be the judge of that," Father Schmidt said. "She is being mentioned at every mass in the prayers for the sick. As soon as she's awake, I'll bring her communion, if she's ready, and I'll visit her every day until she's well. Julie, that's the least we can do as a parish for Tillie. She means a lot to us and I don't know if you will ever know what she has done for us quietly and without fanfare. She's always in our prayers."

"Thanks, Father," she said. "That means a lot to me and Tillie. By the way, Father, I really don't want to ask you for help but Tillie's accident was no accident. She was deliberately run off the road. We asked the 'sheriff's department for a guard for her room, just in case whoever hit her tries to see her at the hospital for any reason. They do not have the manpower to cover her 24/7 they said. The security staff said they would cover her room on a regular basis, which they are doing, but I'm not so sure it's enough until we really know what happened. Is there any way we could get volunteers from church to sit with her in her room, at least until she regains consciousness?"

"It's why we are here, Julie," Father Schmidt said. "I promise you that within two hours, Tillie's room will have at least two people at all times watching her until she wakes up. They will have cell phones programmed to the hospital security office and 911 if they see anything suspicious."

"Thank you, Father, that's quite a relief," Julie said.

She left for the hospital and then would go home to get dinner ready. They would eat, go to the beach, come back for dessert, and make a full day of it. *How much dessert can I buy with $300,000.00*, she thought, shaking her head.

cɔcɔ

Joe made it to the Hertz rental office, right outside the Fort Lauderdale International Airport. Mark waited for him right at the entrance where he checked in his car would have his final inspection papers stamped so everything was good to go. Joe saved one day's rental, which would be credited back to his VISA account. It wasn't much, but it paid for gas and a case of beer on the way back. *I forgot to pick up beer. Can you imagine the crap I'll have to take from Mark?* He'd tell Mark he wanted to wait to get his favorite, Joe decided, which was bullshit. Mark would know but since he was getting the beer anyway, he wouldn't call him on it.

Mark had wanted to at least make a day of it. His wife, Louise, was off from the Hard Rock and the kids wanted to come down to Key Largo. They had never been there before and they looked forward to it. Joe would buy some steaks, hot dogs and hamburgers, and they would have a cookout after bringing the kids to the beach. At least it would take his and Julie's mind off the situation.

Mark had been Joe's partner in the Coast Guard for a

full decade. He was a former gangbanger, growing up in San Diego, and had to join the service to stay out of jail. He turned his life around while in the Coast Guard, married, had two children, and worked with Joe during his entire stay in the Coast Guard. It looked like they would be reunited once again during Joe's assignment over the next few months in the Florida Keys. What Joe had learned from Mark was never taught in any classroom. He could pick a door lock in under one minute, thanks to Mark.

"Hey, Joe," Mark said as Joe hopped in the passenger side, papers in hand, good to go. "Louise and the kids are ready to go, we just have to pick them up and head out." He hesitated. "Okay, what's going on? I haven't spoken to you in two days."

"What would you say if I told you we found $300,000.00 in cash in the attic yesterday, all in bricks of one hundred dollar bills?" Joe said.

"*What*? Are you kidding me?"

"I wish I was." Joe sighed. "I need to talk to you when the kids go to the beach. I believe Julie's father was a drug runner for the Russians. The money had a band wrapped around each brick with a symbol in Cyrillic. We looked it up. It is the symbol for $10,000.00 in Russian, or Cyrillic, if you will. Let's not mention it to Louise, please. Not yet."

"Okay. Do you think this is tied into Tillie's hit and run?" Mark asked.

"I don't know. I don't see how, but you never know," Joe said. "We need to discuss how to proceed. I'm not ready to tell the sheriff's department anything yet, but I don't want Tillie or Julie in jeopardy either. I'm armed and ready. They are not. I have not told them of the connection, not yet. I am sure Julie will catch on quickly. She's a quick study, you know."

Mark grimaced. "I know."

Mark and Joe picked up Louise and the kids. Joe had missed them, especially his only goddaughter, Jennifer. Yes, Jennifer. That name reared its ugly head, once again. She was named after Mark's sister Jennifer from California, not Jennifer Alvarez, Joe's ex-girlfriend.

But does it really matter? It's one hell of a coincidence and a constant reminder from Mark as he so politely pointed out. It's a really good thing we are so close.

Joe hit the beverage mart on the way, picking up the most expensive case of beer in the place.

Mark chuckled. "This will hardly put a dent in Julie's $300,000.00 inheritance."

Smart-ass, Joe thought with a smile.

The cookout went great. Louise and Julie took the kids to the beach while Joe and Mark stayed back for another beer and talked. Julie knew why. And Louise suspected something.

The men said they would meet them in a half hour after they finished. Joe showed Mark the package of $10,000.00 with the Cyrillic band around it.

"We moved the money to a safe deposit box near the Coast Guard facility in case there was a problem," Joe told him. "I'll ask Dan about the statute of limitations on the money, finder's fees, and if they have any personal issues about holding the money. Neither Julie nor I believe Tillie was involved."

Mark nodded. "I don't believe Tillie's involved, either."

"Julie doesn't want anything to do with it if it was tainted," Joe said.

Mark smiled. "I'll take all the tainted money and feel

bad for about ten seconds with thoughts of college for the kids looming in a few years."

"I feel the same about expectations for Tillie's care if needed. Hopefully not, but you never know what the future holds."

"Ninety percent of the one hundred dollar bills floating around in circulation within the United States show traces of cocaine," Mark informed him.

Joe nodded. "I also want to see if I can pull up any fingerprints on the bills. I doubt that Julie's father was ever fingerprinted being that he was only twenty-four when he died and didn't work for any business or government agency, nor was he ever arrested that I know of. Julie didn't seem to think so and I can't ask Tillie in her current state. The only other thing is if there are any fingerprints on the packages or on the bills, and if those fingerprints are on file, they could possibly prove the money came from the Russian mafia, which, as you know, is now fully established in Florida and the Keys. The problem is I have to figure out how to get the fingerprinting done without raising any questions from the authorities, including the Coast Guard, the sheriff's department, or the FBI." He would try to keep it quiet for now, and he would do it on his own, maybe with Mark and Jack Forest's help. "Mark, it looks like I'm going to need your help and Jack's as well if we are going to solve this."

"No problem, Joe. You know we will be there for you," Mark said. "Jack, too."

Julie took Louise and the kids, MJ and Jen, to Cannon Beach, only a short drive from her house. In fact, every beach was a short drive from her house, but this was one of her favorites growing up. She remembered her mother, father, and Tillie bringing her there. These were only some of the few good memories she had of growing up. Cannon Beach was named for the seventeenth-century cannons both on and offshore. It was a prime destination for scuba and snorkeling enthusiasts. Julie loved it because you could just walk out a little ways into the water to see tropical fish and sponges, or swim out one hundred feet to view the remnants of a Spanish shipwreck.

Her father used to take her out in his boat a little farther for a closer look at the living reef and its inhabitants. It was all part of the John Pennekamp Coral Reef Park, the nation's first protected marine area.

"This is so beautiful, Julie," Louise said. "I can see why you came back here to write your book,"

"It was for Tillie too, Louise, you know?" Julie said.

"I know. I know what my family means to me and I know what Tillie means to you. She's your only family, right?"

"You got that right, Louise."

"Other than Joe, of course," Louise mentioned.

"Other than Joe."

"Is he still going with Mary Lynch, up north?" Louise asked.

"Funny you should ask," Julie said. "I think they just broke up, only days ago, but I'm not sure. Joe is so tight-lipped about it. He wasn't happy, that's for sure."

"How long have you known Joe?" Louise asked.

"Since I was ten and he was nineteen. What's that, almost fourteen years? Fourteen long years, I would say."

"Longer than most romantic relationships."

"Louise, can I ask you a question?"

"Sure," she said.

"How many years apart in age are you and Mark?"

"Eight years," Louise said. "I met Mark when I was twenty-one and he was twenty-nine, and we were married at twenty-two and thirty. We had Jennifer a year later and then came MJ a little while after."

"Has the age difference meant anything to you?"

Louise shook her head. "No, it was the cultural difference at first. I am half Cuban, half English, on my father's side. My father was straight off the boat from England. I'll tell you about their whirlwind romance sometime. Mark was Mexican from San Diego. I fell in love with him when I met him at the bar at the Hard Rock Café. It's near where I grew up in Fort Lauderdale, right down the street from where we now live. I'd just started working there when he and his Coast Guard buddies showed up. I guess I am a sucker for a uniform," she said. "We were married the following year. Are you thinking about Joe?"

"Julie blushed. "Yes."

"Does he even know you love him?"

"No, I kind of kept it hidden. I teased him about his love life just yesterday and then he surprisingly asked me about mine. I was very blunt. He gave me a bullshit reason, and I called him on it but he never answered me. I can hear him now, if I mention your age difference. He would say something stupid like, I met you at Career Day while you were in the fifth grade not at the Hard Rock Café."

Louise roared with laughter. "You know that's the truth, though, so live with it."

"I know," Julie said.

"Either drop more hints or ask him outright if he has any interest in you other than as his little sister."

"I know he knows I am grown up, a college graduate, and I have my stuff together, but I think he might be afraid to make the first move. Being under the same roof is okay, now while we have this shared problem with the hit and run, but I have to tell you something else."

Julie needed to talk to someone other than to Joe about the newly found money from the attic.

"Please do not say anything to anyone, but yesterday afternoon, Joe and I found $300,000.00 in our attic all wrapped in plastic in hundred dollar bills. We immediately took it to the bank and opened a safe deposit box, two of them in fact, and took out one brick of hundred dollar bills to be analyzed. We believed it was from a Russian drug smuggling ring. Joe doesn't want me to believe it, but I think my father was a drug runner when he died in 1996 when he was only twenty-four years old. How do you live with that?" Julie said. "I don't want the money if it was from drugs."

She grimaced. "We don't believe Tillie knew a thing about it, but we won't be sure until she wakes up and actually remembers anything. She could sure use the money for her retirement. It's getting very difficult not to jump out of my skin," she said to Louise. "I am so glad Joe is here. Maybe it's why I love him. Please keep it to yourself, Louise."

"I will, I promise," Louise said. "Is that what Mark and Joe are talking about right now?"

"Talking about me?"

"No dummy, about your father."

Julie snorted. "Yes, sorry, wrong brain being used."

Louise laughed. "You really do have Joe on your mind, don't you?"

"Yes."

"As a matter of fact here they come," they both said at the same time.

"Thanks, Louise," Julie said.

"Anytime. You know Mark and I would do anything

for you," Louise said. "Can both of us and the kids all be in the wedding party?"

"Asshole," Julie whispered to Louise who couldn't control her giggles.

"What are you two laughing about?" Mark asked.

"Wouldn't you like to know?" Louise answered.

"Not really, save it. We're going for a swim with the kids. Dessert is in the refrigerator for when we get back. Louise, we should head out by 7:00 p.m. and no later."

"Okay," she said.

Joe and Mark met the kids at the water's edge and had a ball. They toweled off, hopped back in the car, and headed to Julie's house. They had dessert and said their goodbyes. The kids were getting sleepy. Louise put them into their pajamas for the ride back to Fort Lauderdale.

Julie and Joe waved to them. "Tomorrow is the big day," Julie said. "Father Schmidt prayed for Tillie at mass and he said he would come to visit after she was brought out of her induced coma, and then he would be there for her for as long as she wanted."

"I believe she'll be fine," Joe said. "Please don't worry, she will be fine."

"I certainly hope so," she said as they walked back to the house.

CHAPTER 10

As soon as Julie entered the house, she noticed the light flashing on her answering machine. She pushed the button to see who called. The machine came on and a robotic voice stated she had two calls. The first call was from Jan Marino who said she had gotten Julie's message about Tillie being taken out of the coma early Monday morning and not to worry about coming in early for school. She had everything done for this week's lesson plans. The call came in today while they were at the beach. She quickly called Jan at home and left her a message that she would be there a little after 11:00 a.m. They had a meeting with the principal at noon during lunch and she did not want to miss it.

The second call came from Maddy Malone, Julie's old roommate from Brown University. After graduation in the spring, Julie and Maddy had made plans for Maddy to come down to Key Largo so they could spend the week after Christmas together. Christmas was on a Wednesday this year and Maddy would fly from Boston's Logan Airport with one stop at the Tampa Florida airport and then she would take a puddle jumper flight to Key West the day after Christmas, coming in around 5:00 p.m. Maddy would spend New Year's Eve with Julie in Key

West and then would fly back the day after the holiday. She'd already booked a room for New Year's Eve at the Best Western on Simonton Street off Duval, the main drag and party central for Key West.

Maddy had to spend one extra semester for her Masters of Arts in Education to fulfill her obligation to do student teaching in the Wakefield, Massachusetts School District, prior to receiving her degree. She was guaranteed a teaching job for third grade, starting after Christmas recess because the third grade teacher was having a baby in late January. Come September, for the new school year, Maddy would have her own fourth grade classroom, due to a retirement. Actually, just like Julie, the Wakefield School District would be lucky to get a Brown University graduate who was on the cutting edge of education for the twenty-first century. Not only pedagogically sound, Maddy had advance technology training. She was able to fully integrate technology into the classroom and embed the technology right into the curriculum. Her interview at the school district, attended by several long term teachers and administrators, was duly impressive due to her technology presentation using Power Point. And then she'd demonstrated the actual technology-based lesson plans she personally developed through her research.

At Brown University, students studied the field of education from a variety of disciplinary perspectives, including anthropology, economics, history, political science, psychology, and sociology. The faculty included social scientists, historians, and field-based experts who taught a wide array of undergraduate courses that comprised the Education Studies Concentration. Maddy majored in psychology and hoped it would relate directly to student learning and teaching. This led to her pursue a

Master of Arts in Education and Urban Education Policy. In her final year, Maddy was allowed to conduct research on important educational issues as related to students living in poverty and equity in education for children of color. The greater Boston area changed dramatically in demographics, not only in terms of poverty, but also in terms of mass immigration to the region from Mexico, South American, and the Caribbean Islands. Maddy wanted to be ahead of the curve and it appeared she was very much ahead of those within the district.

As Julie was talking to Maddy, Joe called Dan Simmons' attorney friend in Miami. Jane Swanson went to Albany Law School and upon graduation, both she and her now husband moved to Miami after he finished his internship at Albany Medical Center. He was in training as a neurologist and accepted a position at Jackson Memorial Hospital in Miami. Jane got on with a very well-known law firm and was specializing in estate planning. She was the perfect choice to represent Tillie in dealing with her solely owned property, her house of forty years in Key Largo. It would have been tricky several years ago with estate taxes but now, the limitation on estate taxes was well within the valuation of her house which would go tax free to Julie upon Tillie's death.

The most essential element was to have Jane hold all the legal paperwork at her office, especially with Tillie's future unknown condition. Once the paperwork was signed and notarized, all they had to do was FedEx it to her overnight and she would handle the rest. Joe would convey this to Julie after she hung up from speaking with Maddy. It was also quite useful to have Jane's husband informed of Tillie's condition if there were issues after they took her out of the medically induced coma Monday morning. Timing was everything.

Joe conveyed the information to Julie and they would get the paperwork done as soon as Tillie showed cognitive functioning and as soon as it was clear she was fully competent to sign the paperwork. They ate dinner and Joe went to do his laundry that had piled up. He didn't have time to get his civilian clothes cleaned until today and he was running out of socks and underwear. At least he got clean uniforms at the Coast Guard station. He had to switch out of his dress uniform to his everyday working uniform to actually function in his new position as the intelligence officer on staff.

ဗာဝာ

As Julie finished up the dishes, her memories of her time at Brown came flooding back to her. Five years was a very long time. It was mostly spent away from home, except for most summers and Christmas breaks. She had no idea how she would have made out if it were not for Joe and Maddy, and especially Maddy's family. It was quite clear early on during their freshman year that Julie was barely making it financially, even though she was on scholarship. She had to do work-study and pick up extra hours as a waitress in the faculty-dining hall a few nights a week. It was also clear that Maddy came from money, maybe not of the very rich, but very well off was not out of the question. Instead of being in the Hall of Fame rich, she was from the Hall of the Very Rich, Second Team.

Her father, Arthur T. Malone, Ph.D., was a full professor at Harvard Law School and he served as a town councilman for Reading Massachusetts, as well. Maddy's mother did not work but certainly had the credentials to do so. Marilyn, her mother, had a master's degree from Boston University and was previously a full time teacher in Wakefield, the next town over. She gave up her full time position a few years ago and now filled in as needed at the elementary level.

That connection, as well as her father's position in Reading and at Harvard, didn't hurt either. Maddy got her student teaching assignment through her mother, but due to pure luck, she was able to take over an existing third grade class for the teacher going on pregnancy leave. She was assured of another position in the fall, obviously based on how well she performed this spring. They were very impressed with her presentation and advanced educational technology skills.

In any case, regardless of the status of the Malone family in the Reading-Wakefield community, Julie felt they were probably some of the nicest people she had ever met. When Maddy brought Julie home with her during their freshman year, they treated Julie like their own daughter. Julie felt comfortable for the first time. Maddy was her only friend during her first year. Julie had felt like a fish out of water. She was the redneck from south Florida and really did come from a pickup truck and blue-collar family. It took Maddy and her parents a little while to pick up her southern expressions and accent. Many Brown students, whose parents graduated from Brown, were considered a "legacy." They felt entitled and were fully expected to attend Brown after high school. Unlike those Brown students, Julie had had no such expectations and had no other agenda, other than doing her best to hang in to keep her scholarship. She had to maintain a 3.4 cumulative grade-point average to continue on full scholarship. She maintained a 3.75 and graduated Magna Cum Laude. It was hard, but working to pay bills added to her difficulty and prevented her from doing those little extras that added up to a 4.0. Julie never thought grades equaled intelligence nor would it somehow give her extra insight into writing her first book. She may not have had city smarts, but her blue-collar smarts certainly helped her inform her daily decision-making. Thinking back to her high school days, let alone her childhood, getting to Brown University was truly a remarkable feat for a fisherman's daughter.

At the start of Julie's junior year in high school, she, Joe, and Tillie would all go through college brochures to see how she might fit in. Julie was going to settle for a Florida state school but Joe and Tillie both told her that her grades were good enough to go anywhere. After all, Joe got a full scholarship to MIT after doing so well in high school. He wasn't prepared and joined the Coast Guard after his first semester. It wasn't that he didn't do well. He did okay getting all C's in his five courses while playing on the MIT varsity baseball team for the fall schedule. He'd just had enough of school and wanted to do something different. He felt Julie was much better prepared than he was and she was a lot more mature for her age.

Back then, every Saturday night he was in town, while stationed in Miami and in the Keys when she was now in high school, they would have dinner and watch college videos that showed the campus, the professors speaking, the curriculum, and the "how to pay for college" speeches. Those videos were all aimed at middle and upper class white America, knowing those parents valued education and they would pay for it. Joe saw it as an opportunity to show everyone that someone of her background and financial status could perform as well, if not better, than the entitled crowd. Julie settled on five schools but when she read the curriculum and actually spoke to the dean of the department at Brown, she was sold. Joe helped her with her financial aid package application and Julie wrote her own application narrative on why they should accept her at Brown. In fact, Julie worked with her own high school English department to ensure that her paper set the right tone and truly stated the feelings she wanted to convey. She was obviously hoping for a full scholarship or she would never have been able to attend for financial reasons alone.

౭൦౭൦

Joe was finishing up in the Coast Guard and, when Julie started college, wherever she would go, Joe decided to return home to Troy and get his MBA from Rensselaer Polytechnic Institute at age twenty-eight. Rensselaer is an unheard of university sitting right in Troy, New York. Unheard of in the sense that everyday students and high school guidance counselors were unaware of this prestigious university, but heard of by the top corporate recruiters in America. Rensselaer was rated in the top ten in America for engineering and technology right behind MIT and Cal Tech, and it was considered in the top fifty universities in the world. It was a mile and a half from Joe's home. This presented an opportunity he could not pass up. If RPI was good enough for an astronaut, Joe thought it was certainly good enough for him.

Joe chose Rensselaer, not only because it was in his hometown, but also because there were many graduate students who had been sent to Rensselaer by the United States Army, Navy, and Air Force to receive degrees that were not offered by their military institutions. Joe was probably the first Coast Guard graduate to enter Rensselaer's MBA program. Upon their graduation at Rensselaer, they would take positions of importance back in the military once they received their advanced degrees. They actually had special student housing for these military students and their families.

Through the years, Joe had met several of these individuals and had gotten to know their families when they resided in the apartments right on his own street in the north end of Troy. Most of these military personnel, attending RPI, wanted their kids to live in a neighborhood and attend local schools in the neighborhoods where they resided. It would round out their education. When he was growing up, Joe was friends with a few of these kids who went to Catholic High with him, which was located, only blocks from his family home in Troy. So when Joe went to class, he could look around and see faces resembling his own face now, as an adult, not like when he was only eighteen years old attending MIT for the first time.

ฌฌฌ

In the fall of Julie's senior year, she made her applications to five schools with Brown as her top priority. She applied to Brown in early November for early admissions and received a positive response. However, she could not afford to go without a scholarship. She received her financial aid information in December and she would be receiving a full academic scholarship including room, board, and tuition. She still had to pay all the fees and be responsible for all her own personal expenses and books, which cost a small fortune. Her personal essay sealed the deal. She was accepted into the Brown University Literary Arts program in the School of Humanities, quite a coup. Her letter told her of her acceptance and, basically, that she was considered for the Honors program, only one of thirty-five accepted for this prestigious program. Upon graduation with a B.A. degree, the MFA program would accept approximately twelve graduate student writers for the year and one half program. Julie knew her work was cut out for her. She could complete the MFA in one year by going to class during the summer, following her graduation from the undergraduate program.

In the acceptance letter she received, the president of Brown went on to explain Brown's status in the world of education. He stated, "Known internationally for excellence in academics and innovative research, Brown offers a wide range of undergraduate concentrations, master's programs, and doctoral degrees. The 6,000 undergraduates, 2,000 graduate students, 400 medical school students, and nearly 700 faculty members at Brown hail from every U.S. state and more than one hundred foreign countries. Together, the members of the Brown community create a dynamic living and learning environment on a picturesque urban campus in historic Providence, Rhode Island."

Last year, there were over 28,000 applicants for the undergraduate Class of 2012. Brown admitted approximately 2,800 or less than 10%. Ninety-four percent of applicants to the Class of 2012 were in the top 10% of their high school class. Julie was second in her class in her high school and would be the salutatorian for graduation. For 2008, the Graduate School at Brown received more than 9,000 applications and admitted 1,400, or 15% of applicants, yielding a matriculating class of 620. Selectivity for Ph.D. programs was 10%. After reading the letter, Julie was actually in awe. She showed Tillie first and then Joe when he arrived from his duty. Tillie and Joe were extremely proud of her and Joe took them out for a dinner celebration.

Julie left for Brown in late August, for her freshman

year, one week before school started to get her dorm room set up and go through orientation. She was a wreck, never being north of Miami in her entire life. She had never been on a plane before either. She landed at the Providence Airport on Southwest out of Fort Lauderdale, the cheapest and the most direct flight she could get. All her worldly possessions were in her two suitcases by her side. Joe met her at the luggage carousel in Providence, helped her with her bags, and jammed the luggage into the trunk of his 2005 Ford Focus he'd picked up a few weeks earlier to attend Rensselaer for his MBA. They drove to campus, only a short drive away, and checked in. Everything was ready for her. *Thank God.*

Everyone had heard the horror stories of students who showed up without even knowing if they were accepted or even had financial aid packages. But everything went smoothly. She found her dorm and then her room after speaking to her dorm leader. Sitting on her bed, already checked in, was Maddy Malone from Reading, Massachusetts. She was an education major, and she seemed very nice. They exchanged greetings and Julie introduced Maddy to Joe. All Julie had in her two suitcases were her clothes and some books. Julie and Joe went to Wal-Mart and got her sheets, pillowcases and the normal necessities of life that she couldn't bring with her. Joe had a used computer for her that he got on the cheap from his consulting group. Maddy had a TV, stereo, and printer so they were good to go. Maddy said Julie could use anything she wanted. *What a nice girl.* Little did Julie know they would wind up as lifetime friends and close confidants. Meeting Maddy's parents was a bonus.

Through the first few years, they both did well. They met new friends but they stayed close, as close as sisters. Julie would go for weekend visits to Maddy's house in

Reading, even spending Thanksgiving and Christmas one year. Maddy came down for two summers and spent a month each time with Julie in Key Largo. She loved Key West but would never leave the four seasons of New England. Upon graduation after four years, both receiving their bachelor's degrees in their respective fields, Julie spent the summer between graduation and her MFA start up in the fall taking three critical graduate courses, which would allow her to graduate in one year instead of an extra half or whole additional year. This was true of Maddy as well. By taking three courses as well, she could do her student teaching in the fall and graduate six months early. This allowed her to take the full time third grade position due to the teacher's pregnancy leave at the Wakefield School District near her home. They both were fortunate enough to get their courses scheduled on Tuesday and Thursday and they drove to Providence from Reading early in the morning, coming home well after 7:00 p.m. at night.

Joe had surprised Julie by giving her his car at the start of her junior year. The older Ford Focus he drove while at Rensselaer was sound, had good tires and only 70,000 miles on it, well below her old VW Rabbit that was left in the Keys to die a slow death. Instead of transferring the car and title to her, because she would have to register it and get plates and insurance in Florida, which didn't make sense, Joe simply handed her the keys and said have a ball. He left the title in his name. He paid for the insurance, and it simply had New York plates and registration.

Every year, he drove over, specifically to switch his new leased car for the Focus. He would drive it back for the annual New York State inspection sticker and then right back to Providence the following weekend. She was good to go for another year. Hell, half the cars at Brown had plates from other states.

In the greater Boston area, it was the same thing. New York plates were an accepted reality with kids going to the twenty plus colleges in the greater Boston area. Joe told her if she had an accident to please hit something inexpensive. The good thing was when she got her MFA and headed to Key Largo, she didn't have to drag the car down with her. She drove it for almost three years and only had to pay for the gas. Julie offered to pay for the insurance but Joe said not to worry about it. The car was insured for the minimum liability only and had no collision insurance. If the car was in an accident, they had to take a chance. As Joe told her, "Hit something cheap."

After graduation, she would leave the car with Joe and he would give it to his brother as a construction work vehicle. Joe was able to lease a car after graduation from Rensselaer since he started a new job at the Albany Coalition for Families, and he got his fully furnished apartment in Troy, through the Troy Education Group where he worked part time, to partially pay the rent. He only leased it for 7,500 miles a year because he was so close to work and home and really didn't take any long trips. The only long trips were by plane to see Julie in Key Largo for the holidays.

Julie still had to make money during the summer so on her off days from school, she got a waitress job at a fine Italian restaurant on Main Street in downtown Wakefield. She made a lot more money on the weekends and on a few days a week than she ever did helping out at the Waffle House in Key Largo. She saved almost $2,000.00 for her MFA year. She liked living on campus so much that when the fall came, both Maddy and Julie signed up for the new Brown University Condo campus, a few blocks away. She retained her scholarship for tuition, room, and board, while Maddy's mother and father simply wrote Maddy a check for the fall. While Maddy could have been pretentious with all her affluence, she never appeared that way to Julie. Maddy knew, due to fortune and good luck, she was one of the privileged, but she also knew Julie would rise above her current status and be successful in any endeavor she encountered.

Julie told Joe, when she got off the phone, that Maddy had dropped a bomb on her. She was getting married and wanted Julie to be her maid of honor. The wedding wouldn't be until next fall but there were a few things Julie had to go to, to be part of the wedding. Joe was certainly invited as well as Tillie if they could make it. Maddy understood that under the current circumstances, Julie couldn't plan ahead too far, with Tillie's condition, but they would play it by ear.

They hadn't scheduled the wedding date but would wait until Julie had answers for Tillie's condition. Julie had never met Maddy's fiancé and it had happened pretty quickly. He was a teacher in the Reading School District and Maddy met him at an education conference required for new teachers. He taught science at the high school level and was the assistant baseball coach, so he and Joe would probably get along famously. His name was Kevin White. He was twenty-five, grew up in Reading, and was two years ahead of Maddy in high school. She didn't even know he existed when they were at the Reading High School. He was actually in one of her art classes when she was a sophomore and he was a senior. He needed one class in art that didn't interfere with his baseball spring schedule. They never spoke. They didn't even sit near each other but he remembered her at the conference.

You never knew what life would bring. Maddy's parents were thrilled to say the least.

Julie finally hit the shower and said good night to Joe. It was late. She wondered if Joe ever even thought about her other than as a little sister. She knew how Maddy felt about Kevin, who never gave her the time of day until he walked into the conference that morning. She felt like she was on the Walton's TV show, "Good night Mary Ellen, Good Night John Boy." She sure hoped Tillie would wake up tomorrow and tell them what had happened to her. Julie thought she'd better start doing her Hail Marys again. It couldn't hurt.

She was out like a light.

CHAPTER 11

It was early Monday morning, around 6:00 a.m. Julie and Joe were both very anxious to get to the Mariner Hospital. Today, Doctor Robinson would be taking Tillie out of her medically induced coma. The plan was to perform all the necessary tests on her to ensure it was safe to bring her back to a normal state. She would be getting an MRI test first, head to toe, and then an X-ray to ensure her bones were mending properly and were fully aligned. They would check her pelvis to make certain everything was stable, take all her vital signs, and continue to monitor her, right up to, and through, Doctor Robinson's procedure.

Doctor Robinson had induced the coma through the use of pentobarbital, a barbiturate. The coma should be completely reversible, and it should cause no permanent damage itself. These barbiturates had a profound effect on the cerebral metabolic requirement of oxygen, much more so than any other sedative. Brain activity was essentially shut down so the injured brain had lower requirements for nutrients and oxygen and would better tolerate the injury. Tillie's fractured skull was the main issue causing the internal swelling had to be reduced. Medically-induced sedation and/or coma was used to protect the brain while the initial period of swelling and increased intracranial pressure passed, hopefully preserving as many normal brain tissue as possible. Once these cells were severely injured there was no treatment to restore them. This was why so much was done to preserve the healthy brain tissue after an injury.

The monitoring during this medically induced coma was exceedingly important. One way the staff routinely did the monitoring was by electroencephalography, which measured brain waves. By merely looking at the brain waves, they got a pretty good picture of how deep the coma was, even if the person was unresponsive. There were other types of monitoring as well. They could measure intracranial pressure directly.

The other monitoring was done in the intensive care unit, where Tillie had been for over a week. It would be done to make sure she was not suffering any side effects of this therapy.

Doctor Robinson had patted Julie on the shoulder. "Once there's improvement in Tillie's general condition, the barbiturates will be withdrawn gradually and she will regain consciousness. We'll start the process Sunday night and complete the procedure early Monday morning. She'll be groggy and nonresponsive for a while, but all her vital functions will be her own. It might take several days to several weeks before she's fully conscious and has her complete faculties back. It might take several months to complete her recovery." He shook his head. "She's extremely lucky, for being over age sixty. Most individuals would not have survived, or would have been severely handicapped. She's in great shape due to her daily physical activities and routine. But prayer wouldn't hurt."

They arrived at the Mariner Hospital about 7:30 a.m.

The procedure was well on its way. They had started last night and they completed their task as Julie and Joe arrived.

A little while later, around 8:30 a.m., Doctor Robinson came out of surgery into the waiting room to see Julie. "Everything went as well as could be expected. Tillie's starting to come out of the coma but is still in a semi-conscious state and that will take quite a while to clear. It might take a day or two or even a week. Any longer and I would be concerned but I am extremely hopeful that all went well."

Julie reached out and hugged the doctor and then Joe. She smiled from ear to ear and thanked God for this day. "When can we see her?" she asked the doctor.

"Give her another hour in the recovery room and then she will be back in her bed in the critical care unit," he said. "Don't forget, she's still in critical condition but stable."

"Thank you doctor for everything," both Joe and Julie said at the same time.

"Let's get some breakfast, I'm starved," Julie said. "Can you eat?"

"What kind of a question was that?" Joe asked. "I can eat anytime."

As they were going to the hospital cafeteria in the basement, they ran into Mike Kenny. "Hi, Mike, she's going to be okay," Julie said. "Is that why you are here?"

"Actually, yes and no," Mike said. "I have another victim brought in this morning after a robbery went bad. I planned on seeing Tillie right afterward."

"What happened?" asked Joe.

"It was a 7-11 robbery last night. The clerk was hit in the head with a metal pipe and robbed. We have it all on video from the camera, so it won't take long to solve, hopefully," Mike told them. "Is Tillie awake? Can I talk to her?"

"Not yet." Julie shook her head. "She won't be fully conscious for a while, and then it will be determined what she remembers. We will keep you posted."

"Joe, we ran the paint from the vehicle that hit Tillie and, as you know, we found out it was a 2002 Ford F-150, and the truck was obviously white," Mike said, changing the subject. "There are over 750 trucks exactly like this in the state with half down here in south Florida and the Keys. So, next, we are running the registration ownership names to see what's what. Thank God we can download to an excel computer file. You are an expert in this area are you not, Joe?"

Joe nodded. "As much as anyone."

"If I send the file to you, can you do some excel sorts? I think we want to separate male from female ownership first. Then separate by county, with local counties first and then the rest. Not to discriminate, but the man in the truck from the gas station video, looked like he had a white arm. Can we run a report that separated last names as close as we can by ethnicity? We are looking for a white guy, I think. It's just a guess at this point," Mike said. "However, this will never be reported or every do-gooder organization in the state will be after me."

Joe nodded again. "I can do it but it will take some time. From the data I looked at, 90% of trucks are owned by men. It would bring it down to a little over 650-plus vehicles for men. Sorting the names may bring it down by another 20%, leaving about 500 trucks to look at. In addition, we could start locally and work our way back through the state. We're also not even sure it had Florida plates. We guessed it did, but I think it's a good guess. I'll get it started tonight."

Joe and Julie went on to the cafeteria. The nurse came down to get them. Evidently, Tillie seemed to be coming around. They ran up the stairs instead of waiting for the elevator, which was always crowded on the first floor and seemed to take forever to get to the fifth floor. When they walked into the room, the Nurse Supervisor was looking down at Tillie.

Tillie's eyes opened and she started to look around. "Water," she said.

Anticipating the request, the nurse had a cold cup right next to the bed. She gave her the cup with a straw and told Tillie to drink slowly at first so she wouldn't get sick.

After her sip, Tillie turned slowly to Julie. "Julie?"

Tears were forming in Julie's eyes. "Hi, Grammy, how are you?"

"It's Tillie to you," she said.

Joe laughed. "She's back."

"Joe, is that you? What are you doing here?"

"Hi, Tillie. Yes it's me. I came to see you. How are you?"

"Not too good," she said. "What happened, why am I here?"

Julie looked at Joe and then at Tillie. "You don't know what happened?"

"No, what happened?" she asked.

"You were forced off the road last week by a pickup truck and you have been here in the hospital ever since."

"I don't remember," Tillie said. "My head really hurts and I'm tired."

Tillie suddenly went to sleep. Julie panicked. "Nurse, will she be all right?"

"Yes, she will be all right. Don't worry. She needs her rest. Her brain is still catching up. If she doesn't remember now, she will when she gets better. Don't worry everything will be okay."

Julie looked at Joe. "I can't lose her now, Joe, not with what we went through."

"She will be okay but she obviously doesn't remember anything at this point," Joe said. "Give her time, Julie. She needs rest."

As Joe walked out of the room, he called Mike Kenny who picked up his cell immediately. "Mike, it's Joe. Tillie just woke up but doesn't remember anything about the hit and run. The doctor said it might take a while. She was groggy and went to sleep. You would be too if you got hit by a truck."

"Let me know when things change. In the meantime, if you can run the excel spreadsheet, we can still move forward. Thanks, Joe, got to go."

Julie came out of Tillie's room. "What do we do now?"

"Go to school and get your mind off of this. She's alive and breathing on her own. She needs time for her brain to recover. That's clear. We need to do what we can do. We need to figure out about the money, who hit Tillie, and why. All these things may be connected and we have to be careful for Tillie's sake and yours," he said. "I carry a gun and have friends who carry guns as well. You have to be on your toes. I don't believe this is an isolated incident. Also, I have been shirking my duties at the Islamorada office. I have to go there now, Julie. I'm way behind."

Joe had five investigations he was working on and he had to go to sea for at least a week and check out some of the data he had already translated that had come in earlier this week.

He believed there was a big shipment coming into

the Keys in the next few weeks. It meant millions of dollars in raw cocaine from Columbia by ship. He needed to be on top of this to keep his edge.

Julie nodded. "Do what you have to do, Joe. I am not on my own. I have a lot of friends and I have to get my book going again. The nurse thought we should come back after dinner tonight, and not before, or we will be wasting our time. We should take her advice. I'll see you tonight. We can get something to eat on the way back to the hospital." She hugged him. "Thank you for everything."

ⰽⱁⰽⱁ

Julie headed out to the Key Largo school and stopped to see her pastor on the way. Father Schmidt opened the door to the parish house at St. Justin's and immediately asked Julie how her grandmother was.

"She woke up and she is out of the coma but she doesn't remember a thing about the accident, Father," Julie said. "She went right back to sleep five minutes after she said hello. She knew who we were but she doesn't know what happened. The doctor said to give her time to let her brain recover and adjust. It may be a day or several weeks. We're hoping for the best. She's the only one who knows what happened and we don't know if her life or ours are in jeopardy. So we're quite anxious about everything, Father. I hope you understand."

"Perfectly," he said. "Do you mind if I go now to see her and at least give her the last rights? Remember we didn't do it yet. It's always for the best."

"Sure, Father. You can go ahead. That would be nice."

"Nice." He smiled. "It's a straight shot to heaven, after Extreme Unction, you know. Not that she really needs it. She's on the express train anyway."

She shook his hand, gave him a hug, and said she would see him in the hospital or at least at mass on Sunday. "Thanks, Father, for everything."

Julie headed for school and pulled into the school parking lot around 10:30 a.m. She headed right to her classroom. The district had been so kind to her that she would never be able to pay them back. First, they let her put Tillie on her health insurance. Thank God, they had let her take this time now for Tillie. Julie had to dedicate her book to the district as well as to Tillie and Joe.

It was funny. She'd never thought about it very much with all this on her mind, but Joe mentioned several times he would be more than glad to help her school write a few grants while he was here. He won over a million dollars in three years at the Coalition in Albany before he found out about the money-laundering scheme by Luis Hernandez. Joe's grants were legitimate and not to some phony foundation but to the New York State Education Department and several New York State agencies, including Child Protective Services. He had the grants on his computer and he looked up what Florida had to offer school districts.

He had written a grant for a technology classroom for the Coalition that could be easily transported to her fifth-grade class and to her entire school building, grade by grade. The Florida State Education grant, coming up shortly, was only for $100,000.00, but it would be enough to start the school on the right path. Joe had given her the grant he'd written, that they could submit to Florida, to show to the principal at her meeting today. *Maybe this will take some pressure off the situation. The grant is due next week and is virtually completed. All that's need-*

ed is the Superintendent's signature, the principal's signature, and the school union representative's as well, and it's a go. Joe had told her that the same grant could be sent to other Florida state agencies and foundations as well. *Why not? Let's see what happens. What have we got to lose? This will pay my salary and benefits back almost double.* Joe was very smart.

Julie almost walked into Jan, and the near-collision pulled her back to the present. "Hi, Jan, how are you?"

"I wasn't expecting you back so soon. How's Tillie doing?"

"She's out of her coma and is stable. She's very tired and had a severe headache but that was to be expected, they said. She can't remember anything. Hopefully, in a few days she will remember what happened and we can move forward. It's going to be a while before everything is back to normal, but she is alive and awake. Before we meet with our principal, I wanted to show you a grant Joe Traynor had written and successfully won for $100,000.00, up north. He found a similar grant through the Florida Education Department and it's due next week. Do you have a few minutes? I wanted you on board before we met with Mrs. Black."

Jan laughed. "Of course I have time, Julie. Especially when you want to hand me money."

"Don't count your winnings just yet, Jan, old girl."

They met for a half an hour and Jan thought the idea was great.

"It's about time I earned my money," Julie told her.

"Don't worry about it. We need and want you here. When you're wildly successful as a nationally recognized author, you can show up in my class, anytime, and give me all the credit for helping you along the way."

They both laughed.

"I promised to make you look good, Jan."

They met with Mrs. Black and Julie outlined the proposed grant and how it would work if they won. There were no matching funds required or any cost to the district. It was for school buildings that had high free-and-reduced lunch numbers, identifying high poverty levels. The grant was a way to give equity back to poor kids. This school had a poverty index of almost seventy percent. The same kind of kids attended today that had attended when Julie went there. She was one of them. Julie handed Mrs. Black the completed grant to get the signatures and copies ready to be sent next week by certified mail, return receipt requested.

"Julie and Jan, thank you for moving this forward," Mrs. Black said. "This is great. It's so exciting. We've never had a grant before. I don't know why. But we sure will from now on. Again, thanks, you two. I am so pleased, and, Julie, don't worry about your present condition. We are happy to have you here." Mrs. Black laughed. "If we win the grant, it will pay for your salary and benefits for the year, probably twice over."

Bingo. Joe was absolutely right. I have to tell him when I get back.

సౌసౌ

Joe was at his desk for the rest of the day at the station. He outlined his five cases and how he would have to resolve them through interdiction and through his intelligence gathering. There was nothing worse than boarding a ship and finding nothing. It had happened exactly once with Joe and it never happened again. He had a few meetings with the station Chief, with Joan, and with several other team members who would be participating in the eventual takedowns in the next few weeks. It was getting close to 5:00 p.m., so he called Julie and asked her to meet him at a restaurant near the hospital in a half hour. They would go see Tillie from there. *Hopefully, she will be better and more awake and with it.*

After a quick visit to the hospital, they went home. Julie had to continue writing her book. She had deliverables due by early December. She'd been living off of the stipend and her teacher's aide salary, which barely covered the bills. And without Tillie's paycheck looming, it might just get worse before it got better. She owed it to herself, to her grandmother, and to everyone else, especially to Joe, who had helped her along the way to move forward in spite of this setback. She put water on the stove to make a cup of tea. Joe was busy reading his case files in the living room. She went to her office cave to spend a few hours and restart the process all over again.

CHAPTER 12

O nce again, Julie was deep in thought at her desk, surrounded by memories. It was almost 11:00 p.m. She wanted to really think about what Joe had meant to her and Tillie, especially for her book but also for the record…

༺༻

In the fall of 2000, Julie had been in fifth grade. Her mother had died two years earlier when she was eight. Tillie did not have the proverbial "pot to pee in" but they remained happy and together. It was all that mattered to Julie as she looked back over the years. She and Tillie were dealt a bad hand and a terrible blow but it did not keep them down. They pulled together.

Tillie made it possible for Julie to join her every night for dinner at the Waffle House. She picked Julie up before the crowd became too big, around 4:30 p.m. Julie was on her own a few days a week after getting off the bus, right in front of her house. The neighbor had looked after her if there was a problem. Then they drove back to the restaurant to eat dinner together, sitting on two stools at the end of the counter. Julie stayed there until the

crowd thinned, then she cleaned off one of the used ta-
bles, brought the dishes to the back, and started her
homework. They left together at 7:30 p.m. every night,
which was the deal that Tillie had made with the owner.
Julie was in bed by 8:30 p.m. Watching TV was a luxury
on the weekends only on the little thirteen-inch black and
white TV with tin foil for an antenna. Reception was not
much to speak of in the Keys. The dinner and breakfast
time together was a deal breaker for Tillie with the owner. It was that or she had to quit.

Tillie was an institution by that time, having worked
there since she was fifteen years old. Thirty-five years
and still going strong—they owed her. The other deal was
Tillie that would bring Julie with her at 5:30 a.m. for
breakfast. They would eat together at the counter and
then Tillie drove her to her school by 7:30 a.m. every
morning. Tillie would go back to the school at 3:00 p.m.
to pick her up. They went home. Tillie did her chores, the
wash, and then they went back for the same routine five
days a week. Julie didn't have to stay alone much of the
time. Tillie worked Saturday morning as well and the
next-door neighbor watched Julie until she was old
enough to take care of herself.

It had been a Tuesday morning in early October 2000
when Joe showed up at Key Largo School. He arrived
right at the very same classroom that Julie now served in
as a teacher's aide. Joe had joined the Coast Guard the
winter before, went to basic training, and, after graduation and additional training for the Intelligence Division,
he was assigned to the main Coast Guard facility in Miami. Part of his training was on a 33-foot Special Purpose
Craft Law Enforcement (SPC-LE) vessel, serving out of
the main Florida Keys Coast Guard headquarters in Islamorada, about ten miles from the school. It was Career

Day and Joe and two other of his fellow *Coasties* were doing public service and recruitment as well as serving their country. Who better to recruit than those students growing up in the Florida Keys? *Get them while they're young*, was their motto. The ocean salt water was in their blood, growing up in the Keys, and these kids wanted to be on boats. Who would be better to recruit?

With Joe was Mark Silva, who was older, and was Joe's closest friend. He and Joe joined the Coast Guard together and went through basic training together, winding up in Miami at COMMSTA headquarters. They seemed to be inseparable. Joe learned Mexican-dialect Spanish from Mark and this led to their careers together and their close personal friendship. When alone, all they did was speak Spanish. Mark gave him the idioms he needed, street smarts, and the language of the barrio. Without that, their success at drug interdictions, mostly from South America and Mexico, would be a lot more challenging. They were now considered to be the experts within the Coast Guard at taking down drug runners utilizing Spanish intelligence language resources.

With Joe and Mark was Joan Talbot who was in her mid-thirties, at the time, and assigned to the Islamorada Station as the Information Systems Technician (IT) and was the Chief Warrant Officer's main assistant. She was an E-4 and the only other full time staff at the station other than the chief warrant officer. She was married, lived in assigned Coast Guard housing, and had two small children who were just about ready to start school at Islamorada Elementary. She was also the liaison to the community and local schools and set up Career Day events to put the Coast Guard in a favorable light. Many viewed the local Coast Guard with much respect because of their search and rescue missions but many were just as wary of them because of local family involvement in the drug smuggling trade. They were the "cops" for the region and locals with ill intentions did not speak to the cops. The Coast Guard tried to improve local relations through these events.

Joan, Mark, and Joe showed up at Julie's school to tell the fifth-grade students all about the Coast Guard as a career and what it meant to be a *Coastie*. Joe was the youngest by several years. After just turning nineteen, he looked like he belonged at the Coral Shores High School. In fact, he was the same age as many of those who were seniors at the high school. What was he doing in the Coast Guard? she wondered.

They made their presentation and Mrs. Carson, the fifth-grade teacher—there were no teacher's aides in those days—asked if there were any questions from the students. Several of the boys wanted to know how old you had to be to join. Joe, as the youngest, answered the question. The girls asked Joan what it was like to be a girl in the Coast Guard. Laughingly, she told them was no longer a girl but it was great. It was her career and she loved it. It allowed her to stay home in the Keys and watch her children grow up in the same place where she was raised. The girls in the class liked her answer.

There were a few Hispanic boys in the class and Mark asked them how they were, in Spanish. They looked quizzically at him because they barely understood a few of the words. Come to find out, they were third- and fourth- generation residents of the Keys. So Spanish was a long forgotten memory for their families. In fact, one of the boy's mothers taught third grade at the school.

Mark looked kind of sheepish. "Oh well, there goes the neighborhood."

They laughed.

To say Julie was independent was an understatement. Living with Tillie since birth, and since it was only the two of them for the last two years, it gave her a sense of self-worth and an inner strength that was not quite shared by the rest of her classmates.

As soon as the presentation ended and they started to say their goodbyes, Julie went up to Joe. "How old are you, Joe?"

Joe looked a little surprised to say the least, but a big smile came over his face. "I'm nineteen. How old are you?"

"I'm ten."

"What's your name?" Joe asked.

"My name is Julie Chapman," she said.

"Nice to meet you, Julie Chapman."

Julie hesitated.

"What?" Joe asked.

"Can I come visit you on your boat?"

"I'm not sure, let me ask Joan." He went over to Joan and asked her if they had visiting days or tours of the station in Islamorada.

"No official tours, but when you are off, you can take anybody around the facility you want, as long as you stay with them."

"Good to know," he said. Joe went back to Julie. "Joan says there are no tours. I can take you around the facility anytime, but I have to stay with you. Obviously you have to get permission from your mother or father and one of them would have to come with you."

Julie looked pained.

"What's the matter?" asked Joe.

"My mother and father are dead," she said.

"Oh, I'm so sorry. Whom do you live with, then?" he asked.

"I live with Tillie," she answered.

"Who's Tillie?"

"She's my grandmother but she wanted me to call her Tillie instead. She said she's too young to be a grandmother."

Joe laughed.

"It's her name, Tillie Carpenter," she said.

Joe smiled. "I'll tell you what. I will give you the office number for Joan. If you have Tillie call me, I can set up a tour for both of you on Saturday afternoon. My schedule is strange with two days on, two days off, then three on and three off. Then I go back to Miami headquarters in between."

"What does that mean?" she asked.

"I'll explain it to Tillie and she can explain it to you. I have to go now but I hope to see you, Julie Chapman. Let me know," he said.

That afternoon, when Tillie picked her up after school, Julie said, "I had a great day Tillie, just great."

"Wow, you are so happy. Tell me what happened," she said.

Julie explained how she met Joe and about the invitation to meet him on Saturday at the Coast Guard facility. Julie gave Tillie the phone number for Joan and asked her to please, please, please call right now.

Tillie smiled. "Boy, I haven't seen you like this in a long time."

"Just call, please Tillie, call now, please, Tillie? P-l-e-a-s-e?"

"Okay, give me a minute to get my coat off." Tillie dialed Joan's number and Joan picked up almost immediately.

"United States Coast Guard, Islamorada Station, how may I direct your call?" she said.

"Is it Ms. Talbot or Seaman Talbot?" she asked.

"Either or," Joan said.

"This is Tillie Carpenter. I am Julie Chapman's grandmother with whom you visited on Tuesday at the Key Largo School's fifth-grade class."

"Yes, of course, Mrs. Carpenter. I remember Julie asked Joe if she could visit our station," she said. "Joe is back in Miami at the COMMSTA headquarters but he will be back for the weekend, coming in late by ship on Friday night around 9:15 p.m. He gave me his Miami number to give to you. He said he would be there on Wednesday night at 7:00 p.m., if you wanted to call him. If you can't, he said to come anyway on Saturday for 2:00 p.m. and he will meet you at the front door."

"That would be great," Tillie told Joan, and wrote down the number. "If we don't connect, we'll still be at their facility on Saturday." Quietly, Tillie added, "I haven't seen Julie this excited in a long time."

"Well we look forward to seeing you then," Joan replied. "I am in on Saturday until 4:00 p.m., and then on to soccer practice with the kids. Please stop in and say hello. Tell Joe I will be here Saturday."

Tillie thanked her and thought *what a nice lady.* Then she had to calm Julie down.

"What did she say? What did she say?"

"We are welcome to go on Saturday. Joe will meet us at 2:00 p.m. but I want to call him first in Miami. I don't know him and I want to talk to him just to make sure. I am in charge of you and I want to make sure you are safe at all times. I can't call until 7:00 p.m. tomorrow night. He said he would be there and we will call him then."

"Okay," Julie said, reverting back to a ten year old.

Funny how that works, thought Tillie. *She must real-*

ly have a crush on this guy. Puppy Love. "Okay, Julie, now can you tell me all about your day?"

They talked for an hour and then went to dinner at the Waffle House. Some things never seemed to change.

As Julie reminisced, she remembered when Tillie called Joe the first night.

Joe answered his phone, "Seaman Traynor speaking, may I help you?'

"This is Tillie Carpenter speaking. I am Julie Chapman's grandmother from Key Largo. What should I call you?"

"Joe is fine. It's nice to hear from you. How is Julie doing?"

"You made one big impression on her. I haven't seen her this happy in some time."

"Wow, that's great," Joe said. "I don't think we did anything special, but I'd love to see her on Saturday, if it's possible."

"Before that happens, I would like to ask you a few questions and then give you some of Julie's background. I really don't want to build Julie's hopes up and have her let down. She has been through a lot in her young life."

Joe didn't know what to say. He then told Tillie all about himself and then said she could tell him anything she wanted.

"Fine," Tillie said.

"It's Wednesday and the only time I have off is from 5:00 p.m. to 8:00 p.m. and then it's back to my office until midnight." He went through his short nineteen years, culminating with his dropping out of MIT with a full scholarship after his first semester and then joining the Coast Guard. He told her about his construction family background up in Troy, New York, and his great love for baseball and how he was a pitcher at Catholic Central High School and then for one semester at MIT.

"When I met Julie, I thought she was very special and very much together for a ten year old. You did one hell of job with her." He went on to tell her that he had an older brother, two years older in fact, and they both worked for their father until Joe left for college and then to the Coast Guard.

"It wasn't easy. I learned to be very independent at a very early age and it was both good and bad. I had to learn to trust others, which I'm doing with my best friend in the service, Mark. I liked Julie's spunkiness and I laughed when she came right up and asked me how old I was. I'm nineteen by the way, just turned in April and joined the Coast Guard immediately after my fall semester at MIT. I'll elaborate after we meet."

Tillie liked Joe almost immediately. He seemed like a decent guy who would be kind to Julie. She told Joe about the family background and history and deaths of Julie's father and then mother two years later.

Joe was quite taken by Tillie's frankness and admired her very much. "I would be glad to do anything I can to help her. I'll meet you on Saturday afternoon at 2:00 p.m."

"I work until noon at the Waffle House on Saturday and we will be there at 2:00 p.m.," Tillie said.

"Can I speak to Julie for a minute?" Joe asked.

"Of course. She would love to talk to you. Just a second. Julie, Joe would like to talk to you" Tillie said.

Julie was all excited and took the phone from Tillie's hand. He spoke to her and told her all about what he had planned for Saturday for her and her grandmother. "I have to get off the telephone now because I have to go to work."

"Great. I can't wait until Saturday."

"I have to be back on the ship by 6:00 p.m. Saturday but I'd like to take you both to dinner around 4:30 p.m. if it's possible.

Julie asked Tillie and she said it would be fine.

"My treat," he said. "Tell Tillie. And tell her that I'll explain about my days on and off and how I can be reached every Wednesday at 7:00 p.m. unless I'm on emergency duty or on the ship for some reason. Julie, if I don't call you on Wednesday at 7:00 p.m. every week, there is a reason, not that I forgot. I hope you understand and some day when you are older I will tell you what I am doing in the Coast Guard. I can't tell everyone what we are doing. It's classified," he said.

Tillie got back on the phone. "Thanks so much for your kindness, Joe. We are both looking forward to meeting with you on Saturday."

෧෨෧

On Saturday at 2:00 p.m., Joe met Tillie and Julie at his station in Islamorada after Tillie finished work. He had until 6:00 p.m. to get back to his assigned boat. Unmarried seamen, non-officers, were not assigned housing and had to stay on the ship or obtain their own housing options on shore leave. Joe tried to make his time with Julie as meaningful and as much fun as he could. He only had an older brother and no sisters. He didn't quite know what to do or say to Julie or even to her grandmother.

When he got back Friday night, he asked Joan what he should do.

"Be nice. Be yourself. Be her friend, and be respectful of both of them and you won't go wrong," Joan advised him.

"Thanks, Joan. I appreciate it. I am a little nervous about this."

"Don't be. This is a good thing you are doing for this little girl and her grandmother."

Joe had spoken to Tillie by phone during the week and she had given him the lowdown on Julie's life, and hers, since Tom and Annie died. This was harder than meeting a new girlfriend for the first time, or even her parents. He was not only representing himself but the Coast Guard as well. He had only been in less than a year but was catching on quite well. He was smart enough but his inexperience showed under trying circumstances and he wanted to be as prepared for this as for his duties.

As soon as they met on Saturday that year, Joe handed each of them a Coast Guard baseball cap and a Coast Guard T-shirt with Islamorada on the front. Julie put her hat and shirt on right away. Tillie put on the hat and put her T-shirt in her oversize pocketbook.

I don't think Tillie wears T-shirts. Joe had put together a binder on the Islamorada facility, which Julie took home and then to school to show her teacher and friends. Joe didn't have much money so he talked Joan into giving him the Coast Guard hats and T-shirts for both of them out of her promotional funds. Julie was thrilled and Tillie smiled from ear to ear.

The Coast Guard binder began with an overview of the Islamorada facility. The cover sheet stated that the United States Coast Guard Station Islamorada was located adjacent to Snake Creek just off U.S. Highway 1—87 miles north of Key West on Plantation Key and only ten miles south of Key Largo. The unit served the surrounding communities of Islamorada, Tavernier, Key Largo, and South Miami/Dade County. Station Islamorada was a multi-mission unit with a challenging area of responsibility, spanning from Long Key to the South West, Biscayne Bay to the North East, and to Flamingo Florida to the North West. On a daily basis, they conducted the Coast Guard missions of drug interdiction, aids to navigation, marine environmental protection, and other law enforcement activities. These missions were performed using five distinct vessels: one 41-foot Utility Boat (UTB), three 33-foot Special Purpose Craft Law Enforcement (SPC-LE), and one 24-foot Special Purpose Craft Shallow Water (SPC-SW).

He had placed several pamphlets into the binder and a video of the Coast Guard in action. He really didn't even know if they had a DVD player at the time, Julie now thought, wow, fourteen years ago almost to the day. There were no coincidences. It was meant to be.

※※※

Julie remembered the day and the tour Joe had taken them on, through his vessel docked at the facility and then through the different offices. They wound up back at Joan's office early. Joe was assigned to the SPC-LE boat with his crew as a Seaman E-2—first year. He'd been trained in Miami at the COMMSTA Center as an Intelligence Specialist but had to field test these classroom courses with actual "in the field" training, hence, his time in Islamorada. He was assigned to partner with Mark Silva who also had graduated with Joe in his classes. Mark was also at work and would meet up with them during the day around 3:00 p.m.

Mark was twenty-seven and would be twenty-eight by the end of the year. Twenty-seven was the oldest you could be to join the Coast Guard. His joining was not necessarily voluntary. Living in San Diego, Mark had gotten into serious trouble. Now his gangbanging days were over. It was the Coast Guard or incarceration.

Joe was assigned to work with Mark, permanently, as Chief Petty Officer, Tom Jones, told him. Joe was to be fluent in Mexican Spanish as soon as possible to really make an impact as an Intelligence Specialist. Most of this was left unsaid. No one was to know of this role, outside of his Miami COMMSTA headquarters. After less than a year, it was clear Mark had a purpose and had turned his life around from his days in San Diego. His purpose was Joe.

At the end of the tour, Joe, Tillie, Julie, and Mark went to Joan's office where Joan gave them the video and gave Julie several Coast Guard patches that could be sewn onto her jacket. Joan gave her an application to join the Coast Guard when she was eighteen and she told her to hold on to it.

"Julie, will you be available for babysitting in a few years?" Joan asked, handing Julie her card.

Julie thought it was great. The Coast Guard actually had a babysitting and life-saving course that girls, and boys, could take starting at age twelve.

"I'll slip you in early if you really wanted to get started," Joan said. "If that's all right with you, Mrs. Carpenter?"

"That would be great, Mrs. Talbot." Tillie was amazed at the time everyone was giving them and grateful to them for making Julie's day, and evidently her life.

At 4:00 p.m., Joe asked them if they were hungry. When they said yes, they all hopped into Tillie's Escort and drove the short distance to Bentley's Restaurant, right on Overseas Highway. They had a children's menu for kids under twelve but Joe said they were all ordering from the main menu. Julie ordered the stuffed shrimp,

Tillie ordered lobster/shrimp crab cakes, and Joe got the St. Louis BBQ rib special. Tillie glanced at the prices and looked at Joe.

He simply nodded. "My treat."

It was about half of what he was paid every two weeks. He couldn't think of a better way to spend his money or his time.

At dinner, he gave Julie his number for Miami, and for the one in town at the Islamorada facility. "You can call me at any time but I may not always be around. I'll call you every week on Wednesday at 7:00 p.m. without fail unless there's an emergency. So don't get upset if I'm not there. I can't help it. That's the deal. I'll also meet you every other weekend on Saturday if you want. I'm around on Tuesday all day and in the morning on Wednesday before I leave for Miami."

They shook hands. Both Julie and Tillie gave him a kiss on the cheek. They drove him back to his cutter and said goodbye.

Tillie had a tear in her eye. "This was the nicest thing that has ever happened to me and Julie. It's most appreci-ated. The kindness and respect we received shows what kind of guy you are."

"I promise I won't let her down," he told Tillie quiet-ly.

As far as he was concerned, his family was 1,500 miles away and he had no one in Florida. He could not think of a better friendship than what had occurred that day. On ship, he spoke to Mark about what happened and could see that Mark understood the kind of person he was dealing with.

"How did it go?" Joan asked.

"Great. I gave them my number and I'll stay in con-tact with them if they want me to."

"That's great. I'm sure they will."

He left for an assignment around Key West, would be back in the early morning and then on to Miami.

"Did you enjoy yourself?" Tillie asked as they drove home.

"Oh, yes!" Julie had a new idol, a Coast Guard rock star. "I can't wait until I see my friends in school on Monday, and my teacher. I'm going to wear my hat and shirt. Will you wash my T-shirt because it's a little big and I want it to fit?"

"Sure. Of course."

At the time, Tillie hoped Joe would keep all of his promises to Julie. She wanted Julie to be happy, and that day had been the happiest she had ever been since she was born.

Joe kept every promised he ever made to her.

♥◑♥◑

Before going to bed, Julie got misty remembering all the kindnesses shown to her and Tillie by Joe and the rest of the Coast Guard crew. Not only that day but throughout her school years in Key Largo. Joe called her at 7:00 p.m. every Wednesday night, ever since she met him at age ten, ever since he was only a nineteen year old first year Coast Guard seaman. He called every week for the last fourteen years, not only when he was stationed in Miami and Islamorada in the Keys, which was only ten miles away, but also he continued to call her when he went back home to Troy.

He continued to see her and Tillie when he got vacation time. He even called the week his father was rushed to the hospital with a concussion coming from a home invasion at his house in Troy. As Julie nodded off to sleep, she could not think of anyone else in this world that kept his commitments like Joe Traynor. Making a commitment to a ten-year-old girl, whom he didn't even know, had changed the course of her life for the better. Tillie thought of him as a son, and Julie knew in her heart that Joe would always be there for both of them.

CHAPTER 13

All that week and into the next, both Julie and Joe had work to do, in addition to visiting Tillie and making plans for her ultimate return home. They would have to set up a schedule for the Visiting Nurses Association to spend time during the day, when both Julie and Joe were working, and then have Father Schmidt's volunteers from church sit with Tillie over the weekends when Joe would be at sea for an investigation and Julie attending cross-country meets and practices. If the church volunteers could cover Julie so she could work on her book, it would help as well.

Thank God, Tillie was covered under her school district health insurance plan to cover these additional expenses.

Neither Julie, nor anyone her age, would even think about coverage for home visits, rest homecare, or even for critical care. At age twenty-four, and even for Joe, those situations would never have occurred to them.

Joe was asked by Mike Kenny to analyze the results of the downloaded truck file that included all ownership of Ford F-150s, year 2002, painted white. The sheriff's office investigators were actually able to pinpoint the make and model through the color analysis. All vehicles had very specific color codes for each make, model, and year. For the 2002 year, Ford's white color was designated as Oxford White, specific to the F-150 pickup truck. However, Joe discovered, after lengthy research, there were two types of Oxford White that included designations YZ and Z1. The YZ and Z1 designations also pinpointed not only that it was a Ford F-150 pickup truck but also depending on the features, it was painted either color code YZ or Z1. So now, Joe had a list of 750 vehicles designated as 2002 Ford F-150s, painted white, but the paint scraped from Tillie's Escort was of the YZ designation. Unfortunately, this was the most popular truck. It had the fewest features for the model year, compared to the Z1 painted vehicles which had roof racks, special bumpers for plowing, and were undercoated for rough winters. There was no need for those features in South Florida, although Joe could have used them back in Troy. Nonetheless, many bought the truck with the higher priced features anyway. Dressing up a pickup truck in Florida was like buying a new Mercedes up north.

Joe went back into the Florida registration file, extracted YZ paint designation as part of the vehicle description, and sorted these vehicles, in order, by county, and then in alphabetical order, by owner. This dropped the ownership in question to 550 of the 750 vehicles. Evidently many owners in northern Florida still wanted the heavy-duty features of the Z1. The next step was to sort by first name, then last name, and to sort out all female truck owners who had obvious female first names. Then these remaining 450 vehicles were reassembled by county and last name of owner to remove obvious last names with a Hispanic origin. The resulting names were again alphabetized and sorted by first name, looking for the same results, obvious Hispanic first names. The final pass with potential Caucasian truck owners came to 402. These were sorted by county and by last name. The final county sort including Monroe and the two closest counties to Monroe covering the greater Miami area came to 245 potential hit and run drivers. It was a substantial amount. Joe would leave the 157 in the northern counties for the next run. At least now, a proper truck description with the proper paint code would be circulated to all Ford dealers and truck body work companies to see if any trucks had come in within the last few weeks with body damage, specifically with scrapes to the passenger side. That would also take some time. He doubted any hit and run driver would bring a vehicle in for repair as soon as the incident happened. They would most likely wait a length of time to let the news die down and have everyone forget about it. A lot of truck owners would either spray paint it or just leave it alone. He didn't believe there was a lot of damage to the truck in question, maybe a gouge or two and a five or six foot scrape mark on the passenger side.

Joe was also in the process of trying to figure out how to get the plastic wrapped package of $10,000.00 in one hundred dollar bills, along with the bills themselves, tested for any potential fingerprints. He brought home a fingerprinting kit and tried to work at the kitchen table to see if any would appear. He could then transfer the fingerprints to specialized fingerprint paper and send those prints electronically to either Mark in Fort Lauderdale or to the COMMSTA Center in Miami, or to Jack Forest up at the Atlantic Coast Intelligence Center in Virginia. No matter what, Joe had to be careful and it would take a lot of time. This was time he didn't know if he had.

Julie was back full time as a teacher's aide at her elementary school and still assisted the coach, her friend

Jimmy Smith, of the cross-country team, preparing for the last three meets and for the state events coming up in a month. She also submitted the $100,000.00 grant to the Florida Education Department for the Key Largo School to get a new technology lab. In addition, she could only work on her book at night, due to time constraints, usually right after they got home from visiting Tillie in the hospital. Tillie wasn't ready to come home yet and it looked like it would be a few more weeks. By that time, hopefully, they would be ready for her and have everything in place to get her through the day.

Julie would also sign Tillie up for the Lifeline connection, once she got home, so that Tillie could wear the Lifeline beeper around her neck when Julie and Joe were not there. If Tillie had a problem or an emergency, she could simply press the beeper, if she was able to, which sent an automatic call message to the company office. They, in turn, would call back immediately, through their own digital call box, usually placed near the customer's home phone. They would ask her if she was okay, and if not, they would immediately call one of four individuals designated to assist her during an emergency. It was usually a next-door neighbor who had a key. If they could not get through to any of the designees within ten minutes, they sent an ambulance to respond. They would send her to the appropriate emergency room at the hospital of choice, in this case, the only hospital for Key Largo, the Mariner Hospital in Tavernier. The total cost was $36.00 a month for the service. It was a real bargain.

Tillie improved every day but she was still not steady on her feet and needed physical therapy and cognitive conditioning to improve her mental functions. No one came out of head trauma cleanly, immediately, so it was an uphill battle. But in Tillie's case, she was lucky. She remembered new things every day, just not what had happened to her the night of the crash. Her long-range memory appeared to be fine. However, she had difficulty with certain words and could not recognize certain commands. She was frustrated, as only Tillie could be. She wanted to get out of bed and get back to work but even she understood this was not a quick fix or easy process.

Julie actually brought flash cards from school. Tillie thought the cards were useless until even she knew there were certain words and pictures she could not quite recognize. As soon as those cards were reviewed, the meanings seemed to pop in her head. She was having difficulty when she walked through the hallway, even though they wanted her to get up and walk about to keep her active so there would be no bedsores or other issues related to a bedridden condition. Julie and Joe brought her favorite foods most nights. She didn't complain about the hospital food. She ate most meals at the Waffle House anyway, previously, so she certainly didn't mind a little diversity in her food choices.

Doctor Robinson suggested having her moved to the longer term care facility connected to the hospital for a few weeks so she could be in a more appropriate home setting. Tillie said no, she wanted to be home as soon as practical. She knew it would be a burden on Julie but she was not going to be in a home for old people. She was sixty-three not eighty-three, and she let everyone know. Her appetite was getting better. She started to walk better on the walking cast and her pelvis was not an issue. Her headaches were subsiding and most of her nausea had passed.

Doctor Robinson felt, with her daily improvements, she would be able to leave the hospital almost one month to the day from the day of the accident.

ೞೞೞ

Since their schedules were completely full, Julie didn't want to get Joe upset, but she was getting a little worried about the money they found and it made her feel apprehensive in general. She couldn't put her finger on it but she wondered if she was being followed. It was nothing in particular but she had noticed for a while that after she pulled into school, or into the high school for cross-country practice, it felt like someone was watching her. When she turned around quickly, whoever was there disappeared. Julie wasn't sure what or who but she had an uneasy feeling.

She decided she would tell Joe tonight when she got back to the house. He was working every day, some days later than others, due to his investigations. He told her something big was coming down in the next week or two so not to expect him home on a regular basis for a while. She wasn't happy but what could she possibly say to Joe? She wasn't his wife, or even related to him. He gave both Tillie and her everything he had and more and he had to work or he would lose everything because of them. She certainly didn't want that to happen and she didn't want to alarm him—that was the last thing she wanted.

When she got home around 4:30 p.m., it was dark and winter seemed just around the corner. It was not the fall like in Providence with the trees becoming bare and snow starting in late October or early November. It was becoming noticeably fall in Key Largo since daylight savings was over. They lost an hour of light and it was mild but chilly at night. She would take late fall in the Keys anytime over New England. The only difference was the fall in New England was spectacular, a burst of vivid color, compared to the bland texture coming over her hometown of Key Largo. Key Largo changed gradually, with the trees starting to shed their leaves. New England *burst* into color. Joe used to kid that fall in upstate New York looked like his grandmother's couch. It seemed like every grandmother in the region had an autumn-season-colored couch in the living room. There was no escaping it. He laughed and said even Mary Lynch, at age twenty-eight, had a Grammy-couch in her living room. Florida Keys wicker furniture was a much better buy.

Julie opened her side door as always, dropping her keys on the kitchen table along with her books from school and her pocketbook. She reached into the refrigerator and grabbed a Pepsi. She did this almost every day, even when she was in college at Brown. Habits were not easy to break. She then hung up her coat and went into her makeshift office. It certainly was roomier since they threw out all the junk before finding the money. As she looked around, she had a funny feeling that someone had moved her stuff. Who? Why? How?

She went back to the kitchen and looked at the door. There were no marks of a break-in. Same with the front door. No jimmy marks or scratches on the lock. The chain was still on the front door. Everyone came in the back. She looked at her desk. The computer was not sitting right.

Yes, she knew she was anal retentive, but that's not exactly where her computer went. Files were not lined up straight, one on top of the other. The top page was from yesterday's work. She always left her work for the next day on top with her little notes attached. Those notes were not where she put them.

She opened her drawers and went into her files. The files were slightly out of sequence. She kept her documentation for the book in precise alphabetical order, not one file out of place.

Now three of them were not where they were supposed to be. The history files with the dates were out of sequence. The interview files where she kept her comments were at the bottom of the drawer. She was starting to get a little panicky.

When's Joe coming home? She called him on his cell. He said he was just leaving and would be there in twenty minutes.

As he pulled in, Julie quickly opened the back door and waited for him.

"Are you okay?" he asked. "What's wrong?"

"I think someone has been in the house. Someone has been searching through my files. Several of them were on the bottom of the file drawer."

"Did you check your computer?" he asked.

"Not yet, but it's password protected and I don't think anyone could figure out the password in a million years," she said.

"Is it T-i-l-l-i-e?" he asked.

"No, smart ass," she said and smiled.

"Let's go look around."

They searched thoroughly throughout the house, including the attic. Nothing was missing.

"I think we're both nervous about the money we found," he said. "If someone knew about it before now, it would probably already be gone."

"Who would know?" she asked.

"Your father, whom I believe hid the money in the attic, his two friends who drowned—and that was proven—and maybe whoever else was in on it."

"But everyone believed my father drowned," she said. "No one has come around since I was six years old that I know of. I would love to ask Tillie but who knows what she remembers now."

"Julie, who has been in this house for as long as you remember?" Joe asked.

"Believe it or not, just you, Tillie, and me," she said.

"No one else?"

"No one," she said.

"Here's what I am going to do," he said. "I am not leaving you alone for one minute. We are heading to my office and we're going to get my fingerprinting kit. And tonight, we'll turn this house upside down for prints. At least we threw out all the junk to make it easier," he added. "If anyone came in since we cleaned a few Saturdays ago when we found the money, there could be prints lying around." Joe paused and scanned the room. "My prints are on file because of my Coast Guard affiliation. Your prints are on file because of your new job at the school, and I don't believe Tillie ever had any reason to be fingerprinted. So on the way back, we'll stop and see Tillie and I will discreetly fingerprint her if possible. I will cover this house with fingerprint powder and use my light sensitive equipment that will pick up prints in the dark. We can then separate out our prints from anyone else's, and since no one that you know of has been in this house, we might just find something. Let's go."

They headed out to Joe's office for the fingerprinting kit and then immediately went to the hospital to get Tillie's prints to compare and eliminate from those in the house. Tillie was sleeping when they got there so Julie nudged her to wake her up. It took a few minutes but she was finally fully awake. Julie explained to Tillie they wanted to get her fingerprints to compare those with her Escort in case anyone got near the car or if the person who pushed her off the road got out and touched her car.

Joe had decided this was a reasonable explanation as he didn't want to go through the rest of the situation, including finding the money and the possible break in at her home. They wanted to wait until she was in better condition and could understand the possible ramifications of what had happened—and what could happen.

"Joe why doesn't the sheriff's office do my fingerprints instead of you?" Tillie asked.

"I was asked to do a potential search on the truck that hit you, and they also wanted me to eliminate your prints on your car from any others," Joe said.

It seemed reasonable to her so she put out her hands and let Joe do his work. They left right after, telling Tillie they would see her tomorrow and she fell right back to sleep.

On the way out, Julie said to Joe, "How did you concoct the story?"

"It just seemed reasonable to me it would occur that way if I was working for the sheriff's department. Eventually, I will take her prints and see if anyone else touched her car but I doubt it," he said. "I hope she doesn't mention it to Mike Kenny. In fact, I hope in her condition she forgets all about it. I'll tell him what I'm doing in time, just not yet."

They headed home.

CHAPTER 14

On the drive back from Joe's office, after getting Tillie's fingerprints, Julie thought about where she grew up and where she had lived her entire life before she headed north to go to college. She remembered her grandparents, Tillie and George Carpenter, had purchased their first and only home on Glendale Drive, right off Route 1, the Overseas Highway, on the southeast side of Key Largo, back in 1971, only a few years after they were married. They paid $12,500.00 for the three-bedroom cottage that sat on a postage-stamp-sized piece of a property. The house was only 1,100 square feet but was plenty big to shelter all those who came after them, including their daughter Annie, her husband Tom, and Julie herself.

Now, over forty years later, the property was worth twenty times what they paid for it. This was a big problem for natives to the Florida Keys. If they were not left property by their family, they could never afford to pay the current prices.

Taxes were not too bad. The upkeep on the house, without a mortgage payment, could certainly be paid by Tillie and Julie now. Electricity was very costly in the Keys so they were very careful how and when they used

heat in the winter and fans in the summer. Air conditioning was a luxury they could not afford.

Most cottages, like theirs in Key Largo, had ceiling
fans when it got really hot and the electric heat was
turned on for only about a week a year around Christmas.
Again, air conditioning was a luxury and used only during those really humid days. The thermostat was left on at
80 degrees and no lower. You could see the electric meter
outside the house moving at breakneck speed when the
AC was left on for an extended period of time.

Julie also thought about her first few days as a teacher's aide at the same elementary school she attended so
many years ago. She had to be at Key Largo School at
7:30 a.m. in the morning, every day. Back at Brown, 7:30
a.m. was the middle of the night. She worked late as a
waitress and scheduled classes for late mornings and early afternoon before her 5:00 p.m. waitressing shift. Now,
thank God, Tillie had gotten her up until she got used to
the changed hours.

It was only a short seven-mile drive out of her street,
Glendale Drive, down Atlantic Avenue, and then north
onto Overseas Highway. The Waffle House and her
school were only a few miles apart but Tillie had to leave
earlier for the breakfast crowd so she was up before Julie.
Tillie still had her old 1990 Ford Escort. The car had less
than 100,000 miles on it and it was still going strong. Julie leased her car, a Ford Focus, when she came back to
Key Largo, and she picked a plan for less than 6,000
miles a year to keep the monthly lease payment down.
Neither of them went anywhere other than to work,
home, or church. She used part of her cash stipend for the
down payment and sales tax on the car. She had to keep
an eye on the stipend because she needed all of it and
made ends meet with her small teacher's aide salary. For

now it worked fine. If she ever got to sell her book, she would probably have to double the mileage for her lease plan, just to get to an airport in Key West or Miami to make appearances. *One day at a time*, she thought. When and if her book sold, she could probably afford the changes necessary to become a full-time author. She would still keep her teacher's aide job in the meantime.

Julie had made it to her school at 7:20 a.m. every day, parked in the school lot, and walked to the fifth-grade class to which she was assigned. Jan and Julie got along fine since both attended St. Justin Martyr Church. Jan had two small children, a little girl in daycare, Madison age three, and her five year old son, Tony, who was in Kindergarten in the same school. Her husband dropped off her daughter before work and her son went with Jan to and from school every day. It was quite convenient.

"Hey, Julie."

"Hey, Jan."

The normal early morning conversation always began before the bell rang. Jan knew the reason Julie was only a teacher's aide and not a teacher, especially after she had graduated with honors with an MFA from Brown University. She was a writer first. The administration, being quite proud of Julie's accomplishments, also placed her with Jan in the exact same classroom Julie was a student in, way back when she was in fifth grade at the very same school. Talk about full circle. Jan knew Julie had an affinity for the school, the community, and that she wanted to give back after all the opportunities she received growing up with only her grandmother by her side.

Jan was not a native Conch but, in fact, grew up outside Harrisburg, Pennsylvania. She went to the University of Miami in Coral Gables and did her student teaching at this very same school during her senior year at Miami.

She fell in love with the area and with her now husband, Tony Marino, born and raised in the Keys. Julie and Jan had more in common than they could have ever imagined before they were placed together by the school principal, Mrs. Black.

Julie remembered one night in mid-October when she first started.

It was still warm by most standards, but the locals felt the change with the cooler nights and lower humidity during the day.

It was football weather and the Coral Shores High School Hurricanes were doing well this year. Jan loved the Hurricanes name because that was her college's nickname, the University of Miami Hurricanes.

"Julie, are you going to the game Friday night?" she asked.

"Are you kidding? Tillie wouldn't miss it for the world," she said.

"Tony and I are taking the kids if they can stay awake that long," Jan said and smiled. "Any dating prospects?"

"No." Julie said half-heartedly.

Julie remembered the conversation vividly.

"Everyone knew you were back," Jan told her. "Any calls from ex-boyfriends?"

"No. You know I didn't have time for all that back then," Julie said.

"How about now?"

"No."

"Was Joe coming down for Thanksgiving or Christmas this year?" Jan asked Julie.

"He's not sure. Joe has a new job at the consulting firm in Troy, and he had two calls from Homeland Security and has taken on a new assignment," she said. "He said he would let Tillie and me know as soon as he could."

"Is he still dating Mary from the Albany Coalition?" Jan asked.

"Yes, I think he may have found someone after all," Julie answered. "His previous Miami girlfriend Jennifer was a disaster, but I don't want to get into it. Talk about the jealous type. I met him at ten years old down here when he was only nineteen in the Coast Guard. He was like my big brother and Tillie's son, for God sake. What the hell was wrong with Jennifer? Mary was nice. I never met her but I spoke to her on the phone several times."

Jan thought Julie had held back her true feelings for Joe but it was intuition and nothing she could have put her finger on. "Are you ready to meet the fifth-grade holy terrors?"

"Bring them on," Julie said.

Just then, twenty-five ten year olds steamrolled over both Julie and Jan, and took their seats about ten seconds before the morning bell rang. While 7:30 a.m. to 2:30 p.m. every day might not seem like much for regular working stiffs, if they tried it for a whole year with twenty-five kids, they'd change their minds.

Every day, after watching their assigned school buses leave the premises, Julie and Jan met with the other fifth-grade teacher and aide, along with the principal. They compared notes and saw what worked, what didn't, and then they compared lesson plans and student evaluations. It had only been a few months into the school year but some kids were already behind, some were bored to death, and then you had to deal with those in between. School only seemed to work for those in between. Really smart kids were bored. Other students—due to a variety of issues—just didn't care, even in fifth grade.

Everyone had asked Julie how her book was coming, as soon as she started at the school. It was an open topic of conversation. She had made significant progress over the summer but then had to stop for three weeks to acclimate herself to her new role as a teacher's aide, meet the other faculty members, the staff and administration, and bone up on what a teacher's aide could and could not do at any given time. It was exhausting but she was now comfortable in her assigned role. At the time, she thought she could get back to the book without feeling overwhelmed. But now, with Tillie the way she was, Julie was inundated and not sure if she would ever finish what she started. She was about 150 pages into the book for now, on hold, with only a few hours a week currently devoted to new chapters. She felt the new book would be around 400 pages in length and approximately 50 to 70 chapters, more or less. She had 15 chapters done and it was a good start. But now, she wasn't so sure.

Julie remembered the old Yiddish proverb, "Man plans and God laughs." She knew where she was going. She had a road map, but would she ever get the time to meet her deadlines? Maybe, but not now, not until Tillie was home and feeling better. Julie believed, at first, it was just a matter of time before she was comfortable fitting in all the pieces. She remembered writing down some important questions that were at the heart of her book. *How do you talk about your mother dying of a drug overdose? What was it like living with your grandmother who didn't want to be called a grandmother? How about mother and daughter talks that never happened but became grandmother and granddaughter talks which were significantly different, coming from completely different generations and years apart?*

Growing up in the 1960s and 1970s was not the same

as the 1990s and the new millennium. Julie was the first Carpenter or Chapman to go to college, let alone an Ivy League university. *Receive a Masters in Fine Art, for what? Be a waitress, a mother, or a fisherman's wife? How did Joe Traynor fit in?*

Could she have written in her disguised memoirs that Joe was almost as influential in her life as her own grandmother who raised her, almost since birth? Would Tillie be mad when she read the book? Julie did not have any answers for the questions she'd proposed, not until she actually asked those most influential in her life what they really thought about everything. *Conch Town Girl* was going to be quite a project, if it ever happened.

With this new crisis of Tillie's hit and run, the money found in the attic, and the possible break-in at their house, her other questions that had filled up the pages of her notebook seemed irrelevant now. Just maybe, those questions would serve as the basis of what had already happened and what now appeared to be happening. Julie sure hoped Tillie had no involvement with the money in the attic—hoped to God she never knew anything about it.

But where the hell did it come from? Julie also wanted to know if they were in danger. How would she or Joe even know?

CHAPTER 15

As soon as Joe and Julie got back to the house, they had put their heads together and devised a plan of attack.

"There must be thousands of fingerprints all through this house, Joe," Julie complained. How do we attack it and keep it to a reasonable amount?"

"Let's think about this for a minute," he said. "We only cleaned up a little while ago and junked everything you wanted to let go. The attic should have no fingerprints in it except for ours. It should be the same for the attic drop down stairs and anywhere near where we cleaned everything and placed it in garbage bags to be thrown out."

They decided they would dust her office space because that's where she had noticed her things being moved. They would dust the entire kitchen and the back door area, since if anyone came in, they would have used the back door because the front door had the chain and the top security lock turned.

"I believe you Julie," Joe assured her. "I just don't know how anyone could have gotten in. All the windows are locked. I checked. But we'll go around each window in the back, not the front, because someone had to break in during the day when we were not here, and definitely not through the front, where someone would have noticed them while driving or walking by."

Joe took his time and showed Julie how to take fingerprints correctly. He had been trained by the best and he had done it himself on many of his own cases. Going to trial, if necessary, would be no problem because everything to be done would be by the book.

"No offense to Mike Kenny, or his investigators, but quite clearly, I am much better at this than they ever would be," he said. "I'll share the evidence, if any, with them, if we find out anything, depending on what we find out."

He went on and explained fingerprinting methodology, the whys, the how, and what to expect. "Properly identified fingerprints can uncover information used to identify an unknown victim, witness, or suspect, to verify records, and to establish links between a suspect and a crime. Since no two fingerprints are alike, dusting for fingerprints is a highly accurate method of identifying individuals at a crime scene."

He then told her to take some yellow post it notes and place the notes near, but not on, the surface she thought they should dust, starting with the attic as they needed to identify the surface area that they wanted to dust for fingerprints.

"Fingers are coated with perspiration and oil," he went on to say. "When fingers have touched any relatively smooth surface, the friction releases the oil from between the ridges of the fingers and a print is left."

He showed her how to pour a small amount of powder on a piece of paper and to use a powder whose color contrasted with the surface color. He carried several colors for this purpose. He started by trying a white powder on a dark surface and a black powder on a light surface. They needed special paper, the dust in various colors, and a soft bristle brush to obtain proper fingerprints.

He showed Julie how to shake the brush so the bristles spread apart, how to dip the tip of the brush into the powder, and then gently tap the brush's handle to remove excess powder. Then he had her run the brush's bristles lightly over the powdered surface in short and quick strokes. He showed her how to unroll the cellophane tape and how to gently press it on top of the print. He taught her to pull the tape away from the print in one quick and fluid motion and apply the tape with the print attached to a piece of the special paper from his kit.

"We should get around fifty samples from the areas we outlined, starting with the attic," he said. "It's a slow process, almost three hours long, but we have to do it to find out who came in."

For one last review of the attic, they needed to re-inspect the pull down stairs area and her office.

"Because oils and residues typically reside in the skin, fingerprints can be transferred easily to almost any surface a person touched," he continued. "Some surfaces create more of a challenge when fingerprints are detected, such as a highly contrasting printed page or porous surfaces. We'll also use ultraviolet light, also called a black light, with fluorescent powders, to help bring out the prints and then photograph those prints."

Joe was concerned about being able to see any prints on the papers in her office that consisted of the bright white copy paper she had been working on for her book. In his kit, he had the black light and fluorescent powder needed and the required camera that had utilized yellow or a 2-A haze barrier filter. He wasn't as familiar with this technology but he had the instructions printed out in his kit, so he could follow the instructions step by step. Julie stood right next to him like she was a surgical assistant in the operating room, handing him the scalpel when needed.

"Camera, chemicals, black light. Anything else, doctor?" she said, laughing.

The scalpels in this case were the camera, chemicals, and black light. The instructions said to spray or submerge the object to be fingerprinted in a fluorescent solution for five seconds to two minutes. He decided to spray. Submerging could be a problem. He had the proper ardrox system, versus the other acceptable lighting systems that included basic yellow 40, because they reacted to lower wavelength ultraviolet lights. He then followed the specific instructions for the chemical to be used. Next, the directions said to lower the ambient light in the area, put on the ultraviolet protective goggles, and then shine the black light on the object to look for fingerprints. The prints should glow from the reaction between the fluorescent solution and the black light. It said to place the yellow or 2-A haze barrier filter on his camera to enhance detail. Finally, it said to photograph the prints in close detail for later review.

After they were done, they picked up an additional five prints in her office, captured digitally by the camera, that the original dusting hadn't picked up. Joe had a special envelope to hold all the fingerprints they found and he included his prints he downloaded on line.

"Hand me the envelope on the coffee table, please," he told Julie. "We need to make sure we get everything together and shipped to Jack."

"No problem," Julie said as she handed Joe the special envelope.

Each fingerprint was placed on a separate page and

labeled as to exactly where it was taken from, specifically from the attic, the attic stairs, in the living room where they repacked what they found and threw out in garbage bags, in the kitchen, and in Julie's office area. Joe added Julie's prints to the package separately. They were the prints that were taken from her by the school district when she started working. He added Tillie's prints, which they'd just taken, and then separately placed the $10,000.00 in one hundred dollars bills with the Cyrillic strap attached. He sealed the envelope and would FedEx it immediately tomorrow morning to his friend Jack Forest up in Virginia, to be tested.

ဢဢဢ

During Joe's basic training in Cape May and at Yorktown, he made friends that had remained with him for the last fifteen years. They had built a trust system and watched each other's backs, even though they were all as different as night and day. Joe was the youngest in his class but they all got along pretty well. There were four others beside Joe in his immediate group including Mike McGreevy, who came from Seattle, Mark Silva from San Diego, now his best friend, Sean O'Neil from Boston—they came down together since they both signed up together in Malden, outside of Boston—and Jack Forest from Charlestown, South Carolina. They went through basic training and Yorktown together, ate, slept, and breathed the same air.

Jack originally grew up in New Jersey, the Cape May area, but his family transferred down to South Carolina when his dad's company moved. He still had family in Cape May and while in basic, on weekend leave, saw his grandparents, on both sides, as they lived their entire lives in Cape May. Jack had just turned twenty-two when Joe was eighteen and he wanted to attend Officer's Training School since he just graduated from Rutgers University—New Jersey's State University—at Camden with a BS in computer science. Jack's computer science degree allowed him to pick the intelligence field and he wound up in Joe's training group. Now at thirty-seven years old, and a Coast Guard lifer, Jack had his own department. Jack was still at the "A" School in Yorktown, Virginia. He was in charge of the Artificial Intelligence Training Program and responsible for testing all new innovations in intelligence for the Coast Guard, for the entire Atlantic Coast region.

Jack had been testing and had used the new fingerprint technology called FIF—Familial Similarities in Fingerprints. It was an amazinge breakthrough in fingerprint technology which isolated information on parenthood with fingerprint whorls and loops that were remarkably similar to both mother and father. The top of the fingerprint "matched" the father's, while the bottom half "matched" the mother's. This methodology proved parenthood on both sides for the first time ever.

Joe was very curious to see what the results would be. *Who would break into a house where there has only been the same occupants for the last forty years?* Until Joe, the only people ever in the house were Julie and her grandmother. *If there were a break-in, it would have to be the most successful in history since no one could find anything. Nothing was taken, Julie believed things had been moved, but there was no damage anywhere. There was no attempt to pick or break the locks on the doors or even the windows. It was as if someone, if there was someone, walked right through the door.*

"Julie, have you ever had your locks changes since you've been here?"

"Not that I know of. We have had the same key since I was ten years old," she said, "Why?"

"I was just thinking out loud," he said. "We should change the locks tomorrow first thing just in case. What if Tillie ever lost her key? Someone could have picked it up and used it."

"I don't believe so, but you never know," she said.

"I'll call in the morning and have the locksmith come over when I get back later in the afternoon." *Another Visa charge coming up.*

"That really is a good idea. I know I'll feel safer," Julie said.

They cleaned up all the mess and went to sleep around 1:00 a.m. in the morning. Joe had to move all the junk off the couch where he slept. Julie headed to her room. They were both tired but they felt better knowing they were actively doing something about finding the hit and run driver, not just sitting around and waiting for the sheriff's department to respond at their leisure. Joe called Jack as soon as he could, and told him to expect a FedEx package no later than tomorrow morning with all the evidence, if it could be called evidence.

"I'll do it as quickly and as quietly as I can," Jack said. "I have some discretion because I'm in charge but for my final report at the end of the month, I will have to justify my time and expense. I'm sure I can come up with some stupid reason," he told Joe. "I won't lose much sleep over it."

CHAPTER 16

The next day, Joe and Julie had breakfast and headed out to work. Both had long days planned. There was nothing specific to do at home, other than wait for the test results of the fingerprints from Jack. So they went back to their normal routines.

Julie called the hospital to see how Tillie was but she would be unable to see her today. Joe would miss her as well. He had already completed his outline of the list of the Ford F-150 white 2002 trucks registered in the state of Florida, sorted every way he could. He put together a flyer on the truck description, and the potential damage, to be sent to all the truck bodywork companies in the state, not expecting much from the effort but you never knew. He emailed the list and the flyer to Mike Kenny at the sheriff's office and headed out the door for Islamorada to catch his ship to Key West for a meeting. He told Mike, in the email, about his upcoming schedule for the Coast Guard and, if anything came up, he gave him several phone numbers to call. They would do ship-to-shore and vice versa contacts. His cell phone would not work out at sea. He would have to use his intelligence encrypted satellite phone instead. He didn't give this number to Mike because it was classified.

Julie had to go to a cross-country meet at 3:30 p.m. and catch the team bus at the high school at 2:00 p.m. As soon as she got out for the school day, she ran to her car and just barely made the bus for the trip to Marathon High School, which was about forty miles away. With one-lane traffic going both ways, it took about fifty minutes to get there since buses were not allowed, by law to pass others, leaving little time for the boys and girls to warm up. There were four other high schools competing that day, and they waited another fifteen minutes for the last bus to arrive. It gave them enough time to go through their warm-up routine. They had already run this course earlier in the season, before Lucy really started to get the hang of running and pacing herself. She came in sixteenth in that earlier race. She was now considered an up-and-coming runner and came in second in the last race. So she was starting to be noticed.

The race went off fifteen minutes late, but toward the end, Lucy was really moving and passed the one girl in front of her with about a half-mile to go. She took the lead and never looked back, winning by over twenty seconds over the runner-up. The girls won the meet and the boys, still in a rebuilding year, actually came in third. This was their second non-last-place finish of the year. Everyone was happy and jumped up and down. *You would think they won the Olympics,* Julie thought with a smile.

The bus ride back was very pleasant. Lucy came up to the front and sat with Julie before the bus left. Julie smiled. That was a really nice gesture on Lucy's part. Julie had been her babysitter forever, but this was the first real sign they were really good friends as well. Most kids didn't want to be considered a kiss up, but Lucy couldn't have cared less.

രുന്ദ

Joe spent the day on the ship going into Key West. He set up a plan for the following week with the other Coast Guard vessels stationed there. They talked about timing and logistics. Joe knew from the chatter in Spanish that a big shipment would be coming. They just didn't know exactly where, but they plotted out a reasonable plan of attack, knowing all the major drug runner lanes used around Key West. They had the helicopter pilots review the takedown plan and determine their involvement as well.

Logistically, the soon-to-be-drug-laden, go-fast boats came one way and the big ships came another. Joe knew from the chatter the shipment would be coming in near Key West, about twenty-five miles southwest, and a ship would be meeting a go-fast boat sometime next Wednesday. He tried to pin it down closer by continuing to review the transmissions. He believed it would be closer to 4:30 p.m., since they normally wanted to do the ship to go-fast boat transfer in the dark. Like everyone else, drug runners were creatures of habit, which helped Joe immensely in his planning. He wondered if they ever thought about their own patterns when doing drug runs. He hoped not.

Joe had to be very careful about the actual search of any vessel he believed was carrying drugs. One aspect he had to be extremely careful about, in all cases, was how the search of the boat came about. Just thinking the vessels looked "suspicious" was not enough. Coast Guard authorities were not allowed to search a person's vessel at will.

They had to follow certain rules, even if it meant establishing probable cause for getting a warrant. If authorities performed a search illegally, it could render any evidence obtained during the search inadmissible in court.

Joe's intelligence work played a key role since the transmissions from the ship served as a means of getting a warrant to search the vessel, once he knew the actual name of the ship. He traced the transmissions back to the actual vessel and then pinpointed the location at sea. He had a helicopter fly over and the pilot took pictures of the ship to find out the name, which was located on its side. This showed cause and was the basis for the warrant. That was what he worked on. He would have until next Wednesday, when the transfer was supposed to take place.

He came down to Key West from Islamorada on one of the first of six brand new 154-foot Sentinel-class ships called Fast Response Cutters that arrived in the Keys in mid-August, only a few months ago. The crews of the new vessels were in training to operate the new ships and this drug runner case of Joe's would be a perfect addition to the training schedule. Earlier last week, he'd heard the ship carrying the drugs could contain over thirty-nine bales of cocaine. That much cocaine was estimated to be worth about $24 million dollars. He also believed there would be four people on the boat. They would likely face drug trafficking charges.

In addition to the Fast Response Cutters now training in the Keys, fifty-eight additional Fast Response Cutters were being built in Louisiana that would eventually go through Key West, specifically within the next few months, en route to their home ports, mostly located around Florida. Those ships were to be outfitted and made sea-ready. Joe would be very busy. He was only one of a few that was fully experienced in the intelligence sector, especially with his language skills and expertise.

All these new ships would replace the aging 110-foot Island-class cutters nationwide. In Key West, that included the *Pea Island, Kodiak Island, Knight Island,* and *Key Biscayne*. It was decided to replace them after a failed retrofit in 2004 that continued to be plagued with structural problems. The new ships, with room for 24 crewmembers, cruised at twenty-eight knots and sported a remotely operated twenty-five mm chain gun and four fifty-caliber machine guns. The cutters' go-fast boats could be deployed via their sterns, as opposed to the cranes used now—a big improvement in the hunt for drug submarines. The Coast Guard now had the technology, the equipment, and the crews but still needed people with Joe's experience. It would not be long before Joe got more than a temporary assignment.

୧୬୧୬

Joe got back late, around 8:00 p.m., to the Islamorada station. He called Julie and then picked up submarine sandwiches for her and himself at the 7-11 store on the way home, along with a twelve-pack of Sam Adams *Oktoberfest* beer. Julie had gotten home around 6:00 p.m. and had some cheese and crackers while waiting for Joe.

They really needed to go grocery shopping. It had been almost three weeks since she picked up any real groceries. They seemed to have been living on snacks forever.

She heard his car pull up and looked out the window. Joe opened the kitchen door, handed her the beer, and said, "Let's eat."

She smiled. "I'm fine, Joe. How are you as well?"

"I'm sorry, I'm starved. How are you, Julie?" he asked politely.

"Good. The plates are out and the glasses are ice cold for the beer."

They ate quickly. Evidently, Julie was as hungry as Joe. She picked up the leftover bags from the subs, put all the remnants into the garbage bag, and then took it outside. In the Florida Keys, due to the weather conditions, if you missed one week of garbage pickup, you would smell it forever, especially left over submarine sandwich wrappers.

As soon as Joe walked into the living room with his second bottle of *Oktoberfest,* the phone rang in the kitchen. Julie picked it up. "Hello."

"Hi, Julie, it's Jack. How are you?"

"Good, Jack. Do you want to speak to Joe?"

"Why don't you put it on speaker phone," he said. "That way you both can listen in."

"Great," she said and moved the phone closer to Joe in the living room.

"Can you both hear me?" Jack asked.

"Yes," they said at the same time.

"Well here it goes. Of the fifty-five fingerprint pages you sent me, I found four distinct matches. I found Julie's fingerprints on twenty-five of the matches, with five of them labeled 'The attic.' Most of yours, Julie, were on the sheets labeled 'Julie's office.' Joe, your fingerprints were on fifteen of the samples, mostly in the attic and stairs, as labeled on the sheets. Tillie's fingerprints were on the kitchen and back door sheets with five fingerprints that were clearly hers. This takes care of the three of you.

"In addition, there are ten fingerprints, two on the back door window, five on the white sheets of paper in the office, as you have labeled those prints. Two were on the drop down stairs to the attic, and one was on the side of the dropdown door for the attic. However, we have no record of those fingerprints in our system. We also did an analysis using our new FSF testing on those fingerprints that we could not find within the system. As a matter of fact, Tillie's were not in the system either, so I was glad that you went ahead and took her fingerprints at the hospital. Without those, we would not be able to identify her. We had both of your fingerprints on file. Julie's were the most recent, and Joe, your prints were from when you came on board with the Coast Guard, fifteen years ago. Back to the FSF testing," he said. "What it showed was, for all it's worth, Julie, Tillie is your grandmother. Her fingerprints matched the bottom swirl of yours, meaning she was related to you on your mother's side."

"Wow, really?"

"Really," he said. "Now, this is more critical, Julie. The unknown fingerprints also match your fingerprints. The fingerprints are most definitely your father's prints, which matched the top swirl of your own fingerprints. Tillie's are less of a match because it skipped a generation, but clearly the other unknown fingerprints are your father's prints. The prints matched, Julie."

Joe had kind of suspected something like this was going on but never articulated it to Julie. "Can you tell how old the unknown fingerprints are?" Joe asked Jack,

"The prints are no older than three years old, and more likely less than a year old because there was no degradation in the prints."

"He's alive isn't he?" Julie said, turning to Joe. "My father is alive?"

"Yes," Jack agreed. "I believe that is true."

"So he didn't die seventeen years ago?" Joe asked. Julie looked pretty shook up. Joe put an arm around her shoulders. "I believe the hit and run is probably related to this as well. I do not believe in coincidences." However, he didn't want to show the sheriff's department their hand just yet.

"I looked at the one hundred dollar bills as well," Jack told them. "There are so many fingerprints on the money that I couldn't distinguish one from the other. I can tell you there is three times the cocaine residue on all the bills you sent me than there is on bills in regular circulation in the United States. All one hundred dollar bills have cocaine residue but this is clearly worse. I can tell you for a fact the paper wrapper is Cyrillic in origin, at least the stamp was, and it stands for ten thousand dollars. I believe it was the designation for each bundle of one hundred dollar bills."

"I believe that as well," said Joe.

"We also know the paper wrapper around the bills was very distinctive and is manufactured for the Cayman National Bank," Jack continued. "We have seen this before in our drug busts. You probably didn't notice but on the inside of the wrapper was a small CNB logo."

"No, we didn't even really examine the wrapper, Jack. Great find."

"So putting this together, your money came from the Cayman National Bank in the Cayman Islands and had a Cyrillic stamp on it. We know the Russian mafia moved into the Caribbean and then into Florida from Cuba. When the Russian government pulled up stakes in Cuba, the Russian Mafia moved in. Castro had been a transfer station for drug smuggling since he came into power. After the Russians left, this was his only source of income. Joe and Julie, please be very careful. These people don't play by the rules, as you know, Joe. Can you at least fill me in?"

"I am not 100% sure what's going on but this was what Julie and I believe. Julie correct me if I am wrong."

Joe then went on to tell him about the hit and run, the money, and the break-in. "Please keep it under your hat for now until I know exactly what to do."

Joe asked Jack for another favor. He knew the Coast Guard had been using progression technology for the last several years. Through the use of computers and some relatively new recognition software, Jack could take a picture of an individual at a certain age and then age what the person would look like over the years. Joe asked Julie to take the pictures of her father out of the frames in the living room, copy the pictures into her computer, digitize them, and send the pictures to Jack.

"Jack, Julie will be sending you pictures of her father at age eighteen. It's her father and mother's wedding picture. She will also be sending you a picture of him at twenty-four, right before he supposedly died. If he was alive today, as we now suspect, he would be forty-one years old this year. Can you age him to age forty-one, Jack?"

"Well, not specifically age forty-one, but we can age him to be between age forty and fifty, in both good shape and not so good shape. The aging might be completely different if he didn't take care of himself. We did one drug user and, at age forty year old, he looked almost sixty-five."

"How long will this take?"

"Hopefully, I can do it within the next day or two and figure out a way to justify the expense. It doesn't matter if you pay for it or not. Something has to go into my report."

"I understand, and I owe you a big one."

"No you don't, Joe. We've always looked out for each other, the entire old crew, and you know that."

Joe thanked him and hung up. He looked at Julie and, as he suspected, she was still shook up.

"My father is alive and he had been all this time?"

"I believe so," he said.

"Do you think he is responsible for hitting Tillie?" she asked.

Joe didn't want to answer her but reluctantly said, "Yes, I do."

"I do too," she said. "What are you going to do with the pictures?"

"Well, I suspect your father drove the white Ford pickup truck that hit Tillie. I believe he probably owned it in his own right, under an assumed name, since it's a 2002, because it's almost eleven years old. I am going to match the truck registration and the driver's license information. I already did the sort and I have a good idea of owners of those trucks who are most likely white. I will try to match the Florida driver's license picture to the new picture of your father as he might appear in early middle age as soon as it comes in from Jack. I really can't think of anything else to do other than if he shows up at your front door and says, 'Hi, Julie, I'm you father.'"

"Fat chance," Julie said.

"If there is a match, and I suspect there will be, we can get a home address and the name he is now living under. I don't suspect he has used his own name for the last seventeen years. Do you? He would be nuts to run around as Tom Chapman if he stole at least $300,000.00, if not more, from the Russians as I suspect. However, we know from experience, people living under assumed names, even those in the witness protection program, tend to keep their same initials for both first and last names. Out of curiosity alone, I will look for names with 'TC' in them, unless he became Hispanic, which I don't believe he could do since he could not change his coloring very much, but you never know. I will be looking for a forty-year-old white male, living somewhere in Florida, with the initials TC. That's what I hope for, at least."

"Why he left all the money in our attic is beyond me," Julie said. "Other than that it was safe in case he ran into trouble. Maybe he had more and this was the last of it."

"Who knows at this point but, Julie, we will find out," he said. "If he hit Tillie, the son of a bitch is going to jail. I hope you agree."

"Agree? Yes. I would rather see him dead or in jail for what he did," she said. "He doesn't care about us obviously. Trying to kill Tillie proved it."

"Of course, we need to find out for sure," Joe said. "Now we have to wait for the pictures to come back from Jack. It will take some time but I believe we are on the right track."

Julie agreed and since there was little she could do in the meantime, she decided to start working her novel once again.

The whole affair was taking its toll on her and Joe could see it. He had to move quickly as well. He had only sixty days down in Islamorada to resolve all these issues. He could not count on the sheriff's office to help out. They had not been very helpful to date, except for getting Joe the truck registrations data file. He thought they did it quickly, simply because they did not want to spend the time tracking down hundreds of trucks. Joe was looking for a needle in a haystack.

CHAPTER 17

Julie had settled in nicely into her fall semester at the Key Largo School before Tillie's hit and run—and the issues of the money turning up in Tillie's attic—had turned her world upside down. The only training she had in education was her few weeks with the staff before the fall semester started but she was very quick on her feet and learned all the skills required of a teacher's aide. She learned new teaching and learning techniques every day from Jan and the others, with a few helpful calls to her close friend, Maddy. The school wanted Julie there and they wanted her to succeed so they went above and beyond to help her get up to speed. She was very appreciative.

Her kids improved by leaps and bounds in writing, vocabulary, and in expressing their thoughts on paper. She helped out as best she could in the areas of math and science. Those were the areas Joe got her through in her four years at Coral Shores High School. Going to Brown's Fine Arts program meant not having to worry as much about those topics. Her job at Brown was to improve her English language arts and writing skills. Those were her strengths and where she wanted to be both professionally and academically. Her math was certainly good enough for any real world applications, including figuring out car lease rates, down payments, balancing a checkbook, and other meaningful applications. If they taught math like Joe taught her, the world would be better off.

Doing math, especially where addition was required, adding up the numbers from right to left instead of left to right, was much easier to grasp for almost anyone. No wonder people were lost when their calculators weren't handy. It was funny how she actually taught Joe effective English writing and comprehension, even when she was in high school. Joe was math oriented. He didn't know how to structure sentences for his reports or how to write clearly so he was as well understood in written form as he was verbally. Joe was never misunderstood verbally. You knew exactly what he was saying and why.

Her students knew Julie was writing a book and Jan promoted her work as an inspiration and as a model these students could follow as well as achieve. These students were on the same exact educational path, sitting in the same exact classroom as Julie had thirteen years ago. They had the same experiences growing up in the Keys but maybe did not have it quite as bad as Julie's situation. Many were from broken homes, poverty, and a downward spiraling economy that left their parents unemployed or working two and three jobs just to put a roof over their heads and food on the table.

Julie and Jan were very aware of this, especially from working as volunteers on Saturdays at the food pantry at St. Justin's. Parents showing up for food were the same parents of those students in their very own classroom. It was the only show in town both for school and church. Multigenerational families were living under one roof in homes they couldn't afford on their own. At least

George and Tillie bought their place in the early 1970s and now Tillie could at least afford to keep up with the taxes and repairs, especially since Tillie and Julie were on their own for so long a time. Julie's five years in college had also been a burden to Tillie, keeping the house up on her own and sending Julie airplane fare when she could, along with a credit card to pay for absolute necessities. Making minimum payments to cover the bills over those five years had added up. Payments were made on time, but just barely.

With everything that had happened since she'd been home, Julie had to bite the bullet and make quality time every night, hour after hour, so she could continue to write her book, do her research, and review her daily lesson plans that Jan and she would implement every day. She was not discouraged but it was getting there. Julie just wanted some free time once in a while. Writing *Conch Town Girl* could not be a burden to her because then the book would not be very good. It would not flow and it would not tell the story she needed to tell to help young girls who were now exactly in the same place she'd been while growing up. *Make the time, dammit! Can't be any clearer.*

It was now 8:00 p.m. and Julie went to her home office cave, hollowed out from the stacks of memories in the back room. She had written eight additional chapters and about fifty more pages and she had been at this same spot for two weeks. *It's now time to move forward*, she thought.

She continued the tale with her parents' wedding, the shotgun affair at St. Justin Martyr's Catholic Church. Annie's pregnancy hadn't added to the joy of the ceremony but she wore white. Any other color would have raised eyebrows. The reception was held in the church's annex, right next door to the church. Only about 50 family members and friends attended. Everyone there knew the deal. Tom's parents attended the ceremony but not the reception. Tom was an only child so this was a slap in the face to Annie and Tillie. Tom's parents told him he would ruin his life by marrying Annie. Tillie gave Annie away since her husband George was deceased and there were no other relatives to speak of. There were no adult males left. There were several relatives from the south, nearer to Key West. They implied it was more of an imposition than a celebration and that was pretty much the last Tillie and Julie ever saw of their closest relatives. A majority of the guests were the everyday patrons and staff from the Waffle House and a very select few from church.

Julie tried to develop a family tree, downloading information from websites that dealt with genealogy. Every step leading up to her father and mother's life was a dead end, literally a dead end. Everyone was dead. Early death came from working too hard, or the men were lost at sea on a fishing boat. There were several incarcerations for drug running, making it even more difficult. The family appeared to be untraceable, or at least unreliable in getting to the current descendants.

Her father's death was most perplexing to Julie. She had been six years old, in first grade at the time, in 1996. Her father was away most of the time and Julie really never saw him very much. He joined the Florida Keys Commercial Fishermen's Association as soon as the association allowed him into the organization. He began working at the age of thirteen or fourteen—she couldn't recall for certain, Tillie's words not Julie's. He signed up for a crew when not in school—on weekends, holidays, and during vacations. His ship was docked at the Key

Largo Harbor Marina, right down the road on Oceana Drive, right off Overseas Highway, only a mile from their house. He was with the same crew for over ten years. It was really his first family and Julie's was his second. *God, he loved the sea and he couldn't get enough of it.* How he graduated from high school and had time to marry Annie was still a blur. Julie thought her father had loved her, but the way he was raised completely dictated the way he was, the way he acted, and formed the life he led right up until he died. It was sufficient to say he was not very fatherly.

Later on, after marrying Annie and moving in with Tillie, he would be at sea for two weeks at a time, sometimes more, then home for a short while, doing other things, not really with the family. It was as if he was a guest who showed up for dinner and left. He always had something to do—fixing the boats and the nets, or transporting the fish once he was back at the docks. He made good money but no one ever really saw anything from him. He didn't contribute to any of the bills that piled up. Tillie and Annie took care of those. Tillie never said a word. She could tell Annie was not pleased with how her life with Tom turned out. Tillie spent more time with Julie than either parent. When Tom was home, he took Annie out to the bars. What else was there to do in Key Largo? Julie's pictures and stories about the sea, put on the refrigerator, were left unread by everyone but Tillie.

It was a really bad week in the Keys that month in 1996. It was during hurricane season and tropical storms took their toll. The ocean was choppy and deadly. Late on a Wednesday night, Annie got the call that there was a problem with Tom's boat. They weren't sure what had happened but as soon as they knew, they would let Annie know. Evidently it had capsized during a major storm near Big Pine Key, southwest of Key Largo. The boat and two of his shipmates washed up on shore. Both men were dead from drowning. They weren't sure what had happened to Tom at the time and everyone prayed he was safe and sound. Tom Chapman was never found. The two men had their safety equipment locked in but the waves were too large and deadly. They must have hung on for dear life but were overcome. No one knew where Tom was, from Marathon to Big Pine Key. He could have been anywhere in that part of the ocean. Why he was the only one unattached to the boat was still a question to this day. There were no fish on board and the boat was still very much intact. It had cracks and multi-damage stem to stern, but was otherwise still intact, upside down, not far from shore.

Annie didn't take it well to say the least. She didn't see him enough as it was. Now, with him missing, she might not ever see him again. She fell into a very bad state of depression and, after the service, without a body, she went downhill fast. Julie, at age six, really didn't know what was going on. She only knew her dad was missing but she didn't really know what that meant. Kids at school were unkind, teasing her every day, wanting to know where her dad was. Kids can be cruel, really cruel.

Word was that her mom was out and about, in a town where the gossip traveled faster than the speed of light. Annie missed her shifts at the Waffle House. Tillie covered for her as much as she could but someone had to be home at night with Julie. You couldn't just leave a six-year-old by herself. Fine, she was covered during school hours but babysitting her was never enough. She needed a mother and a father and she had neither. Tillie was the only ray of sunshine in her life. The bills were left unpaid so she could be with her only granddaughter and Tillie became the mother she needed. For two years, Annie's the downward slide was just too much to bear, until the woman finally succumbed to the drugs.

Tillie just couldn't go out every night, picking Annie up when she could find her, with Julie in the car sound asleep. Almost two years to the day from Tom's disappearance, the cops found Annie in a coma, slumped down behind the bar's dumpster, in back of the building. Tillie received the call around 1:20 a.m. in the morning. She woke Julie, got her dressed, started her car—it took a while—and rushed to the hospital. They were not told what Annie's condition was, other than it was critical. She was rushed to the hospital but died in the back of the ambulance before reaching the emergency room. The EMTs knew Annie and did everything they could to try and revive her but to no avail.

It was 2:00 a.m. in the morning and Tillie and Julie met the ambulance at the emergency room entrance. The ambulance was still running, so Tillie thought just maybe Annie would be okay. Tillie saw the EMTs who simply shook their heads at her with tears in their eyes. Two of the EMTs had grown up with Annie and they knew all the circumstances surrounding her being in the ambulance. They brought Tillie and Julie to the back, opened the double doors of the van and uncovered Annie's face. Both Tillie and Julie kissed Annie goodbye and went home. They collapsed into each other's arms, looked into each other's eyes with nothing left in the tank. Tillie was broke, had a new funeral to take care of, and an eight-year-old granddaughter to be strong for. No one knew the future, but she was not going to let Julie down, ever.

But how did you raise an eight-year-old child by yourself at forty-eight years old with no benefits, no savings, and limited prospects for the future?

They had the house but nothing else. Time would tell.

Julie finished her thoughts, closed the computer, and decided to call it a night. Real life was depressing enough. Writing about it, made it even worse. She would temper all the bad thoughts with the good times she'd had in spite of all the problems she and Tillie had over the last fifteen years. She was back now in Key Largo, maybe back for good, and determined to make sure nothing happened to Tillie, if she had anything to say about it. Julie knew that Joe felt the same way and she could count on him, not just for moral support, but to do everything in his power to protect both of them. He'd proved it time and again over the years, ever since he showed up at her school so long ago.

CHAPTER 18

The next day, Julie left after school around 3:00 p.m., making the drive home in seven minutes, door to door. Phil, from the Waffle House, dropped off some extra waffles and fried chicken for her and Joe. He knew how much she'd loved the combination growing up and would probably still say it was her personal favorite, with butter and maple syrup poured generously over everything that moved.

She thought carpet would taste just fine if smothered in maple syrup. She and Joe would eat around 5:00 p.m. like clockwork. She changed her teaching attire, put on her running shoes, shorts, and T-shirt over her sports bra and drove a few miles south to her old high school. She stopped in quickly to go to the girl's locker room. She got some water from the fountain and said hello to a few old friends before hitting the outdoor track.

The principal, Gary Myers, wasn't in but she asked his assistant Marlene to say hello for her. Julie walked down the hall and looked in to see her old biology teacher Mrs. Proctor, who was retiring in the spring after thirty-eight years of teaching high school. She had not lost a step and was just as sharp as always, looking forward to retirement.

She told the principal she would help out when she could, tutoring biology students, because you couldn't just replace a biology teacher overnight in this day and age. Biology teachers, like math teachers, were few and far between.

"Hi, Mrs. Proctor, how are you?" Julie asked.

"Hi, Julie, how are you? How is your grandmother? I heard and I am so sorry."

Julie told her quickly and then Mrs. Proctor asked her how her book was coming. Everyone wanted to know how the book was coming, right after asking about Tillie.

"Slow, but I am making progress. It might be in time to hand you a retirement present," she said, smiling.

"That long, huh?"

"Well, I am a teacher's aide now, you know."

"Oh, I forgot! How's it going?" Mrs. Proctor asked.

"Better than my book," Julie said.

"Oh, come on. You should blow through that in no time. You have such a story to tell."

"Thanks. We will see." Julie said goodbye and ran out the door toward the track.

She was meeting the girls' high school cross-country team for practice. They had already started and she was meeting them at the halfway point. The coach, Jimmy Smith, graduated with her, went to teacher's college in Miami, and now was the girls' outdoor and cross-country track coach as well as a history teacher. He was an All Florida Boys' Cross-Country first team all-star in his senior year, breaking the boys' record by ten seconds. His trophy was still in the trophy case at the entrance to the high school.

"Hey, Jimmy, am I late?" she asked.

"They're just rounding the corner and they get a five minute water break. We can join them at that point and finish the run with them," he said. "We should get our miles in anyway."

"Sure, that would be great," she said.

Julie was also a very good runner, at five-feet-ten-inches tall, weighing one-hundred-and-thirty pounds, with miniscule body fat in high school. Now in her twenties, she still weighed the same as in high school. She kept in shape but it was getting harder and harder, especially with all that had come down recently. She lived for cross-country in high school and never had to watch her weight. Working as a waitress right alongside Tillie, before and after practice, meant she could eat waffles and fried chicken by the bucketful and never have to worry. Now, once a week was about all she could handle, especially after being in Providence at Brown for five years. When she asked her friends if there was a waffle and fried chicken place around Providence, they all looked at her like she was nuts. *I guess I'll have to keep grits to myself,* she thought at the time.

Jimmy and Julie joined the girls near the water fountain and exchanged pleasantries. The girls had met Julie a little while ago after Jimmy had asked her to assist him with coaching the girls' team. The girls didn't know her background, except for Lucy, whom Julie had recruited for the team this year. A few of them asked Jimmy who she was and he let them know what she had accomplished at this very same high school. He used her story as an incentive for them to do better both in sports and in school. The girls were quite impressed but kept it to themselves until they figured out what she was really all about. After her grandmother's accident became known, they though more of her for coming to practice as much as she did in spite of her difficulties. They knew she was all about commitment at this point.

They all left together, crossed the football field where the guys were ogling the girls between pushups, and started down the cross-country course for the last three miles of the practice.

Julie and Jimmy followed the team closely, back about one hundred yards so they could talk. Jimmy had just gotten married during the summer to a local girl he actually only met in college. It was amazing how you could meet someone for the first time after going to school with them all through high school. Evidently they didn't hang out in the same circles and they lived on opposite ends of town. She was a cheerleader for the football and basketball teams while Jimmy led his lonely runner's existence and never really attended any other events. When they met in college in Miami, they vaguely remembered each other but knew nothing about each other. It was like having met someone for the first time.

Julie led the same kind of life as Jimmy in high school, in addition to the fact that she worked twenty to thirty hours a week waitressing at the Waffle House. Other than running, her extracurricular activities were limited. She was salutatorian of her high school class and did extremely well on her SATs. She knew she wanted to be a writer and her early admissions application to Brown University was solidified with her essay, which became the basis for her now anticipated book. A thick envelope had arrived before Christmas of her senior year. It relieved a lot of pressure. She still was not sure how she was going to pay for anything. However, like all Ivy League Schools, if you were accepted and had a family income below a certain level, tuition and room and board were free. She still had to pay for daily transportation, airplane tickets, clothes, and books. Those bills were in excess of $3,000.00 a year so she had to do work-study as well and became a Dorm Resident Leader during her last undergraduate year and through her MFA, one year later.

"Jimmy, thank you for everything. I really enjoyed coaching the girls," she said at the end of their run.

She remembered the first day she ran with the team and later that afternoon, Jimmy had asked her to be the assistant coach. She'd been thrilled and accepted on the spot. He knew she didn't have the time every day, especially now after the accident, but he knew she could give the girls a much different perspective than he could, especially on the effects of running on a girl's body. He told her at the time he would be more than happy to split the $1,500.00 annual stipend but she declined. He knew the principal would be thrilled to have her back at the high school, even as a part time assistant coach.

At the time she'd said, "You know, I would really like to, if you don't mind."

"Mind? Why would I mind? I would love having you here as much as possible. I missed you, Julie Chapman!"

"Great. I'll see you tomorrow at the same time, unless there are more complications with Tillie."

"Don't worry," he said. "Whatever time you can spend, I want you here for the girls."

After the run, Julie hopped back into her car, sweaty and hot, but elated at the day's outcome. Coaching track, back in her element, this was the first time she'd actually felt like she had come home, not out of obligation or need, but because she now had something to look forward to everyday. She talked to old friends every day, and now could make new friends who had the same things in common with her, which was wonderful. They knew she could only make a few of the actual competitive cross-country events with other local high schools. "Local" meant fifty miles or more going north toward Miami and the same when going to Key West High School, down on Flagler Avenue. She still had to take care of Tillie when she came home, and work at the Waffle House, taking Tillie's place when possible, to make ends meet.

The stipend she received from Brown was now being squeezed every month. $15,000.00 didn't go very far after moving back, leasing a car, buying an appropriate teacher's aide wardrobe, and purchasing writing supplies. She also paid for a new computer and a printer to write her book and paid for Internet access to do her research late every night, which was very expensive, but absolutely necessary. Her stipend would be at zero in the spring, but hopefully everything would coincide with getting published and receiving an advance for the book. She would never take a dime from Joe, especially after he turned his life upside down to help both Tillie and her. She would make it on her own or not at all.

The nice thing about being a teacher's aide was that she got health and dental benefits for both her and Tillie. Tillie had not been to a doctor in years. It was just too expensive. She had become Julie's dependent and the administrators at the school district approved it. Thank God. After Tillie's car crash, all her hospital and doctor bills would now be paid, less the deductible. The deductible would be considered small potatoes after looking at Tillie's accumulated hospital, surgery, and doctor bills for only the short time she was in critical care and continued to be at the Mariner Hospital.

The bill was well over $50,000.00 so far and climbing. Grateful was not the word. At first Julie thought the school district got a good deal for not a large paycheck for a Brown University MFA graduate working as a teacher's aide.

Little did she realize at the time, the benefits to be

paid out on Tillie's behalf would be over three times Julie's annual salary.

It now looked like it would work out for everyone, at least financially. Now, when Julie had to bring Tillie to her new doctor, she knew it would only cost her the $10.00 copay. Tillie was two years away from Medicare and this was a great way to cover the gap. Thank God she would be covered, at least until then, as long as Julie worked for the school district. Working was hard for Tillie, even before the accident, and Julie knew she would be looking forward to retiring. Thank God she kept in great shape before this. The dentist was something else. Wild horses couldn't drag Tillie to the dentist. Worrying about the dentist seemed silly now with everything going on. Julie was amazed about what went through her mind on a daily basis.

She remembered when she got home the first night, when she was asked to be a coach by Jimmy. It was around 5:00 p.m. She and Tillie ate at the kitchen table and discussed their day's activities.

"Tillie, you are now looking at the new assistant cross-country coach for Coral Shores High School."

"Wow, I'm impressed," said Tillie.

"Really?" Julie said.

"Yes, really," said Tillie. "It's about time you got out more and had friends your own age, not hanging around with a sixty-three year old like me."

Julie laughed. "Well, thank you very much for your support!"

Tillie sat back in her chair and smiled at Julie, just like always when she found her amusing. "How long have we been together?"

"Too long," said Julie.

"A long time to be exact," Tillie said. "You seemed

to be doing just fine. Just get out more with friends. What are you doing tonight? Today is Wednesday, right?"

"Yes," Julie said. "Speaking of friends, "Joe calls at 7:00 p.m. every Wednesday night, come rain or shine."

Tillie laughed. "Boy, do you live on the wild side."

Julie thought then, just as now, that the pattern hadn't changed much with Joe since she'd been ten years old. The questions about her homework turned to questions about her job and book. It was actually quite comforting to know someone cared about her and her family in the same way every time. Joe was reliable, dependable and very much a close brother as anyone could have been. In fact, probably even better, since she'd met him at such an early age. He had always been protective of her. He adored Tillie, especially since she served as his second mother when he was nineteen years old down in the Keys for the first time with no family around.

Julie had laughed to herself at the time. Joe had two mommies before it became fashionable. When Joe's mother died, Tillie picked up the slack and served in that role, different from an infant or a child, but more as an inspiration as Joe got older. Joe had said he was raised by wolves, growing up in a construction family. He'd worked in a crew since he was fourteen. He was pretty much on his own for a very long time.

Since she had been back, and before Joe arrived after the accident, they usually talked for about a half an hour. Any longer would simply be a rehashing of old times and then Julie as usual, being on a tight schedule, had to get back to her book or it would never get done. Tillie had to come on the phone and say goodbye to Joe as well, which made the call last even longer.

Julie always planned her book writing around Joe's call every Wednesday, and afterward, she would work until midnight. She had gone back into her makeshift office in the third bedroom which also housed every item ever owned by Tillie for which there was no room, but everything was "too valuable" to be thrown out. Julie looked around the room, as if by rote, and had a feeling of calm come over her. All of these things meant everything to Julie. At the time, she had never suspected that Tillie would survive a hit and run and be left to die in the bog.

What would Julie do when Tillie was no longer around? Would she give her things away? Would she keep them? It was really hard concentrating on work when surrounded by all this stuff that reminded Julie of the past—some good, some not so good, and some very bad. Pictures of her mom and dad. God, they were so young.

What a waste. She had no idea how she and Tillie had gotten this far with so little, just a lot of determination and pure chutzpah. She laughed when she remembered the story of the boy with "chutzpah." This boy killed both his parents and begged for leniency from the court because he was now an "orphan." Chutzpah, a really good word, and it was very defining. It was probably a triple word score in Scrabble if it could be used at all.

CHAPTER 19

I t took Jack a few days, but he had gotten the pictures developed using the progression technology program. He sent the digitized photos to Joe and Julie by email. The pictures were now shown on the computer screen. Joe had to load them onto a disc and then have them blown up to compare to the licensed drivers in his new file. Since he would not know Julie's father at age forty-one, he was unsure of which pictures were more like him than not. He would have to put those pictures side by side while scanning the driver's license file.

As promised, Jack sent two sets of pictures, one showing more aging, a much harder life if you would, than the other. Both represented Tom Chapman in his forties but there would be almost two separate individuals, when you looked at the aged discrepancies. It would be almost like comparing a shaved head after having long hair, a beard compared to being clean-shaven, and sunglasses and a baseball hat compared to having no hat or other items to disguise facial features. The pictures were like day and night and could be of two very different individuals.

This meant Joe would have to compare two pictures to each of the white male driver's license photos. There

were a potential 402 white male owners with 245 individuals residing in south Florida, including the Keys, and
157 living in the rest of the state of Florida. He guessed
South Florida residents preferred the cheaper unadorned
Ford F-150s, based on the different paints for the two
models that year. Joe was simply guessing but it was an
educated guess. He would look for a white male pickup
truck owner with the initials of TC.

Joe had been trained by the Intelligence Division of
the Coast Guard about hiding in plain sight. People who
changed their names did so reluctantly, and they tried to
keep their new name as close as they could to the old
name, the one their parents gave to them at birth. Re-
views of individuals placed in the witness protection program, or WITSEC, were discouraged from this practice
since it was so commonly understood that people wanted
to continue to use their own initials after changing their
names. It was almost as if they'd gotten a good deal on
monogrammed towels and they didn't want to give them
up.

Going over 402 names to start with would not be
easy. And starting with the obvious TC initials would
save an inordinate amount of time, especially if a picture
hit, as Joe suspected it would. The new sort had to go by
last name first, which had fifty Cs, C being a popular first
letter for a last name. From there, it was easier. There
were only ten Ts. Joe brought up the ten TCs online and
looked at the registrations for the trucks. Then he brought
up the individual drivers' pictures on their licenses. He
had to make sure the truck registration's street address
matched the driver's license street addresses, for further
proof that this was the same individual. The ten names
were from all parts of the state of Florida.

Joe then looked at the driver's licenses pictures.

Three were immediately discounted because the pictures were of African American men. *So much for a theory.*

After reviewing the remaining seven potential individuals, one picture stood out. It was the picture of Ted Champion from Pensacola, Florida. It was as close a match as could be found. The picture matched the healthier version of Tom Chapman in his early forties. "Hello, Tom."

Ted Champion resided at 8060 Lavelle Way, Pensacola, Florida. Joe immediately switched websites, brought up the name Ted Champion with the address from the driver's license, and came up with nothing. No Facebook, no Twitter, no online accounts, no Internet service. Joe then downloaded the address and what popped up was the street address for the Day's Inn.

The Day's Inn site stated: *This Pensacola motel is off of Interstate 10 and fifteen miles from Pensacola Beach. Guests start every day with a continental breakfast in the lobby and lounge by the outdoor pool.* Sounded nice for only $62.00 per night.

Joe laughed and did the math. At $62.00 per night, Ted Champion could have stayed there for over thirteen years, or for 4,839 consecutive nights, 365 days a year. Joe wondered if he had been living there for the last seventeen years. You never knew. Joe had to do the math. He couldn't help himself.

He then went online to the credit bureau sites, using his Coast Guard Intelligence Division credentials. It made it easier to find a social security number. All three credit bureaus came back with nothing of any interest. Ted had no earnings recorded and paid no taxes, ever. Ted Champion had no credit rating. He never borrowed a dime and did not have any credit cards. He owned no property and had no recorded mortgages. Ted Champion evidently had been living in a motel, probably in Pensacola for the last seventeen years, and only spent cash. He had no bank accounts. There was no way of knowing if he had a safe deposit box. He had no recorded jobs, ever, according to Equifax, Trans Union, or Experian national credit bureaus.

He was completely off the grid. Ted had no criminal record nor did he have any traffic violations. He seemed like a model citizen, if you didn't know the situation.

Now, where the hell was he? He had to be in Key Largo or at least down in the Florida Keys somewhere. Where was Ted Champion's truck? At least Joe now knew the license plate number and the VIN number if they ever found the truck. He wrote the numbers on a slip of paper and put it into his wallet in case he ever ran across a truck in similar condition with damage to the passenger side door with the paint scraped off the vehicle. Had he dumped the pickup and was now driving something else? Too many questions and not enough answers.

Joe didn't want to give this information to Mike Kenny and the sheriff's department at this time. If Ted Champion was, in fact, Julie's father, and if he did steal at least $300,000.00 from the Russians, Joe did not want it to be revealed at this point. He could only imagine the damage it would do to Tillie or even to Julie's budding writing career. He was positive it was Julie's father who put the money in the attic. The $300,000.00 was probably only a small portion of what he stole, only a drop in the bucket of what he spent in cash over the last seventeen years. If he didn't work all that time, had no job or any credit cards, how much did he need to live on over the time period? At $25,000 a year in cash, with a motel bill of $400.00 to $500.00 per week, he would have spent at least $425,000.00 at only $62.00 per night. If Julie's father lived relatively well for a single guy, on say at $40,000 a year, paying no taxes, he would have spent around $680,000.00 in total over those seventeen years.

Joe was almost obsessive when it came to math, but it helped him understand why people did what they did, and it would help him to understand what would come next. If Ted had already spent almost $700,000.00 by now, and he left $300,000.00 in the attic, it meant he probably stole almost a million dollars in cash from the Russians and then disappeared. Everyone thought he drowned, probably including the Russians.

Joe now had to prove that Tom was still alive. Ted Champion must be out of cash to go after the money left in the attic. He must be close to broke at this point. He had probably blown through almost $700,000.00 in seventeen years. Joe couldn't imagine living that way, in a motel for the last seventeen years. Where did Ted keep his cash? If the Russians ever found out, he was a dead man and so were Tillie and Julie. Joe and Julie had to find him and put a lid on this somehow.

Joe would tell Julie what he discovered that night. She had the right to know and probably should not be staying in the house, not until Tillie came home, anyway, although Joe would be there—and armed. He would not leave until this was resolved. He would ask Joan if she had any room in the inn at the Coast Guard housing units. He would have to tell her what was going on, at least a little bit. He hoped Tillie was safe in the hospital, especially now that she had awakened and had made progress in her cognitive abilities. She would be home shortly and she would have care and visitors. Tillie would not be left alone to fend for herself. This would be a blessing.

Joe had to pack and get ready for the Wednesday drug interception near Key West. He had to leave on

Tuesday night so he would ask Joan if Julie could stay over while he was gone. Of course she would say yes but would Julie want to go there? The locks had been changed and Joe had set up a camera in the living room area, which showed both entrances as well and an alarm system that would ring right into the sheriff's substation in Islamorada, not that there was anything valuable to worry about. The nice thing about not owning anything was there was very little to steal.

When Julie got home after practice, Joe had peeled the potatoes and made a meatloaf for dinner. He had been on his own for so long, he'd had to learn to cook while in his teen years. It was a necessity. Coming from a construction family, especially during the peak construction season in upstate New York, meant a lot of missed dinners, or no dinner at all on many an occasion. Contractors used to laugh about there being only two seasons in upstate New York, one was winter and the other was construction.

Winter in upstate New York seemed to run from April to early November, regardless of the definition of the seasons. Winter started in early November and then ended in the middle of the following April. The changing of seasons was a myth most of the time. Spring was only in May. Summer began on the first day of June, running through late September, and autumn was only in October, period.

It was why seasons in the Keys were strange to Joe. You could only tell the difference by the changing of the leaves and maybe the fall was only a few degrees cooler. Winter had a few days in the forties but was mostly in the seventies to eighties the rest of the winter. The rest of the year was hot and muggy.

They would eat and then go to visit Tillie, relieving the constant vigilant volunteers from St. Justin's Church.

"Hi, Joe, I'm home," she said.

"I was expecting a 'Hi, Ricky, I'm home,' from the *Lucille Ball Show*," Joe said, laughing. "Right after we eat, I want to show you something. Jack's pictures came back today." He waved her to a chair. "Let's eat, I'm starved and then let's look at the pictures."

They ate and cleaned up, then both went into the living room where Joe had spread out the pictures on the coffee table.

"Is this what my father would like at forty-one years old?" she asked.

"Well, there are two sets of pictures, one aged more than the other, so, he would probably look like one or the other or a combination of both," Joe said. "Now are you ready, Julie?" he asked hesitantly.

"Yes," she said.

"This was a driver's license picture. I want you to compare it to all the pictures Jack produced and then you tell me what you think," he said.

"My God, Joe, is this him?" she asked as she pointed directly at the picture of Ted Champion of Pensacola, Florida.

"I think it's him," he said. Joe then went on to explain everything he found out about Ted Champion, including being off the grid, and his theories of how much he believed her father stole from the Russians.

Yes, she really now believed he was alive. She also believed he hit Tillie with his truck and tried to kill her. "Why, Joe?" she asked.

"I believe he spent the rest of the money he stole, probably almost $700,000.00 and is now broke and wanted the $300,000.00 he put in your attic for safekeeping.

That's what I believe," Joe reiterated. "I also called the Day's Inn and wanted to find out if a Ted Champion was a registered guest there, but they would not give me any information since they said they respected the privacy of their guests. It meant, to me, that yes, he was a guest, and from the tone of the young girl's voice, I think he has been there for a long while. I'm just guessing, getting better at it anyway. I don't want to get a warrant yet because it would reveal it's your father, and he was still alive, and it could bring back the Russians if they found out he has spent most of their money and still had some left. It would not make them happy."

"I agree," said Julie. "What do we do next?"

"We sit on it for now. Keep the pictures handy, and give them to Tillie's volunteers in the hospital, telling them not to share it with anyone, including the sheriff's office. If they recognize anyone that looks like the picture, they should call security and us only, not the sheriff's department."

"Why are we not telling Mike Kenny anything yet?" Julie asked.

"Because, he does not believe Tillie is in danger. They have provided no protection and I fear they would make a big announcement that they cracked the case and would have it all over the news within minutes," he said. "This won't be good for Tillie or you. It places you smack in the middle of danger. It could force your father's hand more quickly or put the Russians on notice that he's back and they could take it out on you. Trust me, I have seen what they are capable of doing when pressed. It's not pretty."

CHAPTER 20

Joe left around 5:00 p.m. Tuesday for Islamorada and hopped onto the brand new 154-foot Sentinel-class ship called a Fast Response Cutter that had arrived in the Keys only a few months ago. It was the same cutter he came down on last week for the initial team meeting. The crew would arrive in Key West a few hours later and would meet two other cutters responding tomorrow for the same drug intervention. Joe got back intelligence from the helicopter pilot only yesterday. He had discovered the name of the ship coming in to deliver the drugs to the go-fast boat, which would be waiting for the ship around twenty-five miles southwest of Key West. The ship was named the *Infinity* and was supposedly from Argentina, but you could never be sure.

The trip down took about two and half hours from port to port, with Key West being on the south west side of Islamorada.

Joe sat on the deck, quietly contemplating all that had happened to him over the last year.

He'd gotten out of the Coast Guard at 28 years old, after getting his degree from the Coast Guard Academy, as a reward for services performed over a ten year period. He went home and received his MBA from Rensselaer

Polytechnic Institute and then found a position at the Albany Coalition for Families.

Joe was the director for institutional research and grants and did an exceptional job over the almost three years he was there. He brought in significant amounts of grant money to support the career services department that placed at-risk youth in good paying jobs. Those students earned their GEDs, and, at the same time, got technology-based certifications in the field of energy efficiency. Technology was Joe's expertise for many years with the Coast Guard Intelligence Division, so he viewed this new assignment as simply a technology transfer of knowledge from the military service to a non-profit organization.

Last spring, Joe had discovered an incredible money laundering and drug distribution scheme, right at the Albany Coalition for Families main headquarters. No one at the Coalition even guessed Joe was fluent in Mexican-dialect based Spanish. He never told anyone because he had his own duties and did not want to be the lone Spanish-speaking member of the organization. He would then be saddled with bilingual requests on a daily basis and would never be able to do what he was hired to do, to raise funds for local Albany at-risk youth jobs.

That spring, the Coalition had been the recipient of a "free" new Vice President for Operations, an individual who was loaned to them by their own national accrediting organization, located in San Diego. The new Vice President, Luis Hernandez, was the son of the head general of the Mexican Mafia, running the organization from the California prison system. An elaborate plan to loot small non-profits and national foundations, including the Albany Coalition for Families, was well under way until Joe discovered the plan and stopped it cold. He heard every word spoken by the gang and Luis, in Spanish, they being unaware of his capabilities and investigation prowess.

Joe had eventually called in favors from his Coast Guard friends, now in high places, and the FBI in Miami, who then introduced him to the Albany-based FBI staff. Joe had eventually discovered this was not just a local money-laundering scheme but had national implications that included dozens of small non-profits across the country as well as prominent national foundations. These organizations were now being infiltrated by the Mexican Mafia. It was discovered that a five-million-dollar grant had been given to the San Diego based accrediting agency to set up a Hispanic outreach program for high school kids in Los Angeles, who were to go on to college, obtain their Master's degrees from Ivy universities, and volunteer their services to small non-profits and foundations for a two year period upon graduation.

It was later discovered by Joe that all the "students" at the Los Angeles high school, participating in the program, were the sons and daughters of Mexican Mafia associates. Luis Hernandez landed in Albany, to the Coalition's detriment.

Through this scheme, they had already stolen and laundered over twenty million dollars in less than a year, using their own Mexican Mafia for-profit businesses to launder every last dollar. By the time Joe had discovered the crimes, the President of the Albany Coalition for Families, Ted Simmons, the father of Dan Simmons, one of Joe's best friends, died in a suspicious car accident, not unlike Tillie's "accident."

Joe proved it was no accident. Ted Simmons was drugged by Luis Hernandez and died on I-90. Luis's gangbangers followed him to make sure he was dead. These were the same gangbangers who were brought in as potential at-risk "students." The only student part was their vast learning experiences in selling dope on the streets of Albany, as well as serving as hit men for the Mexican Mafia.

For Joe to continue his involvement with the subsequent takedown of the Mexican Mafia, in conjunction with the FBI and Homeland Security, after being the key to the entire investigation due to his affiliation with the Coalition, Joe had to re-enlist under special conditions in order to carry a service weapon and to work directly with the FBI, and Homeland Security. He was out of the Coast Guard for almost four years as a Special Agent for Investigative Services, but was signed back up immediately before the bust. During the national bust, Joe led the charge at the Albany location and he was then shot in the arm by Luis Hernandez after this major confrontation. After being shot, Joe was still able to kill Luis, as well as his three gangbanger friends, right at the corporate headquarters of the Albany Coalition for Families.

Joe had received the highest non-combat award issued by the Coast Guard for his valor that day. After the successful close of the investigation, he was offered a commission and stayed in the service, reporting to the Coast Guard but with a direct line of supervision at the FBI and Homeland Security. He was a quasi-member—not a member of the Coast Guard reserve, but also not an active member either—and was used on an "as needed" basis until his transfer to Islamorada to help Tillie and Julie. Until then, this non-official assignment had fit in perfectly with his other duties at the Troy Education Consulting Group. Now it was even more to his benefit than to the Coast Guard, since he got to go to Islamorada to help out Julie and Tillie.

CHAPTER 21

Now at the Key West station, the data Joe got from the chatter came back directly to the coordinates of this ship, *Infinity*, which was now about one hundred miles off the coast of Key West. That meant it would be meeting the go-fast boat around dusk, near 4:30 p.m. on Wednesday if everything went according to plan.

There were three boats and two helicopters, fully armed and ready to go. And there was no question these cutters and their crews were prepared. They met up with the drug ship as soon as it stopped and dropped anchor. From the sky, the helicopter pilot recognized the go-fast boat coming from just north of Key West, around Big Key Pines. It was really moving and would get there within the next few minutes.

As soon as it was spotted, one cutter fell behind the go-fast and the other two cutters and the helicopter swooped down on the *Infinity*. They never knew what hit them. There were four members on the ship, just like the chatter had said, and two more on the go-fast boat. While in cuffs, the captured sailors watched the Coast Guard sink the go-fast boat on the spot, a hundred grand down the toilet.

They picked up over forty bales of cocaine with a

street value of just over twenty four million dollars. It was a good day.

The captives were brought back to the port at Key West and read their rights. The search, once completed, proved the probable cause which had been the basis for the original search warrant, covering the "what is suspicious" aspect of the take down. It was a clean bust. Once in port, the men who'd been arrested starting talking in Spanish immediately. Joe had them write out their confessions in Spanish. Then he witnessed and translated them into English and had verbal recordings as well. He got signatures from the arrested crewmembers for the translation as well, witnessed by the Coast Guard crew. They would stay over the day, completing their paperwork, and would then be back in Islamorada by late Thursday.

Joe would review all the procedures they went through with the new crew. It would serve as the main training lesson in the use of intelligence in this successful exercise. He would be back at Julie's house on Friday.

℃ↄ℃ↄ

Julie worked all day Tuesday and Wednesday, first at school, then on to cross-country practice, and then continued to write her book into the early hours of the morning. It helped her to keep her thoughts intact. And the more she wrote, the better she remembered all the facts, the people, and the incidents in her life that led her to where she was today. She fell asleep on the couch, watching the news, then got up, and went to bed.

She was barely asleep when the phone rang. *It can't be good news at 2:15 a.m. in the morning.*

"Hi, Julie, it's Mike Kenny. I'm sorry to call you in

the middle of the night but I thought you might like to know," he said.

"Know what, Mike?" she asked.

"There's been an incident at the hospital you should know about," he said. "Evidently, someone tried to get to Tillie around 2:00 a.m. this morning. Whoever it was, and it wasn't anyone from the hospital staff because I already checked, tried to get into her room. Fortunately, two ladies from your Church sat right next to her and they were wide-awake. Both were reading," he said. "I was already out on another call, but I was there within minutes of the 911 call."

The women had told Mike they saw a middle age man peeking into the room. They said the intruder was startled when he saw the two of them looking up at him. It was dark so they said they didn't really see his face, but he was white they said, and then he ran down the hall. They both hit their cell phones, one hit 911 and the other hit the hospital's security hotline number. Within minutes security came running in. Tillie had awakened by this time and wanted to know what happened. Mike showed up almost immediately.

Tillie had been sleeping when the intruder came in and was very weak. She really didn't know what was going on at that moment in time. Her short-term memory was a problem, especially surrounding the hit and run. She couldn't remember a thing about that. She could remember past events. She could tell you her Pastor's aunt's name and both his parents' names, after only meeting them once. Tillie was extremely smart and, hopefully, everything would come back to her in time.

The ladies knew they immediately had to talk to Julie, especially after being grilled by the detective, and so they called her and told her to get there quickly. Julie had already spoken to Mike and she knew she had to go see Tillie right now. She grabbed her keys, barely putting her pants and shirt on, hopped into her car, and headed for the Mariner Hospital. She got to the hospital in fifteen minutes, a land speed record.

The church ladies came over to Julie, as soon as she got there, and told her they recognized the man who came in as someone who resembled the picture Julie had placed on the wall, two nights earlier. They originally said they didn't see his features because they knew Julie wanted to be the first to know. She thanked the ladies, hugged them, and told them not to say anything else at this point, especially to the detective.

Mike had already left, after calling Julie, to look around the facility and the parking lot. He suspected the intruder who showed up in Tillie's room might be the hit and run driver, but he was reluctant to say so because the sheriff's department had not provided any coverage for her. He was not going to admit it to either Julie or Joe. They were right. Instead, Mike looked around the hospital and then went to the hospital parking lot. A white pickup truck was just starting up and appeared to be moving out of the parking lot. Mike pulled his gun and ran after the truck yelling at the top of his lungs to stop. Two security men from the hospital surrounded the truck and told the driver to get out. They all had their guns pointed at the driver.

The driver of the truck was scared to death and he said he hadn't done anything. As soon as Mike saw his face, his heart sank. The driver was a young Hispanic man driving a Chevrolet pickup. The only similarity was that the white truck was old and dirty and nobody could tell what it was in the dark.

The driver was in his early twenties and had just

started working in the hospital cafeteria, prepping for breakfast to be served at 7:00 a.m. His shift was clean up duty from 6:00 p.m. to 2:00 a.m., on the third shift, finishing with the breakfast prep, and then would leave by 2:30 a.m.

Who would want those hours? Mike Kenny thought. *Maybe Joe and Julie were right about us. Whoever went into Tillie's room, and if he did have a white pickup, he certainly didn't park in the hospital parking lot. Whoever it was, was very smart indeed. We better start covering the room as well, but I doubt he will come again. Of course, I doubted he would come in the first place. I really don't want to have the conversation that I know I will have with Julie. She must be really pissed by now.*

Julie was pretty shook up and gave Mike a piece of her mind when she ran into him in the hallway later in the morning, which he was expecting. He promised to do the best he could until Tillie was released from the hospital, and then they would patrol near the house, every few hours. It was the best they could do.

When Joe came home from his case, Julie told him everything that had happened. He was mad as hell but he held it in.

It wouldn't do any good to take it out on Julie, but it solidified his feelings about not telling the sheriff's department about anything he found. It just wasn't going to happen. In fact it would probably get them killed.

"Before Tillie's released in a few days, Julie, you really should stay with Joan and her family in Islamorada and I can stay on the cutter," Joe said. "I have lots to do and I have another case to work on, in the meantime."

He called Joan and asked.

"It would be my pleasure. In fact, it will be like old times when Julie would stay over when she babysat on the weekends when she was in her teens, except now she can drink beer with me," she said, laughing.

"Sounds good, Joan," Joe said. "We will see you in an hour. Oh, Joan, do you want pizza? What a question! What do you want on it?"

She told him and they picked it up on the way.

Joe slept on the cutter and Julie stayed with Joan and her family. Julie went to her fifth-grade classroom early. She never got to sleep. Instead of cross-country practice after school and visiting Tillie, she went back to Joan's and took a nap for a few hours.

Joe was busy that night on another case, so Julie had dinner with Joan and the family. She excused herself and went to her room to continue her book. She'd brought her computer and she had nothing better to do. And she certainly could not sleep.

Lucy knocked on her door and they talked about the cross-country meet coming up and what Lucy needed to do to improve her time. Lucy got an overview from Julie about her book and where she was. Julie showed her what she had written to date and then told her she needed to put a few hours into it or she would be way behind. Lucy said good night and then Joan dropped off some cookies and a cup of tea for Julie to help her work through her text. *God, what a nice lady.*

Julie went back to her book with her thoughts still on her meeting Joe for the first time and how kind everyone at the Coast Guard Station had been to her and Tillie.

ℰ∽ℰ∽

Julie eventually wound up babysitting Joan's two kids, Jeff Jr. and Lucy, after passing the certificate course at the Coast Guard facility.

Now, she was in Lucy's room for the week. Who would have thought?

Joan had started her out babysitting during a weekend afternoon. Julie was only eleven at the time. Joan could now get her shopping and household chores done on time and not worry about the kids because she was less than a mile away. It was too hard working full time at the station and keeping up with everything else at the same time. Her husband put in a lot of overtime at the Marina during the peak season. He was the chief boat mechanic and was much in demand, especially by her own Coast Guard personnel. Jeff was the go-to-guy for motorboats in the upper and mid-Keys. At the time, this helped Tillie as well get her own stuff done. Not that Julie was in the way, but it was nice to get some "me" time as well. All Tillie did was work and take care of Julie. She needed a break every now and then, too.

As Julie got older, Joan had her stay over so she and her husband could go to dinner at the beach, and then eventually some dining and dancing, coming back a little later. Movie theaters were too far away and the cell coverage for emergency calls wasn't great. Julie certainly liked the money but even better, she got to eat at places other than the Waffle House, and Joan's forty-inch HD TV set, new at the time, was a thing to behold. Even the kids' movies fascinated Julie because of how clear everything was, and the color was unbelievable. After a while, she hated going home to her thirteen-inch black and white TV with the aluminum foil antenna. She had been spoiled but would never tell Tillie or Joan. Joan had a satellite dish since her assigned housing was right at the dock and her TV was tapped into the Coast Guard satellite system. It was a thrill.

When Julie first started babysitting, Joan brought her

back and forth to Key Largo until Julie eventually got her
driver's license and could use Tillie's car. Joe bought a
used car for Julie when she turned sixteen, which worked
out even better. Looking back, it was a hunk of junk but
to Julie it was the best present she ever had at anytime,
anywhere. She had to pay the insurance, but so what? It
was her car. It was the first thing she ever really owned
that was in her name and in her name alone. It was a 1982
Volkswagen Rabbit two-door hatchback. It got great
mileage, was easy to maintain, and the VW dealer was
right down the street. Jeff did most of her work for free
anyway. Little did Julie know Joe got the car through
Jeff's key connections. He traded boat mechanic time and
$500.00 for the car. Joe gave him the $500.00. It was almost a month's pay at the time. Hell it was her sixteenth
birthday, after all.

☙❧☙

It was getting late but Julie had to tell the world what
it was like living in Key Largo. First, what was Key Largo? Where was it? What did it feel like growing up there?
She'd never felt poor but as she got older, she understood
quite well the differences between the "Haves and the
Have Not's." At the time, she had to park her VW Rabbit
in the high school parking lot next to kids driving BMWs
and Mustang convertibles. It didn't bother her because
she had a plan. It bothered her friends because they grew
up thinking there was a social place in life, the only place
where they fit in, and they would have to stay there forever.

This was never Julie's intention, conviction, or plan.
She would do well in high school, move on to college,
and become a writer, either living in the Keys or some-

where else where she would be accepted. After graduating from Brown University, she would be accepted anywhere on the planet but she would never feel "entitled." It was the "entitled" part of some of her fellow high school students' psyche that really bothered her. Good things were expected. They were entitled. Julie never saw it that way.

She needed to define her hometown. Where exactly was Key Largo? It was made popular by Jimmy Buffet who still lived in Key West and Key Largo was included in the lyrics in several very popular songs that included the Beach Boys 1988 "Kokomo." God, that song stayed in your head forever. It was written for the Beach Boys by John Philips of the Mamas and the Papas; Scott McKenzie, a friend of John's; Mike Love of the Beach Boys; and Terry Meicher, who produced The Byrds. The one Julie liked even better was Bertie Higgins' song "Key Largo" which had a few immortal lyrics.

It was funny, growing up in Key Largo, she thought. She never saw movie stars, singers, or international guests at the Waffle House. She never saw them at her school for career day, ever. It was very annoying to her, especially when she went to Brown University, that she was a "celebrity" herself because she came from Key Largo. By the end of five years, she couldn't bring herself to tell anyone where she was from because all they did was break out in song. It was very annoying after a while. *Do the people who live in New York City break out into "New York, New York"?* She didn't think so.

Back to where Key Largo was. Key Largo was one of the five largest islands in the Florida Keys. It was the most northern island in the Keys and was thirty-three miles long, with Key West, the most southern point in the United States, exactly one hundred and six miles from

Cuba. Key Largo's earlier Spanish name was *Cayo Largo*, which meant Long Key, because it was the longest island at thirty-three miles in length. The island was only forty-eight miles from the Miami International Airport and it was connected to the mainland at Miami-Dade County by two routes, the Overseas Highway—which was U.S. Highway 1, which entered Key Largo at Jewfish Creek near the middle of the island and turned southwest—and at the Card Sound Road, which connected to the northern part of Key Largo at Card Sound Bridge.

The total population of Key Largo was 10,433 as of the 2010 United States census. The government structure for Key Largo was countywide with only one municipality in the Keys, the City of Key West, with an all season population of a little over 25,000. Monroe County ran all local government in the Keys, except for the City of Key West. The County ran the sheriff's department and the county school district, which encompassed the entire Florida Keys. The population of Key West in 1890 was almost 18,000 and it was not much more now, at 25,000 in 2010, since there wasn't any more reclaimed land. Instead of building out, they had to build up.

Once again, stay on track, Julie said to herself. *Let's get back to Key Largo.* The average household income was $77,800.00 with an average net worth per family in excess of $500,000.00. The average home cost $230,000.00. However there were more vacant homes than those owner-occupied—3,688 versus 3,448. What it meant to Julie was the rich living in Key Largo far exceeded the poor, while the poor were losing their homes. Thank God, Tillie and her husband bought their house so many years ago and had paid their bank mortgage in full. The million-dollar homes were paying the majority of the school taxes, which was a blessing in disguise for Tillie who paid less than $1,000.00 a year in taxes. Crime in the Keys was lower than the national average but growing. The biggest problems were drugs through cartels, burglary, and auto theft but it didn't affect her and Tillie much. Who was going to break into their house? Julie thought with a laugh. It was so far set back that no one even knew where they lived, and an old Ford Escort? Come on. Julie turned off the light and felt better about the day. Tillie would be coming home soon and Julie needed as much sleep as she could get in the meantime. Joe, too.

ɞɔɛɔ

They picked up Tillie three days later at the hospital and brought her home, almost two months from the day she was hit by the pickup truck. She was doing well but it would be a long haul and a lot of work on Julie's part. And Joe had to head back home soon. Julie would miss him terribly. She hoped something would break before that happened. They couldn't count on the sheriff's department. She just hoped what they were working on now would point them in the right direction soon. Joe had agreed.

They could not be sure Julie's father was the hit and run driver. However, they knew he broke in to the house. It all had to be related. They would double their efforts to find out who did this. Of course, finding Julie's father would be like trying to find a needle in a haystack.

Where the hell was he? He most assuredly wanted the $300,000.00 but would he kill his own family for it? Would he kill his own daughter? He must be desperate.

Joe hoped to catch Julie's father before leaving to go home. He just wouldn't let it happen. He would never forgive himself if anything happened to either one of them. He didn't care. He probably wouldn't leave until it was resolved. He couldn't have Julie worry about it as well. He would tell her in the morning that he would stay on, regardless if he was still working for the Coast Guard or not.

CHAPTER 22

After Tillie had been home for a few days, she had to go back for a few more outpatient tests to have her blood work checked and to ensure her cognitive functions were still on the mend. Dr. Robinson maintained a satellite office right next to the Mariner Hospital, in addition to his main office at the Jackson Memorial Hospital in downtown Miami. He was at Mariner only one day a week for appointments, in addition to any emergency surgery required for his patients in the Florida Keys. Anything major required a transfer to his Jackson Memorial Hospital office.

Tillie's condition had improved tremendously over the last two months, and she only required a weekly visit to Mariner until she was given a clean bill of health in about six more weeks.

Julie had meetings to attend to at school as well as coaching her next to last cross-country meet that was being held at home at 3:30 p.m. Joe took Tillie to the doctor's office for her scheduled appointment. If all went well, he planned on taking her to lunch, stopping at his office in Islamorada, and then he would take Tillie to the cross-country meet. Joe hadn't been with Tillie separately from Julie except on very rare occasions when Julie was at various high school events or at Brown University. While Julie was at Brown, Joe flew down for the holidays, and then stopped in Miami at the FBI office. He saw Mark and his family and then visited Tillie in Key Largo before he flew back, all on the government dime while he was investigating a drug related case.

Ever since his takedown last spring at the Albany Coalition, that ruined the Mexican Mafia's plans for money laundering across the country, Joe was asked to review some very critical data concerning other potential high profile cases. He worked out of the Troy Education Consulting Group and Johnathon Mills knew whenever Joe was asked by Homeland Security, Joe had to hit the road for a week or two at a time. And then he provided critical insight into various money laundering cases that involved Hispanic underworld networks. Those included the Columbians and the Cubans in the Caribbean basin; the Mexican Mafia in California and Texas, and now New York City; and, once again, the Cubans in south Florida, specifically in Miami and the Keys. When Joe asked to be sent to Islamorada for two months, his bosses jumped on the chance because of the personal nature of his request, hoping he would make it permanent and then he would come back full time into the Coast Guard and its affiliates, Homeland Security and the FBI.

When Tillie got home and settled from her long stint at the hospital, Joe and Julie both told Tillie about what they suspected—that Julie's father was still alive. Tillie was curious as to why they changed the locks on the house and handed her a new key. Her memory might have been impaired, but her critical thinking was coming back to full capacity. She suspected something was not right and it had a lot to do with her accident. She had the same locks since the early 1970s when she and her husband were handed the same keys by the previous owner who built the house originally.

"Joe, was that why you had the locks changed?" she asked him.

"Tillie, I suggested it," Julie said. "I suspected some-one had snuck around the house and had moved my things just slightly, not enough to notice. But *I* noticed. That is why Joe and I, after he taught me how to do it, gathered over fifty fingerprints, fifty-five to be exact, from the house. Since we had thoroughly cleaned the house, we knew the fingerprints had to be fresh, except maybe for yours, Tillie. You probably had hundreds still here from before. Did you remember, or even know we fingerprinted you in the hospital when you had just come out of your coma?"

"No," Tillie said.

"Joe told you but I didn't think you were really with it at the time," Julie said. "I didn't think you had ever been fingerprinted before."

"I don't believe I ever was."

"Yes, that's what we found out," Julie said. "Your prints were never in the system so we compared the prints in the house to your new set and came up with a match. Did you also know with the new type of DNA finger-printing, the swirls on the bottom of my fingers match the swirls on your fingers?"

"No, what does that mean?"

"It means you are officially my grandmother on my mother's side," she said.

"Neat," Tillie said. "But you will still call me Tillie until the day I die."

"Yes, Tillie," Julie said and laughed.

They told Tillie they believed Ted Champion, for-merly Tom Chapman, was the one who hit her in his white Ford F-150 pickup truck and stored the money in her attic for all this time. The look on Tillie's face gave evidence of the fact that she was unaware of any of this.

"Why would he do that?" Tillie asked.

"We believed he kept a rainy day fund here in case he got caught with the rest of it, almost $700,000.00 he carried with him, and $300,000.00 he stored in your attic."

They went on to tell her they believed he had been living under the alias of Ted Champion for the last seventeen years, he was now somewhere in the vicinity of Key Largo, and he probably wanted the rest of his stolen money. He'd resided in a motel in Pensacola, Florida, for all this time and they believed he probably ran out of money and wanted the money he stored in Tillie's attic. He must have been shocked if he came in and didn't find the money.

Until the hit and run was resolved, and after someone tried to get into Tillie's hospital room, the sheriff's department patrolled the house every day but couldn't be there 24/7 as they had already said. Thank God for Tillie's friends from church who continued to sit with her, whenever Joe and Julie were gone for the day. When either one of them got back, Joe or Julie would relieve the volunteers for the night. Julie hoped this issue with her father would not go on forever. It would be impossible to watch Tillie all day long and still have a normal life. It wasn't like they could put her in protective custody or the witness protection program. And they were probably in danger as well.

The sheriff's department was unaware Joe and Julie had found the money or had even identified Ted Champion as the driver. They were also unaware that Ted Champion was Tom Chapman, that the volunteers had a picture of him, and that Joe and Julie were well aware he was around. The sheriff's department, and especially Mike Kenny, were not in the loop. They probably didn't even know there was a loop. Joe told Tillie the reasons for keeping all this information close to the vest.

"Tillie, if the Russians knew my father was still alive, we would be in grave danger and, as Joe reminded us, families suffered as much as the thief," Julie said.

The Russian payback was not something they wanted to bring down on themselves. It was why the money was in a safe place and only a handful of Joe's friends in the Coast Guard were aware of what was going on. Joe knew his time was coming up to end his two-month stay in the Coast Guard and he wanted to see if he could extend it for a month or so, at least until they caught Julie's father and had a plan for avoiding the Russians. Joe had already thought about it and he would not leave them on their own even if he had to quit the Coast Guard. He could only do that under these temporary circumstances. If he had re-enlisted full time, he would have had no say in where he was stationed. Perhaps with his Rensselaer MBA, now, Joe could catch on with some local corporation in the Florida Keys, knowing the pay would probably stink but it would allow him the time to stay and help. This was weighing on his mind.

cococo

Julie's book started to come together but she needed more time to finish the first draft and meet the people at Brown University around Christmas time, if it was possible. She had taken the stipend and now she still had to produce. In hindsight, it probably was not the best idea, but no one ever knew what life brought. No one in a million years would have expected Tillie, driving around at twenty-five miles an hour, would be the victim of a hit and run. Who would have expected that Julie's father would still be alive and looking for money he stole seventeen years ago?

Julie needed free time every night for at least the next month to get her rough draft together. She knew she was expected to go back to Brown University before Christmas and at least go over what she had produced. It just wouldn't look right if she didn't, and it would probably end her career before it began, if she was unable to meet her schedule.

Joe continued to think about the situation and what could happen. As he was taught, "Plan for the worst and hope for the best." *Where the hell is her father?* Why couldn't he find him? He couldn't put an all-points bulletin out on him because they couldn't chance that the Russians might pick up on it and knock on their door at any time. Was her father dangerous? Joe believed, if Tom wasn't back then and simply got in over his head, he probably was dangerous now. He obviously had not worked in a long time and he only had a high school education. He was a fisherman and not a plumber or electrician, or even an auto mechanic. He couldn't go back to fishing in the Keys, even if he owned his own boat. Someone would have recognized him, eventually. He probably ran out of money as calculated by Joe to be close to $700,000.00, making his theft from the Russians those many years ago at close to a million dollars, in hundred dollar bills. The Russians wouldn't take it lightly. Joe and Julie needed to double their efforts to find her father and end the situation once and for all. They could not rest, knowing that danger would come, if not stopped.

While Julie was writing her book all this time, Joe

had been taking Russian lessons at his Coast Guard facility in Islamorada. The Coast Guard brought in a Russian
linguist and specialist on the Russian Mafia to give Joe a
Berlitz version of the Russian language, a full emersion
into the language and culture, for as fast as he could
learn. Over the last six weeks, he'd learned to understand
his mentor's Russian dialect, intonation, and cultural ref-
erences, just the way he learned the Mexican dialect-style
Spanish from his best friend and partner, Mark Silva.

Joe was on his way and while he learned Russian, he
read every Russian newspaper, article, and pamphlet he
could find and started to understand the history of the
Russians in south Florida. He also picked up Spanish
books on the Russian influence in Cuba from the local
library that catered to bi-lingual Spanish library patrons
in the Keys. There wasn't much on the topic.

Joe went on-line at his office, picked up chatter that
was both in Spanish and Russian, and understood the
Spanish end of the conversations and emails. He could
guess at the Russian answers to the Spanish questions.
His next trip to sea, coming up at the end of the week,
would be for three days and it included a Russian pattern
to his chatter he'd discovered only a few weeks ago. The
chatter came out of Cuba. It was actually from Miami to
Havana and back, and it was definitely a mixture of linguistic flavors. He sat with his Russian mentor and teacher and told him what he needed to get out of the emails
and conversations to find out exactly where the shipment
would be coming in. This would be a first, a Russian drug
bust with a Cuban crew, somewhere between Cuba, the
Bahamas, and Miami. Joe called Mark to come down for
the three-day trip so he could concentrate on the Spanish
end, and Joe could gravitate toward the Russian side.

Julie didn't know Joe had to go back out for three

days, and that she and Tillie would be on their own while he was gone. Tillie and Joe wound up arriving just in time at Coral Shores High School for the 3:30 p.m. cross-country event. The meet started without a hitch and would be over in less than a half an hour. It didn't take long on young legs. Joe ran into Jeff and Joan Talbot, both cheering on Lucy who was now leading the pack. She had come a long way, especially now that she closed quickly and started coming into the top ten and then eventually into second and first place. Now, with her confidence soaring, Lucy led the pack from the beginning to the end, in record time, for Coral Shores High School.

Joe turned to Joan. "Can I talk to you after the race?"

"Sure, Joe," she said with a quizzical look on her face.

Joe had never asked to speak to her personally before, not like this. His face was calm and clear but he definitely had something on his mind. Lucy still led the pack on the home stretch. She could have probably walked the rest of the way in and still won. However, she wanted the record and you could see it on her face. Julie cheered, Jeff cheered, and Joan jumped up and down with joy. Lucy broke the tape in record time and was surrounded by her friends and family. Tillie gave Lucy a big hug and told her how proud she was of her. It was Tillie's first attendance at a cross-country meet since Julie ran many years earlier. Julie was a really good runner, and an all-star, but she was not of the caliber of Lucy. Julie was just proud to be her coach.

Soon after, Joan turned to Joe. "Do you want some privacy?"

"Yes, Joan."

They walked over by the bleachers, a short distance from the finish line.

"What's up, Joe?" Joan said.

"I wanted to see if you could pave the way to have me stay for a little longer than planned," he said. "If the hit and run isn't solved before I leave, I can't leave them alone. If you can't do anything, I may have to resign my commission, and take a job down here for a while. Remember my assignment is only temporary, both here and at home."

"Don't get ahead of yourself," Joan said. "Of course I want you here forever, but I have to talk to Jacob Cramer, our chief warrant officer. I don't think it will be a problem. They have already invested in you, to teach you Russian, and it was not a cheap undertaking. I believe they want you to stay. What's going on anyway?"

Joe told her the continuing story of the hit and run and what had transpired at the hospital. He didn't go into detail with her because he didn't want her to be an accessory to anything he was doing. He just wanted to be clear that it was important for him to stay until it was resolved.

"Joe, I'll do everything I can if it isn't resolved before your time comes up for you to go back home. I promise."

"Thanks, Joan. I really appreciate it."

Julie followed Joe and Tillie home in her own car. She stopped and picked up some groceries. Joe started the coals for dinner. He loved cooking on the grill and would miss it when he went home. The months of October and November were about the latest he could grill on his back porch in Troy before the snow flew. The only barbeque he got during the winter was at the Dinosaur BBQ restaurant near the Green Island Bridge, back in Troy, a short five-block walk from his apartment, but it was well worth it. It was better than anything he could ever grill. Sitting at the bar, eating BBQ, watching the New York Giants on the big-screen TV on a Sunday afternoon was as close to paradise as it got for a Troy boy. Being with his friends, drinking, not driving, but walking home, was a gift from God—but only if the Giants won. This year, the too-old-to-play Giants, started 0-6 but won yesterday over the worst team in the league, the Minnesota Vikings, with a new quarterback starting, who was cut by Tampa Bay only the week before. At 1-6, Joe didn't think the Giants were headed for the playoffs any time soon. Even the Miami Dolphins had a better record and a chance at the playoffs after years of being humbled. You never knew.

After dinner, Joe and Julie did the dishes and Tillie cleaned up the living room. They started to get back in the groove. They had a load of laundry going at the same time. *Almost back to normal, and it feels good,* thought Julie.

"Julie, I'll be away for three days and then back in town," Joe told her.

"No problem, Joe. We'll be fine. Don't worry. The volunteers will be coming in for one more day and then they will cease coverage. Who can blame them? Father Schmidt and his church members went far and above anything that ever could be expected. Their love for Tillie is certainly profound and they put their money where their mouths were."

Julie could not have done it without them. The weekend was coming up and she would be home anyway so she didn't think there would be a problem.

⌘

Joe headed out the next day, said goodbye, and packed his car for the three-day trip. It would not be easy, it never was, especially if there were guns involved, and with the Russians and Cubans, there were always guns involved. Julie hid in her office and closed in on her first draft of her book. She needed some heavy editing before it was even close to presentable. She did her first spell check and found over three hundred errors that had to be corrected. She hated doing quotes and quotations. She could never remember where to put the commas and then the quotation marks. She went back to her old English textbooks and boned up on vocabulary and writing skills. She had plenty to do while Joe was away.

In the meantime, she went to work and on one day during the week, she thought someone had followed her to school. She deliberately stopped at the coffee shop and then the pharmacy and picked up a few items, just so she could look around. No one suspicious was ever behind her. Whenever she looked, she could never see anyone following her. When she got home, she used her new key in the new lock. She really couldn't tell if there were any scratches on the lock itself but she did notice there were some marks right where the key would go in to turn the lock. It looked like maybe someone had used the wrong key and it wouldn't fit but left a small scrape mark on the keyhole itself. Tillie was probably asleep and never heard a thing.

Julie got a little nervous. She would tell Joe about it and maybe they could do another fingerprint set on the lock when he got back. At least if anyone ever did have a key to the old lock, it couldn't be used now. *I'll bet my father still has a key to the old lock and let himself in. It's probably why there was no sign of forced entry. Thank God we changed the locks.*

Joe got back safe and sound. Their mission went well and they got their first Russian drug bust, almost all the way up near Miami. They used the same methodology, using a helicopter to take pictures of the suspected ship where the chatter was coming from, and got a warrant as there was a definite suspicion based on data, which they needed to have for a legal warrant. Joe took Julie and Tillie out to dinner, back to their favorite restaurant in Key Largo. They had a few beers and a few laughs.

Things were getting back to normal.

CHAPTER 23

Julie had just gotten back from indoor track practice. The cross-country season was very successful, not so much for the boys, since it was a rebuilding year, but the girls were ranked fifth in the State of Florida. They came in first for Monroe County. A star emerged in the name of Lucy Talbot, only a sophomore, but she wound up ranked third in the entire state. Julie's friend Jan brought her old cross-country coach from the University of Miami and they watched Lucy one Saturday. He was duly impressed after reviewing her progress for such a short period of time. She won the race that day. It was almost like she knew she had to, for Julie. The retired coach predicted Lucy would win at the state meet next year, especially since five of the top ten girls were seniors and would have graduated.

He said it would be her time and he made a call to the current coach at the University of Miami and told him of "his" find, he joked.

Julie stopped for groceries on the way home. Joe would be a little late so Julie said they would eat around 7:00 p.m.

She would start the coals and marinate the chicken breasts once she got home. Baked potatoes and fresh corn

on the cob would round out the meal. That was the benefit of living in South Florida and the Keys, fresh local
fruits and vegetables all year around.

Julie pulled up and parked her car right by the side of
the house. She took her bags and keys, opened the door
with her rear end, and backed into the kitchen. "Tillie,
I'm home." As she turned around, she noticed Tillie was
very quiet and sat in the living room with a gentleman
who had his back to her. "Hi, Tillie, who's this? Are you
going to introduce me?"

As he turned around, Tillie said, "Julie, I would like
you to meet your father."

Julie blinked then stared. "You are Tom Chapman,
my father?"

"That's right," he said as he smiled.

She was all ready to say there was nothing to smile
about when she noticed the gun in his hand, planted firmly against his leg.

"Why don't you sit down, Julie, over there by Tillie
so I can watch you," he said.

"What's the gun for?" Julie asked.

"I don't know. In case I really need it, I guess," he
said. "I asked Tillie where my money was and she appears to not have a clue as to what I was talking about.
So, I'll ask you the same question, Julie. Where's the
money?"

"What money are you talking about?" Julie asked,
playing dumb. She hoped to keep him talking. Joe should
be home shortly and, hopefully, he wouldn't just barge in
like usual. "Was it you who came to Tillie's room in the
hospital?"

"Yes, I just wanted to see how she was, but a couple
of old bats were sitting next to her bed at 2:00 a.m. in the
morning."

"Why did you go there? Did you try to kill her again?"

"No, I just wanted to make sure she didn't recognize me or remember who I was," he said. "I couldn't take a chance. I hightailed it out of there as soon as I saw them. I didn't think they saw me."

"Good for you, Dad," Julie said.

"Sarcasm, huh," he said. "Just like you, Tillie."

"See? I told you she doesn't know anything about any money and neither do I, so why don't you leave us alone like you have for the last seventeen years."

"You are the same old pain in the ass, Tillie, I see," he said.

"Where have you been all this time, 'Dad'?" Julie asked.

"If you get me my money, I'll tell you the entire story. If I don't get the money, I'll just have to shoot you."

"You would shoot your own daughter?" asked Tillie.

"If I had to, I would," Tom said. "Okay, I'll give you little history lesson but I better get my money before I go. Me and my two buddies ran dope for the Russians out of Key Largo. We were supposed to meet a ship twenty miles out to sea but the ship never showed up. There were hurricane winds and a tropical storm headed our way. I had a million dollars in cash in a waterproof suitcase ready to hand to the Columbians for a shipment of cocaine that never came. My two buddies and I made it to shore of Key West. We were going to meet the ship outside Big Pine Key but it never came. They dropped me off with the cash in the aluminum briefcase. It was the perfect size to hold the money in one hundred dollar bills in packs of $10,000.00, one hundred packs in all. I didn't want to get caught on a boat near shore with that kind of money. So, my buddies dropped me off and I rented a car before the storm came, under an assumed name. I had it already planned, just in case of a problem. Good thing too. Little did I know that on their way back, they got caught in a tidal wave off of Big Pine Key and drowned as the ship was submerged. I stayed at a motel on the way home. It had rained so much. I saw on the news the next morning they had drowned and everyone thought I was lost at sea as well."

"So you took off and left us. Is that about right, Dad?" Julie snarled.

"Damn straight, I did," he said. "The Russians thought I drowned with the money, never to be found. I had my new identity as Ted Champion and I left for our house. I took $700,000.00 in cash to Pensacola and put $300,000.00 in a gym bag and hide it in our attic under my old clothes. I took the $700,000.00 in the briefcase and left for Pensacola. In case I got caught and had to do time, I wanted a nest egg just in case. Guess what? After seventeen years of living well in New Orleans and Pensacola, I started to run out of money. My rainy day fund came due. So I came home to get it. I want my money now and I'll leave you alone. If not, you will be as dead to me as I already am to you."

Tillie turned to Julie. "Do you know about any of this, Julie?"

"I have no idea what he's talking about," Julie lied, although beads of sweat were starting to form around her upper lip.

"I guess you can lie as well as your mother did to me," he said.

"She loved you and died because of you, you asshole," Julie said.

"Now, now, this won't get us very far, will it?" he said. "Where's my money?"

Joe had just turned off the Overseas Highway and was coming in the back way as a short cut. He went two blocks in and turned toward Tillie's house, when out of the corner of his eye, he saw a white pickup truck parked at the curb that he had never seen before. Due to his training, Joe was very perceptive about his surroundings and he had a photographic memory for whatever he saw. It was both a gift and a curse. Someone said a lot of left-handed people had this ability. Others blamed it on being an Aries, born in April. Being both sometimes caused real issues for Joe. He remembered details no one else even thought about. It helped him tremendously when he went through reams of data online, even in Spanish. He put things together that seemed not to have any threads in common, solved a lot of cases, and impressed a lot of people.

His memory immediately put him back into an exact moment in time, as it always did, and he recalled everything vividly. He'd driven by here several times and there'd been no white pickup truck previously.

He slowed the car and drove by the truck. It was a Ford F-150 and white. He stopped and looked at the registration sticker on the window. It was a 2002. He looked at the plates and knew the vehicle came from the Pensacola area of Florida. It was not from Monroe County. He remembered after looking at all those license plates that there were only a handful of trucks like this registered from the northwest part of the state. This had to be Ted Champion, age forty-one from Pensacola, Florida. It was his white truck.

Joe was glad that he'd written both the VIN number and license plate number on the piece of paper he carried around.

He smiled because he knew he really didn't need the

paper, he had memorized both numbers anyway. This was Ted Champion's pickup truck.

This is not a coincidence. Joe walked around the truck and noticed on the passenger side door a large scrape where the paint had come off and had left only raw metal exposed. It was gouged out but it was an older truck and these things were to be expected. That was why people owned trucks, to be used as work vehicles without worrying about looks. *This was the truck that pushed Tillie off the road.* He knew it now. *There are no coincidences. Why park here?* He knew why. He bet Tom was at the house.

Joe went to his car, took out his shotgun and his service weapon, and made sure both were fully loaded. He put some plastic flex-cuffs into his back pocket then walked quietly through the backfield. He saw Julie's car was there by the side of the house. Her car door was slightly opened and the car dome ceiling light was still on. It was close to 7:00 p.m. so she should have noticed it by now. There was something really wrong.

Joe crawled to the back wall of the house and glimpsed into the kitchen. No one was there. He went to the other side very quietly. This was no different than any drug raid he'd been on except he was alone. He looked into the living room and saw Tillie and Julie sitting on one side of the room and a man sitting on the other. Voices were raised. There was no shouting, but they were very firm. Joe saw the look on Julie's face. It was fear and anger. He looked at Tillie and she was mad as hell.

He made it to the back of the house. He couldn't carry both the shotgun and his service weapon and be able to open Tillie's bedroom window at the same time. He put the shotgun in the weeds, a few feet back. In case he needed it, he knew where it would be. He slowly opened

Tillie's bedroom window. It was small but he could make it through, hopefully, without any noise. He raised the window slowly, after removing the screen, and went in headfirst. He knew Tillie's reading chair was against the wall right in front of the window. With the gun tucked into his lower back, in his belt, he grabbed hold of the chair, crawled over it, and slowly rose to his feet. The door was partially open. Tillie liked it that way so they could catch a breeze going through the entire house. Coupled with the overhead fans, it cooled off the house at night. The fans on high silenced his footsteps.

From this vantage point, Joe could see the man, who was obviously Ted Champion, according to the progression technology pictures developed by Jack Forest. Jack's facial progressive technology picture looked almost identical to the man who sat in the chair facing Julie and Tillie.

Well I'll be, Joe said to himself. *Ted Champion and Tom Chapman really are one in the same. Well I'll be damned.* The driver's license and the picture were almost the same, but in person this was uncanny.

Joe wondered how Julie and Tillie felt right now. Betrayed, unloved for Julie, total resentment for Tillie, hatred? Probably all those emotions came together at one time. He felt sorry for them, but sorry didn't keep them safe. *So, Tom Chapman or Ted Champion did not die many years ago and more than likely was responsible for trying to kill Tillie. I'll bet it's why she went crazy and drove home so fast. I'll bet she saw him and recognized him. He couldn't have her identify him, because then he couldn't get his money anytime soon. He tried to kill her to prevent anyone from knowing he was still alive. Damn.*

Joe crept slowly down the hall and saw Tom sitting by himself. Joe knew if he shot him he better not kill him because he didn't know how Julie would react. Ted was still her father.

Joe stepped around the corner as Tom was getting up, ready to point the gun at the ladies, and Joe shot him twice.

One bullet hit him in the arm that held the gun and the second in the left calf. Joe had aimed at both places to quickly turn Ted around to face him and not the women. Ted spun around and now had Joe's gun pointed directly at his head.

"Drop the gun or you are a dead man, regardless of who might want you alive," Joe said slowly,

"Not me," both ladies said at the same time.

Joe kicked the gun over to Julie from where Ted had dropped it. He had the flex-cuffs in his back pocket and he pulled out both pair, securing both Ted's arms and legs.

He was bleeding, so Joe asked Julie for a couple of towels. He tore the towels into strips and started to tighten the strips on both Ted's arm and upper leg to stop the bleeding.

"Joe, I would like you to meet my father," Julie said sarcastically.

"My pleasure," Joe said. "Do you prefer Tom or Ted?"

"Ted," he said. "I've been Ted for a long time. Tom died many years ago. You better kill me or I'll be back to get my money. You can count on it."

"How did you break into the house a few weeks ago to look for the money?" Joe asked.

"I still had a key to the house. Tillie never changed the locks. You should have been more careful, Tillie," Ted said, smiling.

Thanks for the advice," Tillie said.

"How did you get in this time, now that the locks had been changed," Joe asked.

"Tillie answered the door, opened it, and I walked right in," Ted said.

"Bad mistake, Ted," Joe said. Tillie looked quite sheepishly at Joe and Julie. Joe nodded "Don't worry about it, Tillie. He won't be coming in again, ever."

"Have you been following me?" said Julie.

"Of course. I wanted to find out what your schedule was and I never realized this guy was protecting you." Ted turned to Joe. "You sure aren't much to look at and you really fooled me," he said. "I didn't even know you were in the Coast Guard. Shame on me. I'll know the next time."

"There won't be a next time, Ted," Joe told him. "Trust me. Ladies, I have a question for you. Do you want me to kill him? I would be more than happy to. It's up to you. I know he's your father, Julie, but Tillie, he's the one who tried to kill you by running you off the road. I believe you recognized him in town and tried to run to tell Julie before he hit you."

"You son of a bitch," Julie growled, looking directly at her father.

"I'm not making this up, Joe," Tillie said. "But I do remember exactly, and I saw his face as soon as he came even with me, when his truck hit my car, as he looked at me through the truck window." She guessed it meant she was getting her memory back. "I guess I needed to be shook up before everything came back. A little trauma seemed to have gone a long way, Joe."

Julie also told Joe it was her father who went to the hospital late at night to see Tillie and was surprised by the church volunteers. He never expected anyone in the room but Tillie at 2:00 a.m. *Another mistake*, Joe thought.

"It doesn't matter," Ted protested. "You aren't going to turn me in. Just get me to a doctor, give me my money, and I'll be out of here."

"I don't think so, Ted," Joe said. "Perhaps before I call the sheriff's department, specifically Mike Kenny, the detective, you should thoroughly understand who I am and what your options are going to be. I'm a little more than just in the Coast Guard, Ted." Joe turned to the women. "Julie and Tillie listen up. They both know I'm a warrant officer in the Intelligence Division of the Coast Guard for all of Florida and the Keys. I was assigned to Islamorada simply to be near Julie and Tillie. I believe several cases have been solved tonight, but it can take several really bad curves for you, Ted. First, you are going to jail for a long time. If you survive in jail, it is really up to you."

"How so?" Ted asked.

"Let me begin telling you about your options. Tillie and Julie, those options include you as well. We found you in Tillie's house, armed and dangerous. I also found your truck, which upon further investigation, someone would have to conclude that you tried to kill Tillie Carpenter. How am I doing so far?" Joe grinned. "Just to ensure that option, Julie, hand me Ted's gun please." He immediately put two bullets into the wall right where Julie and Tillie had first sat. "This takes care of attempted murder."

Ted's eyes went wide, as Joe wiped his prints off Ted's gun. "What's my second option," he asked.

"The first option will be your best one. You will go to jail for a long time for attempted murder, reckless endangerment, and leaving the scene of an accident, as we so choose in the telling. Right, ladies?" They both nodded. "You will then be tried and convicted for attempted murder and armed robbery, as evidenced by the two bullets in the wall where these ladies just sat," Joe continued. "We can prove both at the same time, which means your life on the outside, will be over, give or take a lifetime or two. Make no mistake about it, Ted. Ladies, do you understand where I am coming from? We have already left the station where he is leaving here as a free man. It's not going to happen, regardless. I will call the sheriff's office in five minutes with or without your cooperation, Ted."

Joe shrugged. "The benefit to you with option number one is that you will go to jail as Ted Champion. Everyone will think you are an idiot for holding up two women with no money and even trying to kill a grandmother, but being considered stupid might just keep you alive. The next option is you are tried for these same offenses as Tom Chapman, the person who stole a million dollars from the Russian mob with the money never being recovered.

"You can scream at the top of your lungs about the money, but no one will ever believe you, especially with the reputations all three of us enjoy."

Joe paused, but Ted made no comment. "Now the bad part, Ted. You won't get the $300,000.00, the Russians won't get the $300,000.00, and you will be dead within a week wherever they send you. Do you get my drift, Ted? I will make sure the Russians find you in jail and I will make sure they know there was no money left because you spent it all. You came back to steal Tillie's house out from under her. How's that sound? Plausible right?" he asked. "Do you understand me? Or, with permission, I am more than willing to shoot you dead right now. It is my right as a homeowner in Florida, at least it's Tillie's right. Maybe she can shoot you. She seems mad enough."

Then Joe smiled at Ted. There was a lot of meaning in the smile and Ted finally understood his options in this. He didn't have any.

Both Julie and Tillie said the same thing at the same time. "Joe, we don't want this drug money."

"Fine, I understand, but think of the consequences. If you turn the money in and it means he is arrested as Tom Chapman, drug smuggler, both your lives would be in jeopardy. The Russians have killed families of those who have crossed them, not just the individual. And, your father, Julie, and your son-in-law, Tillie, will be dead within a week, anyway. Let me make one last suggestion before we call Mike," Joe added, "Julie, you are virtually guaranteed to sell your first book, are you not?"

"Yes the University guaranteed me an agent, publisher, and an editor to make sure everything went smoothly."

"Does anyone in the department care how much you make?" he asked.

"Not really," she said. "They wanted their graduates in the MFA program to be published authors. It helped recruitment and gave credibility to their program."

"What if every six months you 'earned' an addition $30,000.00 on which you paid taxes, and then gifted the money to Tillie to do anything she wanted to do with it? Would they mind?" he asked.

"No. They would not mind, I suspect," she said.

"Tillie, can your church use $60,000.00 a year from you, knowing it came from Julie? However, it's probably best to tell Father Schmidt the gifts were from an anonymous donor."

There was no point in having any red flags raised. Neither of them wanted any praise for the donations. So it was best to keep the gifts as quiet as possible.

"This way, it certainly won't be suspicious," he said. "You could buy gift cards or even obtain a bank teller check that will not even have your name on it. It would only have to state to whom it was payable and be signed by the authorized bank signatory. Brown University authors are supposed to excel from the beginning, are they not, Julie?"

"Yes," she said. "Actually it might work. My father would never get it and the money wouldn't go to the Russians. They won't even know it exists with Ted out of the picture one way or the other. Ted, you have one minute to decide. You go to jail as Ted, or Tillie and I walk out of here, and Joe takes you out," Julie said. "If you think I care, I don't. Do you want to live or die?"

"Live," he said. "I'll be Ted Champion. Hell, I may even get out in 20 years."

"You come back here, Ted, and you are a dead man," Joe said. "Now, Julie go get your tape recorder. We are going to tape his confession as Ted Champion in full and hear a full apology as well. He may get off with a lighter sentence for being a moron and having miscalculated the wealth of two poor women. I'll call Mike as soon as we're done. Ted will also write out his confession, sign it, and date it, and we will sign and date it as witnesses as well."

And it was done.

"Mike, it's Joe Traynor," Joe said a little while later. "A man named Ted Champion attempted to break into Tillie and Julie's house. I have him secured in flex-cuffs. I shot him twice but he will be okay. He had a gun, put two shots into the wall, and scared them both. We also have a taped verbal confession and a hand written signed confession, witnessed by all three of us. Can you come and pick him up?"

Mike whistled. "Sure, makes my life easier. See you in twenty minutes."

Joe turned to Ted. "One word about the $300,000.00 and you are a dead man. Do you understand?"

"Yes," Ted replied. "Where the hell did Julie and Tillie find you?"

"I found them and they mean the world to me," Joe said. "It's a shame you were blinded by money. You have no idea what you have missed over the last seventeen years."

Ted hung his head sheepishly and looked at his wounds. He would at least be alive but behind bars for a very long time.

When Mike put him in the sheriff's car, Ted turned to Julie. "I'm sorry."

Julie did not believe him. He was only sorry that he got caught. *He is my father, but in name only. Oh my God.*

"Well now it's over. Do you want to go out to dinner?" Joe asked with a smile. "Tillie, I believe you can afford it now."

"Joe where did the aggression come from?" she asked. "You are the most mild-mannered individual I have ever met."

"Tillie, I have been trained for ten years to take the bad guys out. I was trained that if you have a gun in your hand, use it, and if the suspect has one, you shoot first and get explanations later."

"You never hesitated, not for a second," Julie said.

"You just shot him," Tillie agreed.

"I could have killed him just as easy, Tillie, and it would not have upset me. His having a gun on two people I love meant not stopping until he was down. I don't think you believed I would kill him. You should ask

Mark or even Dan up in Albany. When the gangbangers came through the door and I shot them—after I shot Luis Hernandez—they were surprised, too. So were the FBI guys later on," Joe laughed. "Let's go get something to eat. And it's on Tillie."

The three of them waved at Mike and the other deputies as they pulled out of the driveway and headed out to dinner.

What a relief. Timing was everything and he had only a few days left before he had to leave. Joe didn't know if he really wanted to leave now. It was probably just the high from shooting Julie's father. It had happened before and he had better be careful. Not too many had ever seen that side of him. It was not pretty. Yes his aggression came roaring back to him. He remembered the time he had pitched in a high school game. It was the last game of the season, and the last of his high school career. He had already gotten the academic scholarship to MIT, but as a left-handed pitcher, he was offered a lot of baseball scholarships simply because he was a left-handed pitcher, and they were few and far between. Most players thought lefthanders were nuts, anyway, so his coach told him to warm up by throwing the ball over the backstop to prove he was wild. They didn't dig in at home plate very much.

Joe felt the same about taking down Julie's father. It was what he had to do to win.

CHAPTER 24

Joe, Julie, and Tillie hopped into Joe's car and headed out to dinner. They decided to go to Snapper's Key Largo Restaurant and Tiki Bar, which was the official name for the restaurant, but was simply known as Snapper's, the best Happy Hour Bar in the Florida Keys. It was located at 139 Seaside Avenue, at marker 94.5, right on the water, on the Atlantic side. Snapper's offered an eclectic menu of the freshest seafood prepared with Caribbean, Mexican, and Asian flavors. They offered daily specials based on fresh locally caught fish from the beautiful Florida Keys waters. Joe wanted their Happy Hour $.75 wings, buffalo style to remind him of home at the Ale House in Troy, and a bucket of spicy hot shrimp, along with a few ice-cold beers, any beers as long as the bottles were cold. Tillie wanted the Big Boss Lady Fried Oysters and Julie had the grilled Lobster special. They ate until their stomachs were filled and their hearts were content. Both Julie and Tillie had a Key Largo Blue Coconut Margarita special, about the size of a football with a tiny umbrella sticking out of the quart-size drink.

During dinner, they all had a serious discussion about keeping the money and giving it to Tillie for retirement. She balked at that and Joe's original suggestion to give it to the church was better received. Julie thought about it at length and wanted to offer a compromise.

"Joe, I know you only tried to protect us," Julie told him. "However, having the money near us and having to watch over it until it's gone is not something either of us really wants to do. Do you agree, Tillie?"

"I am nervous about it, and what if any of my friends found out I had money? I would surely be hit up for every fundraising event since I obviously came into money. It's not who I am. I don't want the money."

She was uncomfortable having more than she needed and, quite frankly, she would be happy to see it go once and for all.

"I agree," Joe said. "So what you think we should do, Julie?"

"I have a plan. I want to go to Joan Talbot and Jacob Cramer and turn the money into the United States Coast Guard with a few conditions. Nothing will ever be mentioned about it to anyone. There will be no repercussions about not turning it in immediately because we were afraid for our lives, since we believed the Russians could come back and kill us.

"Nothing is to be mentioned to the sheriff's department. They wouldn't even watch Tillie in the hospital. Finally, I want the Coast Guard to cut a check for $75,000.00 payable to St. Justin Martyr Church for the food pantry and the second-hand clothing store. The funds are to be used for food and clothing only and to pay the costs of the facility's heat and electric, which has always been an expense they can't afford. Half the money will go to food and clothing and the other half for the operating bills."

All three agreed this would be a good idea.

Joe was not to be involved in any of it because of his rank and status in the Coast Guard.

"I will seek out Joan first," Julie said. "And then, upon her agreement, Joan can go to Jacob Cramer to get permission to turn the money in quietly."

They raised their glasses together and made a vow never to discuss the topic again after they turned over the money.

∞∞∞

The following day, after school, there was no practice so Julie called Joan and asked her if she could speak to her privately. Joan was a little upset, thinking it was about Lucy.

"Is Lucy okay?" she asked. "Are you having problems with her?"

"No of course not, Joan. I would want a daughter someday exactly like Lucy," she said.

With her fears behind her, Joan said Julie could come right over to her office. She didn't go home until after 5:00 p.m., anyway. Julie got to the facility and walked into the front door. She asked for Joan and was directed down the hall, after the secretary called Joan for approval.

"Hi, Julie. How are you?" Joan asked. "You made me very nervous at first thinking this was about Lucy,"

"Lucy has never been, nor will she ever be, a problem. You should know that Joan."

"Thank you," Joan said. "Now, how can I help you?"

Julie went through the entire situation of Tillie's being hit and run and almost killed. Joan knew about it. Julie then went on to tell her about how she thought she was followed, and how her house was broken into but nothing taken.

She went through the fingerprinting process that identified her father's prints, even though he was supposedly dead for all these years.

"Wow," said Joan, "please continue."

Julie went on to tell her how they identified her father as Ted Champion, about the money he hid in the attic, and how he tried to kill her and Tillie.

At this point, Julie asked Joan to be sworn to secrecy, if she could.

"As long as there is nothing illegal about what you're telling me, illegal at least on your part."

Julie took a chance and told Joan everything that had happened. The worse that could happen to Joe was that they would ask him to leave the Coast Guard and, with an MBA from Rensselaer, he could work anywhere he wanted as long as he wasn't prosecuted for a felony. Joe didn't believe shooting her father was a felony, but you never knew.

"Joe shot my father twice, once in his right arm and once in the left side in the upper leg area, knowing it would spin him around and it would get him to face him, not Tillie and me. Joe saved our lives. We were afraid if it got out about my father being alive, the Russians would come after Tillie and me," Julie said. "So would you like $300,000.00 in cash, handed to the United States Coast Guard with only a few conditions?"

"What are the conditions, Julie?" Joan asked.

"First, Joe had no involvement at all. It's a deal breaker. This was our problem not Joe's," she said. "My father was arrested under the name of Ted Champion of Pensacola, Florida. No one knows any differently," she added. "He confessed to and was charged with breaking

and entering, attempted murder and hit and run under
Ted's name. There is no reference to Tom Chapman, my
father's real name, anywhere. He will do his time, probably fifteen to twenty years, with time off for good behavior, under the name of Ted Champion. He will look rather
dumb going after two women who were broke. He was
mistaken to think we had any money. It's the way it now
stands with his oral and written confession. He is on his
way to Raiford State Prison for a long, long time, I suspect"

"So no one else knows about the money other than
you, Tillie, and, I suspect, Joe?" Joan asked. "Is that correct?"

"It's correct," Julie replied.

She never mentioned Mark or Jack during the conversation.

"Where is the money now?" Joan wanted to know.

"It's in a safe deposit box in a bank two blocks from
here," Julie said very seriously.

"So if we take the money for our use, minus
$75,000.00 for your church, and say nothing more about
it, that's all you want?"

"Yes. The check has to be made payable directly
from the Coast Guard to the church and no one else is
ever to know why, other than it was a Coast Guard donation, done quietly. Perhaps, you should also let them
know if anyone blabs about the gift, it will be rescinded."

Joan nodded. "That's a good point, or we would be
swamped by every organization in the Florida Keys. Let
me talk to our chief warrant officer, Jacob Cramer, and I
will call you immediately after we get a resolution. Can
we get the money before the bank closes, today?"

"Sounds like a plan, Joan," Julie said with a smile. "I
have the safe deposit key right on me now."

Joan went in and spoke to the chief warrant officer. After about forty-five minutes, they both decided that, although quite irregular, there was nothing wrong with a donation from an individual to the Coast Guard. They also could use the money to upgrade their technology infrastructure and fix up a few offices. The money, $225,000.00, after the church donation, would be a drop in the bucket compared to their total operating budget, less than one percent, so it would not raise any concerns. It would be counted as a miscellaneous donation to the facility. Joan thought it was nice to get someone in charge with common sense and supported the staff, especially since nothing would ever be said to Joe about the entire situation.

She gathered two *Coasties* from a ship that just came in and told their commander that she wanted to borrow them for an hour. He said no problem. Joan called Julie and said she would meet her at the bank in ten minutes. Before meeting her warrant officer, Joan told Julie to hang close. She was at a coffee shop a block away.

Joan and Julie went into the bank, twenty minutes before closing. Julie signed in, gave her identification, and nothing was required of Joan. They went into the vault with a gym bag that Julie brought just in case this could happen. She put her keys into the two boxes and the vault teller did the same and turned the bottom lock on both boxes. Julie pulled out the first box and handed it to Joan, pulled out the second, and both of them walked to the private area where they would be behind closed doors. The two Coast Guardsmen waited at the front door.

"I've never seen $300,000.00 in cash before sitting in a vault," Joan said. "I've seen twenty million wrapped in plastic wrap on pallets but never up close and personal like this."

"Do you think I have?" Julie joked.

They emptied the $290,000.00 into the bag and Julie took out the $10,000.00 from her purse, that had been tested, which started the ball rolling, and added it to the bag. She then took the house title and canceled mortgage documents from the box and put the documents in her pocketbook.

"Just our title and mortgage papers to Tillie's house," she told Joan.

"Where did the one brick come from?"

"We needed to test it first to see if we could find the origin. Do you see the symbol on each of the paper wrappers?"

"Yes," Joan said. "What is it?"

"It's Cyrillic or Russian for $10,000.00. On the inside of the wrapper, there is a symbol for the Cayman National Bank, where the money originally came from."

"Wow," said Joan. She zipped up the bag and they both walked out as casually as they could, with Julie's heart pumping a thousand miles a minute, and met their guards at the door. Joan and the guards hopped into her government car and left. Julie waved to Joan.

"The check will be mailed directly to Father Schmidt, who is to place it into a separate savings account for the purposes we discussed, okay?" Joan asked.

"No problem."

"Tell Father Schmidt that the Coast Guard will audit the account a few times a year, until we are satisfied they are doing the work they were supposed to do," Joan told her. "Convey this message directly to Father Schmidt."

With great relief, Julie headed home. She'd stop and see Father Schmidt on the way.

She pulled into the church parking lot as he was coming out the door. "Father, hi. Can I talk to you for a minute?"

"Sure, what's up, Julie?"

She then proceeded to tell Father Schmidt what to expect from the Coast Guard and the conditions that would be attached to the silent donation. Julie had already told him about this entire situation under the seal of confession. She did that to ensure nothing would ever be said in the future by Father Schmidt. It might have been a little underhanded, but their lives would be in jeopardy if it came out.

Father Schmidt told her not to worry. It would never come out.

He would open the account and oversee it until the money was gone. He had been there for many years and wasn't going anywhere. "Pray I don't leave or die," he said, smiling. "And your next confession better be a true one or you are going to hell, Julie."

"Yes, Father, I apologize and I hope I made it up to you," she said. "And, above all, thank you for your help and the volunteers' help with Tillie and especially thank those who were there when the man showed up in the hospital. It was my father, you know?"

"Yes, I know ,Julie," he said.

"I am sure they were scared to death," Julie said.

Julie hopped back into her car and headed home. Her life could move forward now, or could it? She needed a heart to heart talk with Joe. She'd never told him how she felt. Louise Silva knew. *Why doesn't he? I have to find out for myself*, she decided.

CHAPTER 25

Julie's father sat in the Monroe County jail, waiting to plead down his sentence. In writing and orally, Ted Champion had admitted to the hit and run and that he broke into Tillie's house and held both Tillie and Julie at gunpoint. He also reluctantly admitted to shooting his gun twice at the wall over their heads to make them talk. He'd heard Joe loud and clear. And it would do him no good to admit to these other felonies and not admit to the shooting, even though he didn't do it. He would get the same sentence and, as Joe told him, he would be a dead man if he didn't admit to everything. There would be no extensive trial. He was offered fifteen years for the felonies but would receive twenty-five years to life for attempted murder if he didn't accept the terms. He'll be out in ten.

The district attorney proved the hit and run was no accident and they had his oral and written confessions, so he took the deal, so with time off for good behavior, he would be out in ten years.

It was also in writing he was never to contact Joe, Tillie, or his daughter, Julie, ever again. If contact was made in any form, in writing, a telephone call, e-mail, or even a hang up phone call, he would go back and serve his entire sentence, plus have five years added back on a harassment charge. One call equaled ten years and he knew it. It was a much better deal than dying at the hands of the Russians in his first week in jail as Tom Chapman.

Julie had signed off on the deal for all three of them, including Joe and Tillie. She went alone to the arraignment, which took twenty minutes, and she would not have to go for the sentencing. It was done and over. Julie headed out of the sheriff's department headquarters in Key West, where her father was being held, and then drove up to Joe's Coast Guard office in Islamorada.

She parked in the Coast Guard lot, walked into the facility, and asked for Joe. Joan was walking down the hall and said hello to Julie. Julie quickly, and quietly, told her about the sentencing and terms for incarceration. Joan hugged her and wished her well, then Julie headed to Joe's office in the back.

"Well, the sentencing is done," she said. "He accepted the terms and, more than likely, if he was smart, we will never see him again."

"I'm glad it's over," he said. "Now, we can all get on with our lives."

Julie took it as a less-than-friendly comment. "Are you trying to tell me you can't wait to get home, Joe?"

"No, not at all," he said. "Please don't take it the wrong way. I just meant we could go back to normal, whatever normal means now."

"Let's go to lunch. Do you have time?" she asked.

"Yes, just let me check out and I'll meet you outside in five minutes. I have a meeting in an hour, but this should work out fine."

They went around the corner to a small luncheonette to get a quick sandwich.

"Joe, I know you have to get back, but I really have

to ask you something, and if this is not the time, then I want to make the time to say it right, so there's no misunderstanding."

"Wow, are you all right?"

"Yes, I am fine but I have something to say, to ask you. I am reluctant to say anything but I must."

"Go ahead, ask me anything," he said.

"Joe, do you love me?" she asked.

He blinked then stared. "Well, of course, I love both you and Tillie and you should know that."

"That's not what I meant, Joe, and you know it."

"Oh."

"I don't want to hear about the fifth grade and Career Day or anything else. I am a grown woman," she said. "You may have thought of me as a younger sister, but those days are gone, Joe. Everyone seems to know, at least every woman I know seems to know, I love you, and I want to know what your feelings toward me are, little sister aside."

Joe swallowed and looked into her eyes. "Julie, I loved you the day I met you. My love for you, like yours for me, has changed from that of the love for a little sister, to someone I have fallen in love with, especially since our time together over the last two months. I wanted to keep my feelings to myself because I have never been comfortable hitting on women, especially when my feeling run so deep.

"Please hear me out," he said as she opened her mouth. "I believed I was too old for you. I am thirty-three and you have just turned twenty-four. You have your whole life ahead of you, and a career as a writer. I don't want to be the one who holds you back from everything you deserved."

"Joe, you would never hold me back, and I don't believe the one thing is related to the other. Nine years is not a lot."

"Nine and a half," he said, and smiled.

"Okay, nine and a half," she said. "Before you go on, I know Louise was eight years younger than Mark and their ethnic background was not even remotely the same but it worked for them. I don't want to go on pretending everything is the same. I told Tillie about this situation and do you know what she said to me, Joe? She said it was about damn time."

"So Tillie knows your feelings?"

"She has always known. She knew before I did. She said she could see it in my eyes when we went for the tour of your ship when you were only nineteen years old."

"Wow, I never saw that coming," he said.

"So what do you want to do about this situation?" she asked.

"As you know, I have not talked to Mary since I have been here," he said. "She never called me. I called and left several messages and even asked Dan to speak to her. I've heard absolutely nothing. At this point, I really don't owe her an explanation about why we broke up. When I get back to Albany, I have to stop and see Dan anyway and I was going to stop and see Mary as well and make it formal. This was not like Jennifer Alvarez breaking up with me and then she never even went to my mother's funeral. I thought Mary, no offense, was the one for me. I guess I was wrong. So how do we begin a new relationship, Julie?" he asked. "I am serious when I say I don't have a clue at this point. I do not want to lose my feelings for you or Tillie if this thing between us didn't work out."

"To your point, Joe. Let's allow this 'thing,' as you

call it, to happen slowly. I too have a knot in my stomach. I never thought we would ever have this discussion but I am glad we talked," she said. "My feelings for you run very deep, and I know the feelings I have for you are love. I just hoped it would be enough of a starting point to move forward. I also don't believe you properly answered my question, Joe. Do you love me as a man would love a woman?"

"Yes Julie, I really do love you," he said. "I had thought about you, like this, since I saw you at your high school graduation. You were a woman in my eyes for the first time. It was confusing to me, and I didn't want to feel like a dirty old man looking at some young girl. But you were right, you are a woman now and it has made all the difference to me. I really do love you, Julie," he repeated. Then he smiled. "Can I go back to work now?"

"Yes, you may, dear," she said with a grin. "Now that we have that settled—" She laughed. "—what time will you be home for dinner, dear?"

Joe laughed too as they walked out the door. For the first time, Joe put his arms around her waist and kissed her on the lips, a real kiss.

"I could get used to this, Joe," she said.

"Me, too. I'll see you and Tillie tonight."

Joe went back to his office and stopped to chat with Joan. He let her know what had just transpired and asked her if he would be able to stay on after his two month stint was over. They had discussed it previously but Joe had been reluctant to pursue it because he wanted to get the hit and run and subsequent incidents behind them. Now that those problems were over, Julie's father was headed to jail, and he and Julie had had a heart to heart discussion about moving forward as a couple, he thought he would sign up for another two year obligation—but only if he could be assigned to the Islamorada facility. He would jump at the chance.

Joan thought there would be no problem but Joe also needed housing now that they had declared their intentions. They would not pursue their relationship under one roof, the roof that belonged to Tillie. It was best he separated his housing and, if and when they were ready to move in together, or get married, they would have a place, either on the base or in other housing once he was settled. He also knew that if Julie were successful in getting her book published, she would be spending a lot of time on the road for book signings wherever she would be sent throughout the country. He could look in on Tillie when Julie was gone and be able to do his job better by being on the base, especially since he would be on twenty-four hour call at all times.

Joe knew this might be the perfect time to re-enlist for two years since there had not only been an increase in drug trafficking, but they also had to break in an additional 58 vessels, currently being built in Louisiana. Those ships had to be cleared through the Florida Keys before being sent to their permanent assignments throughout the country. In addition, the crews had to be trained, not just to operate the ships, but new men and women would be assigned to those boats that needed training in intelligence and drug interventions as well. Joan told him she would get back to him before he left for home so he would know what would be coming and then he would be able to make the transition on his thirty day leave.

❧❧❧

Julie had a lot of work to make up both at her job at

school and on her as-yet-unpublished book. She'd taken the stipend from Brown and she felt a real obligation not to just finish the book, but to make it the best book she could. She was writing this book from the heart about her own life. It was to be aimed at young girls growing up poor, for those who had limited prospects for achieving success in their lives. She'd been fortunate, even though she'd grown up poor. She hadn't realized it until high school, when it became clear the more affluent students dressed better and seemed to have better lives. But that was not quite right. It seemed the more they had, the more they wanted, and they were just as unhappy, if not more so, than those who had less.

What Julie wanted to bring out in the book was that it was love, not monetary success, that gave her a feeling of accomplishment. It was Tillie's love, she wanted to emphasize, that had carried the day. Without Tillie, Julie would never have had the moral upbringing and work ethic that had made her a success. She never had a sense of entitlement and worked hard for everything she ever achieved. This was the message she wanted to convey, in a well-written and interesting way that would hold a young girl's attention while delivering the message.

It was also Joe's influence on Julie that made her want to be the best she could be and spurred her to go on to Brown University to become the writer she was now becoming, slowly but surely. There were very few examples of overnight successes, she thought. Maybe a few one-hit wonders, but hard work had to be the basis for achievement or all her goals would have crumbled. Now, having Joe by her side, not as his little sister but as his equal, hopefully his partner, would fill the hole in her heart, the part of her that was missing. All this time she'd been lonely and hadn't known why. Now she did.

ひかひ

Joe received the call from Jacob Cramer that he was approved for two additional years, to be assigned to Islamorada only. And he would have permanent housing when he came back from shore leave. The next day, Joe went back to his office and completed all the tasks he needed to finish in order to hand his caseload over to Jacob. Joe would be going home on Friday, flying out of Fort Lauderdale. Instead of going home permanently, now he had to make plans to move to Islamorada within thirty days. He had to get rid of his car, which luckily had the lease expiring the following month. He wouldn't need a car in Florida. He had to see Johnathon Mills about his apartment. He had been there for three years and was fortunate to have a caring landlord and friend in Johnathon. The apartment was fully furnished except for his bed and new HD TV, which he had just purchased.

He would FedEx his TV, stereo, and excess Florida summer clothes, and leave the bed. He hoped the FedEx delivery person was not the one they caught on camera, throwing a television set over a hedge. Joe decided to give his winter clothes to his brother. The rest of the smaller items he didn't want, he would leave with Goodwill. He would stay in Troy for Thanksgiving and be down in the Keys for Christmas, if everything went smoothly.

After the heart to heart talk with Julie, they decided Joe would sign up for two additional years in the Coast Guard if he were assigned to the Islamorada main facility. The call from Jack Cramer solidified the decision and made his going home a little easier, knowing he was coming back to Julie and a new life. He was thrilled and happy for the first time in a long time. He finally realized what Julie meant to him after all this time. Joe and Julie would become a couple with Tillie's full blessing, already. It would be so much easier living and working near her than thinking about what it meant to be 1,500 miles away in upstate New York. It was time to change his life.

The request to serve an additional two years and be assigned to the Florida Keys by the Coast Guard authorities went much smoother than they both had anticipated. Everyone, including the current chief warrant officer in charge of Islamorada and Joan Talbot highly recommended Joe for this assignment. It would allow the Islamorada facility to come up to speed in dealing with other organized crime elements like the Russians, who had become firmly entrenched in Florida, Puerto Rico, and the surrounding island nations. It was to the Coast Guard's benefit to have a full time intelligence officer of Joe's caliber on staff to work the multitude of cases underway. There was no one else available with the knowledge Joe possessed and no one with his linguistic skills.

In fact, over the two-month period he was temporarily assigned to Islamorada, Joe had become almost fluent in Russian. Being fluent in both languages would give him a leg up when doing intelligence work on the drug trade, not only in the Keys but in the entire southern region of the United States.

Spanish and Russian? Joe mused. *Who would have thought about the combination?* It looked like it was here to stay. Then they all laughed at one of their meetings. Spanish and Russian? Wasn't that what happened for the last forty years in Cuba? Just because the Russian government supposedly moved out of Cuba, they didn't take their Russian mafia cousins with them. They stayed. Why wouldn't they expand into the United States once the Soviet Union disbanded? It was one hundred miles from Key West, one of the most affluent cities in the United States and the rest of the Florida Keys were just there for the taking, along with Miami to the north.

Joe was packed and Joan picked him up at the house for the trip to the Fort Lauderdale International Airport. He secured a direct flight, serving once again as an Air Marshall, leaving Fort Lauderdale at 5:54 p.m., with one stop in Baltimore. He stayed on the plane for a twenty-minute layover, and then would land in Albany at 11:15 p.m. His brother Pete was picking him up at the Albany International Airport. Joe had to get to the Fort Lauderdale Airport one hour before the flight left, not to stand in a security line, but to make sure the plane's staff, once again, knew he was armed and was serving as an Air Marshall.

സ്ക

Joe's cell phone rang and he looked to see who was calling. It was Mary Lynch. She hadn't called him, and he hadn't talked to her since the morning he'd called her from Julie's house and told her the next phone call was hers.

"Hello?" he said, picking up reluctantly.

"Joe, it's Mary. When are you coming home?"

"Tonight. I'm coming home for thirty days, packing, and returning to the Keys for another two-year stint in the Coast Guard. I'll be home by 11:15 p.m."

"Do you need to be picked up?"

"No, my brother is coming to get me."

She was quite put out by the news he was moving back to the Keys. "Why?"

"Why, what?" he demanded.

"Why are you moving back to the Keys for another two years?"

"Why not? You haven't even called me. That speaks volumes, so I made plans without you."

"Were you ever going to call and tell me?"

"Why? I don't seem to matter to you anyway, so I just assumed our relationship was over. The last time I called, you specifically stated that you didn't have time to talk to me. I asked you what you wanted from me, and you said, 'I don't want anything.' So I moved on."

Almost two months, he thought. *Not a call in two months. Now she's on the line. Sorry, you are a little late, Mary.* He was not going to get into a discussion about his new commitment to Julie. It was best to leave that alone.

"Just like that, Joe?" she said. "You are moving and were you even planning to call me?"

"Excuse me, I called you and you never returned my calls," he said. "The last time I called you, you made it very plain you didn't care one way or the other, so I decided to wait for you to call me," he said. "Two months, Mary, two months."

"I'm sorry, Joe, I was busy," she said.

"Why are you calling me now?" he asked.

"I thought we could get together and discuss it," she said.

"It's a little late, Mary, don't you think?" he asked.

"It's her. It's Julie, isn't it, Joe? You're leaving me for her," she said.

"You told me in so many words you did not have a place in your life for me. I took it to heart," he said. "I have never forced myself on anyone and I am not starting now," He sighed. "I'm really glad you are doing well at the Albany Coalition. I spoke to Dan many times over the last two months and I know he told you that I asked about you. He told me he did on several occasions but he never got back a positive response."

She said nothing so he continued. "Mary, I have to leave in a few minutes so I need to end our call. When I get back, unpack, get settled, and take care of my affairs, I will be glad to sit down with you and talk, but you must know, Mary, that I am moving on and I hope you will do the same." He didn't think Mary expected the answer he gave her.

It finally hit her that it was over and she was kind of thrown by the entire conversation. "I'm sorry, Joe, I should have called you."

"Thanks, Mary. I will try to see you when I stop to see Dan after I get back," he said.

And with that thought left hanging, Joe ended the call.

CHAPTER 26

Joe arrived in Albany right on schedule at 11:15 p.m., flying Southwest Airlines. It was a long walk from the Southwest terminal on the second floor to the baggage terminal on the first floor but Joe only had his one carry-on bag and met his brother right outside the front door. Pete was double parked with his lights flashing as if he was waiting for someone important.

Joe wouldn't have been surprised if Pete had a placard reading "Warrant Officer Traynor." Joe gave his brother a big hug and they headed toward the I-87 Northway to go home. They stopped at a Mr. Sub on the way and then at Stewart's for a six-pack. They went directly to Joe's apartment. Pete found a parking spot right next to Joe's car in the back of the building. Pete had taken Joe's car out once a week to make sure it was running.

They'd had a long conversation, right after he and Julie had their heart-to-heart discussion. Joe told Pete he was moving to the Keys and was home for thirty days to settle up his affairs. They would return Joe's car, on the day before he left, to the Ford dealership in Latham. He would stay at his father's house after handing in his house keys to Johnathon Mills and after he shipped what he needed by FedEx.

Pete and Joe got along a lot better now than they had, especially after his father was attacked during the break-in at his house. It left him unconscious and he too, like Tillie, was placed in a medically induced coma to relieve the pressure caused by the beating he'd received from the robbers. It had shaken Pete up enough to change his life and he recommitted himself to the business his father had started. Pete handled all the jobs under contract, seeing them through to completion, and really understood what had to be done. He even started dating a nice girl, Tanya Fields, from the Burgh, whom he had known for years, but never attempted to ask out.

One day, several months ago, they were at a wedding when Tanya came over to him and asked him to dance. She asked him why he never asked her out. He felt quite sheepish when she told him she liked him and would like to go out on a date. She said she had never done this before, but decided to give it a try. Pete laughed when he told the story and Joe conveyed the same message he received from Julie. They both laughed at how truly dumb they really were when it came to women.

Pete dropped Joe off. Joe promised to meet Pete and his new girlfriend for drinks the following day after he visited his father. His father was home and much improved. He'd started going back to work part time, which was a blessing. Joe thought this helped define his father as well. Since his mother died, Joe's father was not the same. Perhaps this wake-up call had helped him see the light.

Joe went to bed after eating his sub and having a few beers. He watched the late-late show and was falling asleep in the chair. He took a quick shower, changed, and, as soon as he hit the pillow, fell soundly asleep. The next morning, Joe met Johnathon in the front of the building at the Troy Education shop. They had a long discussion and Johnathon wanted to keep Joe on retainer to do a few things. Joe told him not to bother with money. He owed Johnathon big time and Joe would do whatever was needed when he was able. They had truly become good friends after all this time. Johnathon wished him well and told him to take his time moving. There was no rush.

Joe went back to his apartment and called Dan who was in his office on a Saturday morning. "Hi Dan, I'm back."

"Welcome home, Joe," Dan said.

"What's your schedule today? Do you want to get some lunch?"

"I'm out of here at noon today," said Dan.

"Is Mary in today?"

"Yes," Dan said.

"Tell you what. It may not be pleasant but can I come down and see her for a few minutes before we go out?" Joe asked.

"You do so at your own peril," Dan told him.

"Bad, huh?" Joe asked.

"Well, she has been in a funk since your phone conversation," Dan said.

"Best to get it over with then. What do you think?" Joe asked.

"I would if I were you."

"I'll be down around 11:00 a.m. then, if it's okay?"

"Fine, see you then. I'll pray for you," Dan said, laughing.

Joe hopped into his car. Pete had taken pretty good care of it since he'd been gone. It started right away and he headed toward Albany, directly south on I-787. He got off at the Clinton Street exit and meandered up toward Central Avenue where the Albany Coalition for Families was located, right at the top of the hill. Joe found a spot on the street. He always carried quarters for the meters. It was a way of life in Albany. He parked about a block away and headed toward the front door. Since it was Saturday, there was no one at the front door so Joe took the stairs two at a time and headed to Dan's office. He popped his head in and pointed to Mary's office. No words were spoken but Dan got the message. Joe walked down the hall and knocked on her door, which was locked.

Mary opened the door and looked right at Joe. Her surprise at seeing him showed. "Hi, Joe, welcome back."

"Thanks," he said.

She pointed to a chair in front of her desk and closed the door. "And to what do I owe this visit?"

"I just wanted to see you in person," Joe said.

"Well, here I am," she said. It wasn't said belligerently, but it was said very succinctly.

"I just wanted to wish you the best," he said.

"Thank you, Joe."

"I told you I would stop by to see you in person when I got home, Mary. That's why I stopped," Joe said, "Thank you for the good times we had together, and I really mean that. I hope that you will be happy and have a wonderful life."

"It's just that you won't be in it, right, Joe?" she said.

"I wish you the best, Mary. I hoped we could stay friends," he said. He bowed his head to her and headed toward the door.

"Joe, wait. I am sorry. I just don't react well I guess," she said. "Please believe me. I wish it was different, but I am who I am, and I guess that means goodbye."

"Goodbye, Mary," he said and left to go to Dan's office.

"How did it go," Dan asked.

"I really don't know. You know her as well as any-one. Her reactions are way off, and I don' really under-stand her. It's probably me," Joe said. "I didn't dump her. She dumped me by not calling me, not even once."

"So tell me about you and Julie," Dan demanded. "That was quite a surprise I guess?"

"Yes, it was to me," Joe said.

"Does Mary know?" Dan asked.

"I didn't tell her but on the phone she hinted that it was the reason for the breakup. It wasn't. She never called me and she was not very pleased with me when I had to leave." He shook his head. "I'm glad that's over. Let's go have a few beers and lunch, in that order. I'm buying."

They headed down the hill to the closest bar that sort of served food. After Dan went back to the office, Joe called Julie to let her know he'd arrived on time and told her his family was fine as well. "I had a very short dis-cussion with Mary that ended okay, not great, but okay, and I feel better about it."

"I'm glad."

"I miss you already, Julie. I love you." *There's a first time for everything,* he thought, and smiled.

"I love you too, Joe," she said. "Oh, by the way, I got a call on Friday from the Florida State Department of Ed-ucation and my school's a finalist for the $100,000.00 technology grant."

"That's great news," he said.

"They asked me several questions and I need to for-mulate my responses by next week. They've never re-ceived a grant application before from my school and they were quite interested in why I'm sending it in now."

"What did you tell them?" he asked.

"I told them about my background and how my best friend will come down and assist the school in developing a turn-key, technology-based embedded curriculum so we can utilize distance learning and communicate directly with other schools throughout the country. More specifically, Maddy Malone offered her school building as a sister school, after clearing it with her principal and District Superintendent, for cooperative teaching and learning. It seemed to make a difference. They could use Maddy's time for matching funds and the Wakefield teachers' as well."

Joe was thrilled. "That's wonderful. I used my New York State grant to fund a Florida school district program. I've always believed a good program can always be funded."

"I have to hang up and call Maddy and then go take care of Tillie. She's planning on going back to work part time at the Waffle House, maybe one or two nights a week, when I can join her there for dinner."

After she hung up, Joe headed home to get dressed and meet Pete's new girlfriend, Tanya, after visiting with his father.

Other than an uncomfortable moment with Mary, the trip so far had gone well.

He had moved his Troy bank accounts to his Islamorada bank where he got his automatic pay deposits, canceled the power company, and went to the Post Office for his mail address to be changed.

He really didn't need the thirty days and he wanted to get back to the Keys as soon as he could. Maybe he would surprise them for Thanksgiving. He also wanted to see Mark and his family and stay for a day or two before going back to Islamorada.

☙❦❧

After hanging up with Joe, Julie called Maddy. "Maddy, hi. Its Julie."

"Hi, Julie, what's up?

"Guess what?"

"What?" Maddy responded.

"I think we were going to win the $100,000.00 technology grant from the state. I just got a call from the Education Department. I told the woman who called what we had planned and about your involvement and I think she was quite pleased. She said we would hear by Thanksgiving but she gave me a little heads up to start planning to purchase the equipment we need. So start planning Maddy," Julie said, laughing.

"Great! When I get down there, after we go crazy in Key West for New Year's, I can spend a few extra days to work with you in the school. I will start asking my principal now for the extra time off."

"You know I put in for equipment for distance learning so whatever you need you can get as well," Julie said.

"My principal will be thrilled and the entire concept of a sister school will be terrific," Maddy said.

"I have to go. I'll talk to you later," Julie said.

With Joe gone for a while and with Tillie now resting more comfortably at home, Julie needed to get back into the groove and develop more chapters to meet her goals for a first draft before Christmas. She was expected to be in Providence in December and she had to be prepared.

She'd gotten the call to set up a time for the meeting and said she would get back to them as soon as she could. It was no more than a stall tactic.

Everyone knew what had just happened in her life,

but a stipend was a stipend and she was still expected to earn it and hand in her first manuscript to the dean. She'd told them she would get back to them by the end of the following week. It would get her back on track, she hoped.

CHAPTER 27

For the rest of the week, Julie worked on her book, getting four more chapters done. With Tillie now home and Joe away, she had to do as much as she could to get back on target for finishing her manuscript. Tillie's church volunteers had been a Godsend. They took care of Tillie while Julie was in her office, pounding out her memoirs, if you will. Brown University wanted to meet her and review what she had before Christmas. They would fly her up three days before Christmas, sit with her and a potential agent and a publisher, and review what she had completed. She had to be as ready as possible. She would work until midnight, she decided, and then hit the sack.

Julie continued into the night, finally going to bed around 1:30 a.m. She'd wanted to get the rest of her thoughts down on paper. She could fix the sentences, spelling, and punctuation later on. She did her corrections off line and then did a new narrative, saving the new document with a date and time stamp, so she could go back and make sure she didn't miss anything.

She saved her work every half hour. She knew about losing power in the Keys and what would happen if she didn't back up her files. She also bought a pack of discs and copied the new material, and the completed narrative to date, on the disc just to be safe. Every once in a while the power went out during a storm, and a major storm in the Keys was not pretty. There was always some damage, roads blocked, power lines down. It was just something you had to live with if you wanted to stay here.

In many ways wherever you lived you had some weather issues. People in the Midwest had to deal with tornadoes. People in the northeast had flooding, ice, and snowstorms. In the west they had wildfires and earthquakes. Julie would take blackouts and an occasional hurricane anytime. In fact, her high school was actually proud of their nickname "The Hurricanes." It was a point of honor, having lived through those storms. It was dangerous, though, and the aftermath could be ugly.

In 2000, when Joe came into their lives, there were no major hurricanes hitting the U.S. coastline but there were fourteen major tropical storms that included Gordon and Helene in late September of that year. Tillie lost part of the roof of their house but she managed to get it fixed quickly with help from some of her friends from the restaurant. Joe brought in a few of his shipmates on a weekend and they finished replacing the damaged sections.

Julie remembered that it was just in time for her eleventh-birthday party. It was going to be at the house but it had to be moved to the restaurant instead. The yard was littered with debris and had not been picked up yet. Since October seventeenth was on a Tuesday that year, Joe and Joan surprised Julie by showing up, since Joe was just back at Islamorada and Tillie only let him know on the chance he could make it. She didn't tell Julie before the party. At the restaurant, for a present, Joan handed her a gift card that held the babysitting class application and a gift certificate for free transportation back and forth to the classes. Her son, Jeff Jr., made up the certificate. It was really cute. Joan's kids came with her to the party, ate cake, and were covered in chocolate. And then they left, sound asleep in Joan and Joe's arms. Joe got Julie a nice card and placed a twenty-dollar bill inside. It was all he had for the rest of the month. At the time, Tillie's friends remarked how nice it was to have new friends in such high places. Tillie laughed and said Joe was as low as you could get in the Coast Guard, but Joan took care of him. They all laughed. For the first time in a long time, Julie felt loved and became part of a new extended family.

As she grew, she did not have to go through puberty alone. Tillie was a great help but was woefully behind in modern thinking on raising a young girl. At fifty-one, Tillie had forgotten what it was like. Her mother was not especially female-oriented and had never read a book about how to raise a daughter. Whenever Julie went over to babysit—with Tillie's permission, of course—Joan answered all Julie's questions and got her through her difficult stages. Julie was well prepared before her first period.

Joan gave Julie a small clutch bag filled with the necessities needed. She was to keep with her at all times. Joan advised her on how to be fully prepared wherever she may be and for any circumstance that might come up. Looking back, Joe was her big brother/mentor/father figure and Tillie and Joan together served as her mother. Julie smiled. *I guess Joe and I both had two mommies.* Then she laughed. Both wore uniforms, one with a waffle on it and the other a Coast Guard insignia. She wondered how they would look together. The United States of Waffles sounded interesting.

Let's see: hurricanes, my first period, clutch bags,

birthdays, uniforms. What did I forget? Julie asked herself. First prom, first love, eighth-grade graduation, first car, Joe as a chauffeur in full uniform for the junior prom. She'd best mention these events as well. She would also have to relive her high school graduation and leaving Tillie for the first time ever. She'd never been away from Tillie, not for one day, since she was eight years old. Not one day. What had that been like?

She remembered being scared to death getting on the plane. Joe's friend Mark drove down from Fort Lauderdale to bring her back to the airport for her flight to Providence Rhode Island. She'd never been north of Miami in her life and had never been on a plane before. How was she ever going to make it at Brown University? God, was she a hick from the sticks or what?

She'd been nervous but she had met Joe at the Providence airport. He drove down from Troy to Providence, met her Southwest flight, and brought her directly to her dorm room at Brown. He stayed for the weekend at a local hotel in Providence and helped her get settled before he went home. They went to the local Mall and picked up wastebaskets, garbage bags, snacks, pillows and linens. These were things she could never take on the plane. As he said, he was only three hours away and would be there whenever she needed him.

Her roommate, and now her long time best friend, Maddy, was from Reading Massachusetts, not far from Providence. She had a TV, stereo, computer, and printer, which Julie used until she got her own. Joe had made a deal with the Troy Education Consulting Group and traded off more of his work time for a two-year old computer. The computer was already written off but in good shape. Joe told his boss what it was for and he got if for $150.00 for Julie.

She used Maddy's printer for a while and helped out with the cost of paper and toner supplies. She got a work-study job on campus for fifteen hours a week to pay for incidentals as her small savings had to last the entire year.

When Julie started Brown, Joe was just out of the Coast Guard and getting his MBA from Rensselaer Polytechnic Institute in Troy. He didn't have any more money than Julie had, but at least Julie was on full scholarship. Rensselaer was not cheap but it was located right in Troy, only a few blocks from Joe's father's house, where Joe stayed until he got his own place in downtown. He bartended several nights a week and worked his schedule around the time he needed to study. After graduation, he moved into a new apartment by himself, for the first time, and traded off consulting to pay part of his rent to the Troy Consulting Group, which was located in the front of the building.

His life was almost parallel in reverse to Julie's current situation. He went home after being away for ten years and moved in with his father and brother but went back on his own once again. Julie was leaving home for the first time ever. Just seemed kind of weird. She was away from home, almost 1,500 miles away, and Joe now lived in his own hometown, a few miles from his university.

Julie made her notes and started to think about how she went from the middle school into the high school. She had graduated with honors from the Key Largo School and went into advanced placement as a freshman at Coral Shores High School. Her math was better, but not great, but she truly excelled in writing and literature, or English as the Florida Education Department had so aptly named the curriculum. No worry about superfluous language here. English for freshman, Grade Nine, advanced or not, was simply English. At the time, she hoped she could continue writing her stories and work on the school newspaper as well. Julie also had to waitress at the Waffle House if she wanted any money. Tillie had done what she could but between cross-country, school, and work as a waitress, Julie was almost as exhausted as Tillie.

Julie wished she could tell her readers that high school was great, but it was not all a bed of roses. Being tall and gawky didn't really change until the beginning of her senior year. She had friends, a handful anyway, that she could count on in good and bad times. She certainly didn't fit into the "Haves" crowd. The clothes she wore, she bought herself from her small earnings from filling in as a waitress and general cleaning staff at the Waffle House. To make money, she took some shifts no one else wanted. Those shifts did not pay well in tips but she saved every dime she could so she could at least be presentable in class. Her friends called her a "Geek Magnet." She seemed to only attract the class nerds who never failed to invite her to a dance or prom way early so she never got a call from someone she liked. By the time someone she liked got around to asking her, she had already said yes to a friend. She carefully explained they were going only as friends. *God that took forever, explaining the friendship role* she thought. She did not want to hurt anyone's feelings, but that always seemed to bite her in the rear. *For once Julie, say no and take your chances,* she'd told herself.

On her sixteenth birthday, Joe, in collusion with Joan's husband Jeff, got her an older VW Rabbit two-door hatchback which didn't look like much, but didn't have any rust—a southern car all the way—and ran great after Jeff tuned it up. New tires, new battery, and the car put Joe in a hole but it was worth it. He and Jeff, with Joan and the kids, following them in their own car, pulled up to the Waffle House that evening. Julie was filling in for the dinner crowd on her birthday. They walked in and sang "Happy Birthday" to her in front of everyone. Joe handed her the keys and said "Happy Birthday."

She was in shock. She took off her apron and went outside to look at the car. She had tears in her eyes. She couldn't believe it. In addition, Joe made a deal with the local insurance agent, paying the insurance coverage for the first year on a monthly basis until it was paid. All Julie had to do was refill the tank with gas. It had been filled to the top. Tillie came by later in her old Escort as planned and saw how happy Julie was. Pretty great day from her adopted family members.

It was really hard trying to remember every detail for the book and still make it part of the overall story of what happened to her and how she and Tillie had survived against the odds. Julie remembered her Junior Prom in 2007. Joe had just gotten back from Hurricane Katrina duty in New Orleans and was quite disillusioned with everything that had happened. He was back in Miami and was no longer assigned to Islamorada. He drove down every other weekend to see her and Tillie. He stayed over for the weekend and then returned to Miami on Sunday night. It wasn't a long trip, only about forty-eight miles, but it took close to an hour and a half on a Friday night on U.S. 1, a single lane highway, with bumper to bumper traffic all the way.

The Junior Prom was in early May. They got out of school in the Keys by the end of May. She went to the prom with someone she actually liked for the first time, Billy Myers, the son of the high school principal. He went to a different elementary school and they met in their freshman year but never really hung around together. He decided to run cross-country and track the previous fall and they became friends. Julie was smitten for the first time ever. When he invited her to the prom, it was almost like meeting Joe for the first time. Billy didn't have his night license yet. Julie had hers but wasn't going to drive the VW Rabbit to the prom. She went on and on during Joe's Wednesday night 7:00 p.m., scheduled telephone calls. Even when Joe was in New Orleans for six months full time and then on and off for the remainder of the year, he did not miss one call. She never knew what number would pop up because Joe would borrow any cell phone he could if his ran out. He must have made one hundred calls a day during this time and he couldn't keep a phone charged. He told her not to worry about a ride to the prom—just look beautiful. And she did.

Joe showed up for Junior Prom night at the high school, in a brand new 2007 candy apple red Mustang convertible. He was dressed in full uniform from head to toe. *It must have cost him a fortune.* He pulled up at Billy's house first. He'd met Gary Myers, Billy's father, on previous award nights so they knew each other. Joe said hi to Billy's mother and gave her a small bouquet of roses to bring to the prom later when the parents were allowed to take pictures. She was thrilled to say the least.

Billy hopped into the car "Wow, is this yours?"

"It is for tonight, Billy," Joe said.

They went to Julie's house and picked her up. Tillie worked late and couldn't get out of it until 8:00 p.m. Joe would pick her up later, bring her to the prom, and she would get a ride home with Billy's parents.

"Wow Julie, you look beautiful," Bill said.

And she did, Joe thought. You could tell Julie was just starting to come into her own. Her features had caught up to her height, she'd filled out, and she looked like an emerging woman.

Joe dropped them off in the front of the high school gymnasium where the prom was held, said goodbye, and went to meet Tillie at their house.

"Tillie you would not believe what Julie looks like tonight," he said.

She laughed. "I believe it Joe. She has my genes,"

"You aren't too bad yourself, Tillie," Joe said, and off to the prom they went.

Pictures were taken, hugs received, and Tillie went home with the Myers. Joe took Billy and Julie out to meet friends at an ocean side restaurant, which was all set up for the after-prom party. He dropped off Billy around 2:00 a.m. and went back with Julie to her house.

Joe slept until 8:00 a.m. and had to get back to Miami to drop off the car by noon or he would be charged an extra day, money he did not have. Both Tillie and Julie gave him a big hug and a kiss. When he went to the car to get in, Julie rushed to him and gave him another big kiss.

"Joe, I love you so much. You are so good to us and we will never forget you."

At that time, this was the best thing that had ever happened to Julie. Brown University had not even been brought up yet. Joe mentioned this opportunity to her in the fall in the beginning of her senior year.

Now at twenty-four, Julie just smiled at the thought of prom night. She found out the following year, right before graduation, that Joe mentioned to Billy that if he tried to do anything to Julie that was disrespectful, Joe would do the same thing to him.

Billy laughed at the retelling of the story but he said he was not laughing then. He was scared to death of this big bad Coast Guard Special Intelligence operator who said he would kick the shit out of him if things went bad.

Julie and Billy went out for a few months afterward but each knew they were going in different directions after graduation. They remained friends. Julie loved his parents and often stopped to see Billy's father, especially now when she was working for the school system.

Before going to sleep, Julie outlined the next day's chores. Tomorrow, she would do all her laundry that had piled up and would put all her research notes into the story. Tillie now walked every day and she was getting stronger. She had fully recovered all her cognitive functions and her short-term memory was coming back. She got tired easily, but that was to be expected. Soon, she would be driving again. She would have to buy another car, something inexpensive but reliable. The State of Florida covered all her medical bills through the uninsured motorist fund but would not cover the collision on her car that was totaled by the hit and run. There was a State of Florida victims fund but since her car was worth less than $500.00, there was no point in applying.

Jeff Talbot came to visit Tillie with his wife, Joan. He said he would scout out a good deal on a car for her and let her know. She didn't need anything until after Christmas because she wasn't going anywhere. Julie was headed down to Key West with Maddy, when she got here. Julie would spend all her time with Maddy when she was here for New Year's, especially, after the holiday, to implement the new technology grant.

"I will need a car by then, but not until then," Tillie said.

In the meantime, for the next few days, she would go in to work only for the dinner crowd. Julie would drive her, have dinner with her—just like old times—and then they would go home together at 8:00 p.m. when the crowd thinned. Julie would be doing homework again, just like she did when she was ten years old, but now it was her book and teaching assignments instead.

കൗൻ

Joe decided he only needed about ten days to get everything settled in Troy. He couldn't see wasting any more time because there was little left for him to do. He went to Maguire's Bar right around the corner from his apartment, where he used to bartend, to say hello and goodbye. He saw his old friends, most of whom didn't even know he was even gone for two months. All they remembered were the headlines about the gang takedown at the Albany Coalition for Families a few months back and him getting shot. They asked him what he was doing and he simply said he was back in the Coast Guard. He said his goodbyes and headed for home.

One night during the last week he was home in Troy, he got a call from Joan who asked him to wait for a call from the Coast Guard brass in Miami.

"What's this all about, Joan? Are they reneging on the assignment?"

"No, Joe. Just wait for the call. Trust me."

Ten minutes later he got the call from Rear Admiral Jake Barnes in charge of the Seventh District out of Miami. "Joe, I would like you to be in charge of all intelligence activity for South Florida and the Florida Keys with Islamorada as your headquarters. You will also have a dotted line to the FBI and Homeland Security in Miami, if you accept."

"Sir, I accept," Joe said immediately.

The rear admiral chuckled. "You obviously know all

those personnel contacts and it makes it easier for you, and us here in Miami. You can keep your new higher rank of warrant officer and we will add chief to the title. That makes you even with the head of the Islamorada Station. Is that acceptable?

"Yes, of course, sir. That's great. Thank you," Joe said.

"You'll get a bump up in pay as well," the rear admiral said. "I commend you for learning Russian. It will be key to your new position. I want you to concentrate on Russian gang activity in the Florida Keys and the Caribbean region. The intelligence gained from your research will inform our decisions on where to place assets in the region, especially with the new ships coming in and the needed intelligence training."

"I'll be back before the thirty day shore leave is up," Joe told the rear admiral. "But I'll need some time down there to get settled."

"You got it, Joe. Just let me know when you get back. I want to meet you personally here in Miami but I won't be able to do so for a while. I will be stuck in Washington for the foreseeable future but then I will be returning. Just do you job and keep your head low. Don't get shot, Joe," he said with a chuckle.

"I'll try not to, sir."

 езеоз

Julie got back to Brown University. She booked a flight for Thursday, December nineteenth, arriving in Providence early in the evening.

She would spend all day on the twentieth in Providence with her dean, the agent, and publisher, both of whom were brought into meet her. She would fly home

Saturday, December twenty-first early in the morning, arriving at Fort Lauderdale by late morning on a direct flight.

Louise Silva would pick her up at the airport and drive her home to Key Largo. The kids would be off for the holidays and Mark would watch them, so she had the time. Louise would also take the night off at the Hard Rock as well, so they didn't have to rush. Maddy would meet Julie on Friday night in Providence for dinner and fly out on Sunday, December twenty-ninth,' meeting Julie at the Key West airport. They already had their room booked for the holiday. She would tell Maddy everything that transpired with her and Joe and then Maddy would update her on her pending marriage.

Joe flew out of Albany on Tuesday November twenty-sixth, two days before Thanksgiving. He had shipped everything he needed by FedEx and was going to spend the day with Mark, Louise and the kids, stay over the night, and have Mark drive him down the next day to Key Largo to surprise Tillie and Julie the day before Thanksgiving.

CHAPTER 28

Joe flew out of Albany on a direct flight, non-stop and on time, and landed in Fort Lauderdale before noon on the twenty-sixth of November, two days before Thanksgiving. His time in upstate New York was now officially done, for at least two more years and probably forever. As his friends in Florida had constantly pointed out, in January, the temperature was minus five degrees and two feet of snow had just been dropped on his hometown of Troy. They also pointed out that in the Florida Keys it was now seventy-two degrees, sunny, with a slight breeze coming in from the Atlantic Ocean, which made it just about a perfect day.

"But don't forget to bring your umbrella because it will rain almost exactly at 1:30 p.m. for twenty minutes," they teased.

It rained just about every day, same time, like clockwork. As he told his friends, "The horse is dead, get off." He got it already.

Mark picked him up. Joe would stay at his house today and Mark would take him to Key Largo the next day, the day before Thanksgiving. Joe had missed MJ and Jennifer. They had gotten bigger and he was happy he would be around more. Jennifer was his Goddaughter, but he loved MJ just as much. MJ looked and acted like his father. Jennifer was the spitting image of Louise and getting smarter every day. Joe didn't want to be her father when she turned fifteen or sixteen. She was an exotic combination of Latina and English heritage with blue eyes as deep as the Atlantic Ocean and eyelashes to kill for. All Joe thought about, after he looked at Jennifer, was how he watched Julie grow up right before his eyes. He remembered he was a ball of nerves when he showed up in the Mustang convertible in his full uniform to drive her to her first prom. He not only pictured it, but because of his photographic memory, he relived every moment of prom night. It was the night she became a young woman, he remembered. It was the night he knew she would do important things with her life. It was the night he thought about her going away to college. It was the night he knew she was probably the most important person in his life. Tillie might have tied with his own father and mother. His brother, at the time, came in a distant last on his scale. *Thank God it has changed now, especially since Pete stepped up to take care of Father, run the business profitably, and finally met a girl who is a keeper—after all these years.*

Joe spent the night at Mark and Louise's. He played with the kids, ate too much pizza, and had way too much beer. They laughed and poured Joe into his bed—a sleeping bag in MJ's room, same as always. He had not relaxed so much in a long time, if relaxing meant getting really buzzed and eating too much.

They got up early the next day. Louise was having twenty people over for Thanksgiving and had to start peeling potatoes and preparing all the ethnic taste treats from both sides of the family. Pleasing her British-born father and her Mexican husband, coupled with pleasing her half-Cuban mother, meant working well into the night to get everything just right. She loved every minute of it. At least she didn't have to bartend at the Hard Rock that night. Seniority had its privileges.

The only guests at the hotel were those visiting friends and family who lived in the area anyway and they would only be back at the hotel late. It really wasn't worth staying open tip-wise she thought.

Little did Joe know, but Julie called Louise shortly after he left for New York and let her know about their new status.

Louise was quite pleased. "That's wonderful, Julie. "If you really love each other, truly loved each other, the way Mark and I do, everything will work out just fine."

"I know," Julie told her.

"What does Tillie think about it?" Louise wanted to know.

"Tillie said she knew I loved Joe from the moment he showed up at my school in his uniform."

Louise laughed. "I fell for Mark when he came into the Hard Rock one night in his full dress uniform."

Julie also told her all about what had transpired with her father going to jail as Ted Champion, and not Tom Chapman, and emphasized the importance of that point because it would be very dangerous for her, her grand-mother, or even Joe, if it got out that Tom Chapman was alive.

Finally, it hit Louise what would really happen and she agreed it was the best course of action for everyone involved, especially for Julie father. He could be out in ten years or so, and even if there was never any contact again, at least he would be alive. And it was Joe, Tillie, and Julie who had kept him alive, to their credit.

Before they left for Key Largo, Joe and Mark

stopped for lunch, had a beer, and Joe told him every-thing that transpired with the hit and run and the eventual incarceration of Julie's father, and the final disposition of the money with $75,000.00 going to the church.

"Nice touch with the money," said Mark. "So do you think Tom or Ted will keep a lid on this and not get killed or put you guys in jeopardy as well?"

"We will have to wait and see," Joe said. "But it is to his benefit, not just ours, to keep quiet about everything. He won't have any money when he gets out, if he gets out, and I told him never to contact us again, under any circumstances, or there would be severe consequences, and I mean it."

"I hear you, Joe, loud and clear," said Mark.

It took about an hour and half, due to holiday traffic, before Mark pulled up at Tillie's house. Joe unloaded his duffle bags and carry-on luggage and he and Mark went into the house. Both Julie and Tillie were there and they were shocked to see Joe back for Thanksgiving. Joe gave Julie a big kiss and hugged Tillie as well.

"Welcome back, Joe. Big surprise, huh?" said Tillie with a big smile.

"You made our holiday," Julie said. "We haven't even started yet. What do you want? A New York Thanksgiving or a Key Largo one, or both?"

"Both," he said.

Mark said his goodbyes. He had to leave to beat the 4:00 p.m. holiday traffic. He had his marching orders, holidays at his house were big events and he was fully expected to pull his weight. "Goodbye, everyone. Happy Thanksgiving," Mark said and left.

Later, Julie relaxed with Joe on the sofa. "I got the call from the Florida State Education Department, Joe, and the Key Largo School will be the recipient of a

$100,000.00 Learning Technology grant. It's to fully integrate technology into the curriculum for the entire school building. My final answers to the additional questions proposed by the Education Department staff solidified our funding request. Having both me and Maddy, as Brown University graduates, participating and having a sister school partnership with an elementary school in Wakefield Massachusetts, carried the day." She went on to say, "Maddy was thrilled when I told her just this morning, and she said she would be available for an extra week after the holidays to work with me at the Key Largo school to set up the program. Maddy's administrators in Wakefield were also thrilled they would be getting distance learning equipment and software as well, and they can keep it after the grant ends."

Joe had very good news as well. "The reason I barely stayed two weeks up in Troy is because I wanted to get back for the holidays and I was informed by the rear admiral in Miami while I was back in Troy that I would be directing all Intelligence for south Florida and the Florida Keys for the Coast Guard, minimally for the next two years, working out of Islamorada. I am to continue Russian lessons, which up to now have already been successful with the first Russian-Cuban drug interception due directly because of my emerging Russian language skills. I have been working non-stop with my Russian teacher and mentor, which will continue until I am fluent orally and in writing."

"Joe, that's great. I am so proud of you. I am also very pleased that you will be here for a while." Little did Joe know how much she wanted him to stay but she was afraid to ask him if he would. "The first draft of my book will be ready by December. I got a lot done over the last month, in spite of all the events that have occurred. The dean from Brown called and set up a meeting for the week before Christmas for me to come up to Providence to speak to an agent selected by him, a publisher who works with the department, and an editor, who has graduated from the same Fine Arts program. My job is to get my book in the best shape possible before heading up to Providence."

"Wouldn't you just know it," Joe scolded. "I move here and you go north as soon as I arrive. Only kidding," he said when she frowned. "Trust me, I will have plenty to do the week you are gone. Jeff Talbot and I still have to scout out a car for Tillie in the meantime. She can't drive your leased car because you are the only one insured for it."

"Right, I forgot," she said. "In the meantime, Maddy and I will get a head start in ordering the equipment we need at both locations. I also have to sit down with all the Key Largo School teachers and administrators to see how we implement the program, grade by grade. By the way, Joe, I forgot to tell you, if the first year of the grant is successful, we can reapply for the same funding for two more years, and everyone in the school, including students, teachers, and administrators, will wind up with an iPad that they can take home at night as well. This is a giant leap forward for this school district. It will be the model for Monroe County and hopefully lead to other school buildings in the district." She grinned. "We are so excited."

"I am excited for you," Joe said and gave her a big kiss.

Thanksgiving went off without a hitch. Joan called them and invited all of them for coffee and pie later on.

"What kind of pie?" Joe wanted to know.

"We have pumpkin, apple, and chocolate," Joan said.

"Before I say yes," he said, "can I have a slice of chocolate and pumpkin on the same plate covered with whipped cream? I'm not coming if I can't have what I want," he joked facetiously.

"Yes, little boy, you can, and I still have your bib here from last year," Joan said sarcastically.

As soon as he said, "Happy Thanksgiving," and hung up Joe settled in for the first NFL Thanksgiving Day football game, which started at 1:00 p.m., as tradition ruled the day. Joe watched the Lions and the Cowboys for the first game.

In his younger days, the end of the 1:00 p.m. game meant touch football in the park, whenever he and Pete were home. Touch football on a Coast Guard cutter was a little more difficult when he was out to sea on the holiday.

CHAPTER 29

The Key Largo School students were released for their Christmas Holiday vacation, which began on Friday, December twentieth. School would reopen on Monday, January 6, 2014. Schools in the Keys didn't have to worry about snow days like up north but they did have to watch out for hurricanes and tropical storms that usually hit in September and October when the new school year began. Christmas was still the major vacation for the school year, especially since they got out in late spring and restarted the new school year in late August.

Julie had planned her trip to Providence perfectly. She could leave Thursday because there was an early student release, and only a party for the kids was planned, so she wasn't needed. She stopped in with a bundle of presents for Jan, other friends, teachers, and her principal. She told everyone about her trip back to Brown University and how nervous she was in meeting all these professionals who were in charge of getting her book published. She was scared to death but she was ready. Her book was as ready as she could make it, and she would only be there for a few days. She would be back for the holidays. It also started to get out around the school building that Julie and Joe were officially an item now, so she took a lot of heat. Everyone wished her well, and no one was surprised by the news. *So much for keeping a secret.*

Julie made it to Fort Lauderdale on time, an hour and half before departure, just to be sure, on the flight booked for her and paid for by Brown University. It was Thursday, December nineteenth, and she was arriving in Providence in the early evening. She would take a bus to Brown and go to the on-campus hotel room reserved for her by the dean. They had a special residence set aside for the program since numerous graduates were in and out all the time to attend meetings with staff about their pending books. Julie would spend all day on Friday with her dean, and the agent and publisher. She would also meet separately with the editor who worked with recent Brown graduates from the Fine Arts Department.

Julie handed in her manuscript to the dean in the conference room at the meeting attended by the agent and publishing representative. She discussed her book. The target market would mostly include teenage girls, ages thirteen to seventeen, and their mothers. She had four copies, for the dean, the agent, the publisher, and for the later meeting with the editor. She had her notebook in front of her and a full pad of sticky notes to attach to her own copy with questions and revisions if any. She was sure there would be numerous updates between now and when—if—it was published. Only time would tell.

All in all, the meeting went very well. The publisher representative made a very sound suggestion. She said, to be a full time writer and to be successful, Julie would need her own niche, especially in the areas of nonfiction. Her work, although it was basically her life story, was nonfiction, and it had many life lessons for younger girls, advice on how to handle life's unpleasant moments, and suggestions for young women as well. The publisher proposed a trilogy, consisting of three books, perhaps to be subtitled, *A Girl's Story*. It would begin with this her first book *Conch Town Girl*, and then proceed in reverse with a book on her high school years, and then finally to middle school or even at the elementary level, where her story really began at the tender age of six years old, when her father supposedly died at sea.

With Julie's permission, the publisher's representative would make the suggestion to her bosses when she returned to New York City. If Julie signed with the agent, with the full understanding that she was represented by Brown University as well, she would receive her first advance with a check for $30,000.00.

Julie was thrilled and asked if she could send a copy of the contract to her attorney first and then let the agent know before flying out on Saturday. They were all in agreement. They were also impressed with Julie already having an attorney on call. Julie immediately called Joe who suggested Dan Simmons and Tillie's real estate attorney, Jane Swanson, in Miami, who also was a friend of Dan's.

After she spoke to Dan, Julie called Jane in Miami who told her to immediately email to her a copy of the contract. She said she would forward it to Dan, as well. Her firm could represent Julie in negotiations for book rights, but for now, a short negotiated contract with Brown and the agent, would be to Julie's benefit.

Jane got back to her on her cell phone and told her to go ahead but put in a one-year commitment, and representation for the first book only.

Depending on the book's success, and if the agent did well by her, she could sign for the next two years, but only for the next two books. That would make them work harder on her behalf. People could get complacent and sometimes lazy and became a hindrance rather than a benefit.

Julie took her advice and before she flew out, signed the contract with her attorney's suggested changes. Dan called her back after speaking to Jane and said they both concurred that it would be a good deal for her.

When the contract was signed, the agent handed Julie the check for $30,000.00. She carefully placed in her wallet and stuck it way inside her pocketbook, where it would stay until she got home. Julie had never felt more successful at something than she felt at that very moment. She'd handed in her book, gotten a check and an agent, had met with the publisher who suggested a trilogy, and had also met with an editor from Brown, who relieved her of the duty of checking all her punctuation, spelling, and word choices without changing any of her thoughts or ideas. It was a good day.

That night, after all her meetings in Providence, Julie met Maddy and, for the first time, was introduced to Maddy's fiancée, Kevin White. Kevin was twenty-five, good looking, and apparently madly in love with Maddy. He was funny and self-deprecating. They laughed the whole night through.

Maddy was great at telling embarrassing stories about both Julie and herself while at Brown. Julie's first attempt at getting drunk was hysterically told by Maddy with Julie being the obvious butt of a long-standing joke. Julie mentioned several un-lady like deeds of Maddy's as well, so they laughingly called a truce. Then both jumped on Kevin and wanted to know his embarrassing secrets. After their outburst of fun, Julie turned to Maddy and told her all about her and Joe becoming a couple.

"It's about time," Maddy said, laughing.

"You too? Julie asked. "What's going on?"

"Well, all you ever talked about was Joe this and Joe that while you were here for five years," Maddy said. "Every time I set you up with a date, it didn't last. So you tell me. I stopped trying after our five years together. I thought it was because you didn't want to meet someone from up north because you would have to live up here permanently if you found someone. Then you find someone who lived up here permanently, and he moved down to you. I believe his name is Joe Traynor, or am I mistaken?"

"I believe you are not mistaken, Ms. Malone," Julie said sarcastically.

The plans for the holidays were set. Maddy would fly in for New Year's and spend the following week at Julie's school to implement the new grant funded program. She would fly in from Logan to Tampa to Key West airport. The hotel was booked and Kevin wanted to know if he could come too.

"No!" the both said no at the same time. "Ladies Week."

"Most definitely, Joe is not coming either," Julie said.

"Got it," said Kevin, "only asking."

Julie and Maddy smiled at each other as if to say we have this covered.

After their goodbyes, Kevin and Maddy left around 11:00 p.m. and headed back to Reading. It was about an hour and fifteen-minute drive late at night.

They didn't drink much but with the "Staties," the Massachusetts' State Troopers, out patrolling, they did not want to get stopped, so they went slowly and cautiously.

♥♥♥

Julie flew home on Saturday, December twenty-first early in the morning, arriving at Fort Lauderdale by late morning on a direct flight. She still had her check buried at the bottom of her pocketbook and she had to show Louise first before she even got home. She was bursting with excitement.

Louise met her at the airport and they drove to Key Largo. The kids would be off for the holidays and Mark would be watching them so she had the time to take Julie home. She would also take the night off at the Hard Rock, as well so they didn't have to rush. They planned the day around the trip. They stopped for lunch on the way down Route 1. They could have taken the Florida Turnpike which would have been more direct and easier but they wanted to catch up and what better way than going the scenic route.

Julie and Louise, separated by seven years, seemed to have become much closer friends over the last few months. It was amazing how tragedies brought good friends closer together. Joe was already Mark's best friend and this would only make them closer.

EPILOGUE

Christmas was on Wednesday this year. Joe was back working full time at the Islamorada Coast Guard facility and had Christmas Day off. Knowing Julie would be tied up with Maddy for the next week or so, he volunteered to work over the holidays and took the place of some of those in the office and on his cutter, who didn't have seniority and had not seen their families in a while. He filled in wherever he could. He covered the office, the technology area, the front desk, and did chores on the cutters while they were in port, for those who were allowed on shore leave. He would work right through New Year's week and then take a full week off.

Christmas went well. Julie and Tillie exchanged gifts and Joe had several special gifts for both of them that he had gotten in Miami when he was up there for a meeting. He had moved into his own officer's quarters at the Coast Guard facility.

While preparing Christmas dinner, before Joe came over, Tillie had a long talk with Julie about their futures, for both of them. Tillie was uneasy staying at her old house while Julie would be on the road at book signings across the country, come the end of May—if her book was published according to plan. The real estate market had come back in a big way in the Florida Keys and smaller houses like Tillie's were now being offered at a premium. She had stopped into a real estate agency just down the road the week before and spoken to a friend of hers that she had waited on for years at the Waffle House. The agent told Tillie there wasn't a better time to sell her house than right now. She also mentioned that a brand new garden apartment complex would be opening on June first, right down the street from St. Justin Martyr Church. The rent for a two bedroom apartment, with plenty of storage, was running around $900.00 a month, including utilities and cable TV. It was small but big enough for Tillie, with room for Julie, whenever she needed it.

The agent did some comparable property prices and told Tillie she should list her house for $279,000.00 and accept anything over $270,000.00. She had bought the house with her husband George in the early 1970s, over forty years ago, for $12,500.00. The house was only 1,100 square feet but it was certainly big enough for someone's second home near the water in Key Largo. With the new tax laws, Tillie could keep the entire amount without paying any taxes on the difference from her original purchase price and the current selling price.

Not a bad deal she thought. Now she would have enough to live on, supplemented by her small social security check when she retired, and a few dollars when she worked part-time at the Waffle House. *God willing.*

When the house sold—which the agent told Tillie should be done quickly, and as a cash deal—at age sixty-three, Tillie could pay for the apartment out of the proceeds and have more than enough to live on for the rest of her life. She would open a joint savings account with Julie and, if she was ever incapacitated again, Julie would never have to worry about taking care of her financially. Tillie could still work at the Waffle House when she wanted to, not because she had to. Besides, Tillie thought her house now had too many bad memories with the incarceration of her son-in-law, the hidden drug money stored in her attic for all those years, and the terrible unnecessary death of her own daughter, Annie. It was time to move on.

At the apartment complex, built near her church, she would be with friends, several of whom would also be moving in when the complex opened in June. Tillie would set up the spare bedroom and office combination for Julie, if she wanted to move in with Tillie. But the way things were going with Julie and Joe, she would probably never move in with Tillie but would stay with Joe when she got back. In any case, Julie would still cover Tillie under the school district's health insurance plan, at least until she could collect her social security and then be covered by Medicare in a year and a half, when she reached sixty-five. *Sixty-five. I never could have imagined I would hit sixty-five.* Tillie and Julie would only be separated by a few miles. But this would be their first separation, other than while Julie was in college, since Julie was born. *As things change, they still remain the same.*

ᏒᎧᏒᎧ

Maddy came down the day after Christmas. She flew into Key West by way of Logan airport, to Tampa International, and then to Key West, arriving at 5:00 p.m. Julie picked her up, and they headed back to Tillie's house for a few days, and then to Key West for New Year's Eve. They stayed at the Best Western on Simonton Street for the night, one block over from Duval Street where all the New Year's Eve action took place. Girls only, no guys. Time to catch up and they both wanted it that way.

The next week was work, work, and more work. Maddy had a list of all the technology equipment she needed and she brought all her technology-based curriculum plans and books with her for the elementary level. Julie and Maddy met with the principal and reviewed all the timelines for implementation of the programs, starting with Julie's fifth-grade and Maddy's third-grade class up in Wakefield, Massachusetts. They met with the teachers after school and went over everything they had planned.

Maddy sat with Julie in each classroom with the teachers and provided input and further explanation on how they would mold lesson plans with technology. They were both exhausted but happy. They completed their initial start-up phase and Maddy would come back in early spring, on the grant's dime, for follow up. She flew home on a direct flight on Southwest to Logan out of Fort Lauderdale. Julie drove her up and stayed for the day with Louise. They had a lot to talk about.

 ๛๛๛

In late March, Julie's book was completed, edited, and sent to the printers for the first edition. It would be released in early May, as scheduled, and as soon as the school year ended, she would hit the road for book signings. Her publisher submitted the book to the National Book Foundation for a 2014 award in nonfiction for first time authors. Just being nominated would be an honor.

Joe planned on meeting her in New York City, on her second leg of the journey. This would be the first time they would be alone together, by themselves as a couple.

Since Christmas, Julie had been on a few overnights at Joe's place, but it was frowned upon by Joe's superior officers in Miami. After Joe's personal call with the rear admiral, Joe knew the man didn't care but the other "lifer" officers had a different opinion. In Islamorada, everyone knew the score and "Don't ask, Don't tell" had a completely different meaning. It had taken Joe quite a while to move beyond their original relationship to what it was now. Now he wouldn't have it any other way and wondered why it took Julie to seize the day and not him. He was still learning and laughed at himself. *God, women are so much smarter.*

Toward the end of the spring, Julie helped out again as assistant coach with the outdoor track team and taught Lucy how to compete in more than one event and what to do to build up her stamina to compete at a much higher level. The Monroe District superintendent had met with the Coral Shores High School principal, Gary Myers and, during the discussion, Julie Chapman's name was brought up.

The superintendent was not aware of Julie's background. He was relatively new to the district. He received a call from the National Book Foundation to gain insight on her application for an award as a first time author. Gary filled him in quickly and also told him about her $100,000.00 technology literacy grant she had won for the Key Largo School. The superintendent was quite impressed and wanted to meet her, so they set up an appointment for Julie to meet both of them after school on Wednesday, right before track practice. An author, a track coach, a Brown University MFA graduate, a grant winner, working as a teacher's aide at the elementary level? the superintendent mused. *Maybe we could fix it for next school year starting in September.*

The three of them met in Gary's office as scheduled.

"Julie, I am quite impressed by you," the superintendent said. "You are a graduate of the Monroe County School District and are a model for those coming after you. I just want to commend you for coming back home." After he found out about her book tour, he wanted to make sure that she came back in the fall. "Julie, with Gary Myer's blessing, we would like to offer you a position at the high school as a career and guidance counselor, as well as allow you the opportunity to work in the classroom at the Key Largo School to continue to implementing the grant with your friend, Maddy Malone, at the sister school in Wakefield, Massachusetts."

"I accept," Julie said. "I can't tell you where I'll be in two years but please know that while I am here, I will give you my best effort every day."

"That's great, Julie, and we know you will," the superintendent said. "We want you here for whatever time you can give us. You have done a remarkable job under very trying circumstances, and we want to honor that achievement. Thank you for accepting our offer."

Julie mentioned she received another advance for a second and third book for her proposed trilogy that she was creating, aimed at young girls and their mothers. With luck, she could keep the same summer book signing schedule and still work for the schools.

❧❧❧

It was now Easter week and Easter was late this year, April twentieth. Tillie had been packing all her clothes and threw out what she couldn't take with her, what she had accumulated over a lifetime. She sold the house for $276,000.00, just under her asking price. With the commission at only 5% instead of 7% because the real estate agent was Tillie's long-time friend, Tillie netted almost $263,000.00, more than enough to pay the monthly rent at her new apartment. She signed up last week for a first floor, two-bedroom unit, with almost the same square footage as her house. The rent was a little more than she thought at $1,000.00 a month, but with the $263,000.00 in the bank, even with minimal interest, she could easily afford the cost of the apartment. She would be moving in, on the first of June. Julie was helping her, because, as soon as school ended, and after Jeff Jr.'s graduation as a senior, she was headed for New York City to meet with her publisher and agent and appear at her first book signing event.

The phone rang and Julie picked up the receiver. "Hello, may I help you?" she said.

"Hi, Julie. It's Mike Kenny from the sheriff's department."

"Hi, Mike, what can I do for you?" she asked. Julie covered the phone and, with a quizzical look at Tillie and Joe, said that it was Mike Kenny, the detective from the sheriff's department.

"I just wanted to let you know we just received word that Ted Champion was killed last night at Raiford prison," Mike told her. "You don't have to worry now about him ever bothering you again."

Julie's shoulders kind of slumped and she dropped to the nearest chair almost falling down in the process.

"Are you there, Julie, I hope I didn't upset you," he said.

"No, I'm fine. How did it happen?" she asked.

"We asked the same question, and no one seems to know," he said. "They are looking into it but Ted was killed, knifed in fact, in the shower last night. I doubt we will ever find out who did it. Sounded like he probably pissed off the wrong guy."

"Who makes up the prison population there?" Julie asked.

"It's mostly white. As you may know, there was death row, and all kinds of murderers and rapists, and you name it. It's the most notorious of all our Florida state prisons. The TV show, the *Fugitive* was filmed there during the 1960s," he said. "There's a minority of African Americans, and now because of the drug problems, they were getting the overflow from the Federal prisons for illegal aliens, like those from South America and even some Russians."

"Thanks for the call, Mike. It is appreciated." Julie hung up, turned to Joe and Tillie, and started to shake like a leaf.

"What did Mike say?" said Tillie.

"He said Ted Champion was killed at Raiford prison last night and they probably will never find out who did it," Julie said.

"They have no idea?" Joe asked.

"No," Julie said. "No one but us knows Ted Champion was my father, right, Joe?"

"Not to my knowledge," he said. "I know for a fact, Mike, the sheriff's department, and the sentencing judge were completely unaware that Ted was Tom Chapman. Jack Forest, Mark, Joan, and everyone else in the loop, never said a word. Julie, I know he was your father and he wasn't such a great guy, but this might hit you like a ton of bricks sooner or later."

"I just can't believe this," Tillie said. "I thought it was over."

"Joe, do you think he was killed because they found out he was Tom Chapman?" Julie asked.

"Only if he said something. Otherwise, there was no other way anyone would ever know about it," Joe said.

"Do you think one of the Russians or Mexicans at Raiford did this, Joe?" Julie asked.

"I was thinking the same thing but I have no idea," Joe said. "We'd better be cautious for a while, though. Tillie is moving, so she will be safe among her friends at the new apartment complex. Julie, you should be safe on your book tour with all the staff helping you, from your agent and publisher. Don't worry about me. I am surrounded with some very effective well-armed individuals, including myself," Joe said then added, "I will follow up on the chatter, now in both Spanish and Russian. If I think for a minute something happened to your father because he was exposed as Tom Chapman, we will take care of it. I will let Joan know as well as our chief warrant officer, Jacob Cramer. In the meantime, try not to worry about it. Go through your grieving process but please don't let anyone else in on our little secret."

"Joe, I won't kid you, I am scared to death and I will be looking over my shoulder for a long time," Julie said. "Please take care of Tillie while I'm on tour."

Tillie started to say a prayer in the living room, to St. Jude, the Patron Saint of Hopeless Cases. *Maybe St. Jude will come through for us after all. I will light a candle every Sunday in church until we can stop worrying. Please, keep Julie and Joe safe and sound.*

The End

About the Author

Daniel J. Barrett was born in Rutland, Vermont and has lived his entire life in Troy, New York, ten miles north of Albany. He is a graduate of both Siena College in Loudonville, N.Y. with a BS in Finance, and from Rensselaer Polytechnic Institute in Troy, N.Y. with an MBA in Management. Barrett has had a varied career with extensive international experience, traveling worldwide.

An avid reader, and inspired by numerous authors, Barrett has read over 1,500 books in the last several years in preparation to write his first novel, *Conch Town Girl*. He continues to work, as a grant-writing-and-education consultant, serving those most at risk in the Capital Region, and is now working on his next novel.

Made in the USA
Middletown, DE
21 May 2015